Choice

ELIZA GRACE HOWARD

ARCHWAY
PUBLISHING

Archway Publishing books may be ordered through booksellers or by contacting:

Archway Publishing
1663 Liberty Drive
Bloomington, IN 47403
www.archwaypublishing.com
844-669-3957

ISBN: 978-1-6657-3499-8 (sc)
ISBN: 978-1-6657-3501-8 (hc)
ISBN: 978-1-6657-3500-1 (e)

Library of Congress Control Number: 2022922971

Print information available on the last page.

Archway Publishing rev. date: 01/17/2023

Chapter One

They had just finished making love on the blanket that Donna had spread out on the floor in front of the fireplace. Now the fire had died down to mostly red-coal-encrusted logs, and it was putting out a nice amount of heat, even though there were no flames licking upward anymore. They lay in the semidarkness of their living room, the only light coming from the waning firelight.

Donna Porter smiled against her husband's bare shoulder, feeling a rare moment of contentment. "That was nice," she said softly.

"Umm-hum," Stanley murmured, running a hand down her flank. "You know what would have made it even better though?"

"What's that?" she asked lazily.

"If there had been another couple lying here beside us, doing the same thing we were."

Donna's head popped up. "What? What did you say?"

Stanley put his hand on the back of her head, urging it back down against him.

She resisted, her mind reeling. What had he said? She cringed— she'd tried so hard to please him, with the romantic setting, making a pallet in the firelit room. What more could she have done?

"Relax," he said soothingly. "I was just thinking how much more exciting it would have been if there had been another couple in here with us, having sex like we were. Don't you think so?"

Donna pulled away from under his arm and sat up. She stared at him in the firelight. "Where in the world did you come up with an idea like that?"

"Oh, I just thought something like that might add a little bit of spice to our relationship. Make things a little more exciting."

"You mean you don't think it's exciting enough anymore, just making love to me?" she asked, her voice quivering with hurt.

He sat up. "Oh, c'mon, Donna," he said in a flat voice. "You know that's not what I meant. Don't be such a prude. Don't *you* ever fantasize about stuff like that?"

"No." She reached up for her bathrobe, which she had discarded behind them on the sofa earlier. "I don't think about anybody but you while we're making love. Are you saying that you do?"

"Well, sure. Sometimes."

Donna swallowed hard. "Do you think that I'm not enough to satisfy you? That you need to imagine that I'm somebody else?" She hated the way her voice sounded—so plaintive and needy. She pulled her robe tightly around her and knotted the belt around her waist, a spark of anger beginning to form.

"No, no," he said. "I'm just saying that it would make it even better between us if we did something like that to make things more exciting."

"And just who would this fantasy couple of yours be? Where do you think you'd find somebody who would want to have sex in the same room with us?" she asked coldly, leaning back against the sofa and hugging her arms around her knees.

"Oh, I don't know." He gave a short derisive laugh. "You'd be too hung up to do it—even if I did find someone. I know you'd never go along with anything like that."

"You're right about that!"

He shook his head. "Yeah, I know." He got to his feet. "Guess I'll just go on to bed. Make sure the fire screen's closed before you come to bed, OK?" He took a couple of steps and then stopped. He kneeled back down beside her and put a hand on her rigid shoulder. "Look, honey, I didn't mean to hurt your feelings. Just give what I said some thought, will you? About us making things more exciting, I mean."

When she did not immediately respond, he got to his feet again, turned, and walked down the hallway toward their bedroom, leaving her sitting on the floor in front of the dying fire.

Donna felt the tears crawling down her face as she stared blindly at the glowing embers. She felt so alone, so lonely. This marriage had seemed so right, such a perfect answer when her parents wanted to make their move to Florida and retirement, leaving her here with a brand-new job and a signed teaching contract. She'd tried so hard to make a perfect marriage, but it seemed like the harder she tried, the more she failed to meet his expectations— and the more he criticized and told her at length how stupid and inept she was. She had read all the magazine articles about how to please your man and how to make your marriage fun, but nothing seemed to work. He was never happy. Look at tonight. Finally, she rose to her feet, gathered up and folded the blanket, and walked slowly back to their bedroom.

Stanley was stretched out under the covers in bed, already snoring softly.

Shoulders hunched, she quietly went into the adjoining bathroom and brushed her teeth. She slipped her long nightgown over her head, crossed the room, and slid under the covers on her side of the king-size bed beside her sleeping husband. She lay there, a feeling of heaviness pressing on her chest, trying not to cry, until she fell into a fitful sleep.

The alarm jolted her awake in what seemed like only minutes. She reluctantly left her warm nest under the covers, belted her robe over her nightgown, and headed down the hallway to the kitchen.

Stanley always demanded that she make a big, hearty breakfast to begin their day, and this was going to be an especially long one. After her day of teaching her class of first graders, there was a parent-teacher meeting scheduled for seven o'clock, followed by one-on-one meetings in her classroom with any of the parents who wanted to talk to their little one's teacher.

"Can you get dinner out tonight?" she asked Stanley as he worked on his plate of sausage patties, grits, and eggs over easy.

He simply looked at her, raising his eyebrows in silence.

"I have a parent-teacher meeting this evening after school."

"So what are you doing between four o'clock when school lets out and when the meeting starts?"

"I was going to stay at school and catch up on some of my paperwork." She heard the defensive note in her voice.

"Well, I get off work at six tonight. Why don't you come on home after school lets out, fix something to eat, and leave it here in the oven? That way, I can eat when I get home, and you can go on back to school after you cook and be at your meeting."

Donna sighed. "OK, I guess I can do that." *There goes my time to do my paperwork*, she thought.

He extended his coffee cup toward her.

Silently, she got up, poured him a refill, and returned to her scrambled egg and toast.

Stanley finished his meal and pushed back from his seat. "Well, I guess I'll see you when you get home tonight after your parent-teacher thing, then," he said as he headed back toward the bedroom to shower and dress.

"I guess so," Donna replied to the empty room. She drained her own coffee and gathered up their dirty dishes. Rinsing them and putting them into the dishwasher, she pulled a package of frozen hamburger out of the freezer side of the refrigerator and left it in the sink to thaw. She returned to the bedroom and quickly dressed.

The sound of the shower told her Stanley was still in the bathroom. Gathering up her purse and car keys, she left for the elementary school to begin her long day.

∾

Donna sneaked a surreptitious look at her watch as little Danny White and his mother left her classroom and little Gina Thompson and her mother, Linda, entered.

Linda Thompson took a moment to look around at the colorful bulletin boards, decorated with cutout balloons and Donna's first graders' artwork.

Donna had worked so hard on the boards to make the room appear cheerful and stimulating. She smiled as they approached her desk and the two empty chairs she had placed beside it. "Hello, Gina," she said to the little girl. "Is this your mother?"

Gina nodded, her light brown curls bobbing.

"Good evening, Mrs. Thompson," Donna said, even though she knew the woman slightly. "I'm Mrs. Porter."

"Hello," said Gina's mother, sitting down and gesturing for the little girl to take the other chair. "How is Gina doing?"

Donna smiled warmly. "Just great. She's a good student, and she is very well behaved. She's doing just fine."

"I'm glad to hear it," said Mrs. Thompson. "She talks about you all the time at home."

Donna looked at the little girl, who was sitting quietly, her face very solemn. "I think she enjoys being in her class here. Don't you, Gina?"

Gina nodded and ducked her head.

"So, you're not having any problems with her?"

"Oh, no! Gina is a fine student. And she's making friends

among her classmates. I think her best friend is Katy Burgess. Isn't that right, Gina?"

This time, Gina smiled and nodded enthusiastically.

"Oh, yes, she's known Katy for some time. We're friends with Katy's parents, and the girls have known each other since they were toddlers." Mrs. Thompson frowned. "That isn't a problem, is it? The girls aren't causing any disruptions, are they?"

"Not at all," Donna said. "I wish I had a whole class like Gina."

"That's nice to hear." Mrs. Thompson finally seemed to relax and permit herself a small smile.

Out of the corner of her eye, Donna saw someone else pause in the doorway. She gave Mrs. Thompson another big smile. "I'm so glad you came by tonight. It makes it so much easier for us here at school when the parents are concerned and involved with what we're doing."

"Of course," said Mrs. Thompson. She stood up. "My husband is here too. He's talking with our son's teacher now. Do you know him? Jim Thompson? He's in the third grade."

Gina stood as well. "No," she said. "This is just my second year of teaching. He would have been in the first grade the year before I came."

"Well, thank you for the good report on Gina. I'll be going on over to Jim's classroom where he and my husband are."

"Thank you again for coming," Donna said. She glanced past them as they walked out, looking over at the man who was leaning back against the doorframe. He was tall—about six feet, Donna thought—lean and broad shouldered, with longish brown hair combed straight back from an intelligent brow, patrician nose over thin, well-shaped lips, and a firm chin.

The small boy who had been standing behind him moved into view, and Donna smiled, recognizing her student Benjie Cavanaugh.

Linda Thompson and Gina walked past them and out of the room; Mrs. Thompson gave the man a slight nod as she passed by him, but she did not speak to him.

He walked toward her, lazy and graceful.

Donna thought of a panther as he approached. *What a gorgeous man,* she thought, and something stirred deep inside her. "Hello," Donna said. "Hello, Benjie. Is this your dad?"

"Yes," the little boy said proudly, clambering up onto one of Donna's empty visitor chairs.

Donna looked up into a pair of eyes that were so light blue that they appeared almost colorless in his hawkish face. "I'm Mrs. Porter, Benjie's teacher," she said, feeling an almost electric shock as their eyes met.

His thin lips curved upward. "I'm Benjie's dad," he said in a deep, melodious voice. "Quinn Cavanaugh."

"Please. Have a seat," she said, sinking back down into her chair. She took a deep breath.

"I wanted to see how my boy is doing," he said softly, taking a seat.

Donna smiled. "He's doing beautifully. Benjie is a wonderful little boy."

"Good to know."

"Benjie participates very well in our group activities. He interacts with his classmates very well." Donna suppressed a small laugh. "And he really likes recess, when he can go out and play ball," she added.

Those pale blue eyes laughed at her. "Yeah, I can believe that. He's got a lot of energy. He's not giving you any trouble?"

"Of course not. Why?"

"I don't know." He gave a little chuckle. "I just remember how I was … didn't like to sit still and pay attention."

"No, no," she said. "Like you say, he's an energetic little boy, but he's really quite good."

"Glad to hear it. You'll contact me if there's anything I need to know, right?"

"Of course I will," she said as he got to his feet.

"I … I'm a single parent," he said. "My mother keeps him after school … when I can't. I just want him to fit in and be a good student."

"He's doing just fine."

He held out his hand toward his son, and Benjie scrambled to his feet and took it. "OK, good. Nice to have met you, *Mrs. Porter.*" His gaze swept over her.

Donna felt her face flush. Her eyes dropped to the open neck of his shirt, where a tendril of a tattoo curled upward at the base of his neck, and she felt a delicious shiver.

"Good to meet you as well," she said as he turned and left the room, hand in hand with his son.

🕉

Donna settled into her busy routine at work. At home, she tiptoed around her husband's volatile moods, trying to keep the peace.

One evening in mid-November, just as she had finished clearing the kitchen and starting the dishwasher, Stanley came back into the room and slid onto his barstool at the eat-on counter. "Come here, honey," he said.

Donna looked across at him, hearing the odd note in his voice. He had some sort of magazine in his hand. "What?" she asked with a smile, walking around to stand beside him.

"Sit down. I want you to see this." He slid the publication over toward her.

Donna glanced down, and she felt her eyes widen as she looked. She picked up the magazine and began turning the pages slowly, and her mouth literally dropped open as her brain began to process what she was seeing. She lifted her eyes to meet Stanley's eager ones. "Stanley?" she said, barely above a whisper. "What in the world is this?"

He took hold of the magazine, turning it slightly so that he could look at it with her. "It's a swingers' magazine. See? It's called *Choice*." There was excitement in his voice. "Look! These are ads for couples wanting to meet other couples. These are their pictures— and look here! They have little ads about themselves, and they say what they are looking for in the people they want to meet."

Donna's hand flew off the magazine, and she stared at him incredulously. "Where did you get this thing?"

He was looking down at the pages. "I went to a little newspaper store ... down in Winston-Salem."

"A *dirty* bookstore?" she asked sharply.

He looked up at her. "An *adult* bookstore," he said.

She clasped her hands tightly together in her lap and stared at him.

He grimaced. "Oh, c'mon, Donna. Just look at it, at least. Don't be such a prude! I think it's fascinating."

"Fascinating?" she repeated tonelessly.

"Yeah, it is," he said defensively. He jammed his finger against one of the ads. "Just take a look, OK? 'Attractive couple in twenties love fun and games. She is blonde, blue-eyed, five foot five; he has brown hair and eyes, five foot eleven. Seeking couples in Piedmont, NC, who share their love of adventure. Waiting to hear from you.' Isn't that great? Wouldn't you love to meet them? Look at her picture." He pushed the magazine closer to her.

Donna glanced down at the photo of a young woman, smiling brightly into the camera, unselfconsciously nude to the waist. Donna felt mildly shocked. She looked back up at Stanley—he was watching her intently—and she pushed his hand away.

"What?" he asked. "What don't you like about this?"

"Stanley, what's the matter with you? Don't you realize this is against everything we've been taught?"

"Yeah, I know it's super conservative here."

"Yes! Didn't they teach you in Sunday school that this is wrong?"

"What's wrong with it?"

"It just is!" She shivered. "Everybody knows it is."

"Well, I don't happen to think so."

Donna shook her head. "I'm a teacher," she said. "I can't do things like this. Why, they'd fire me if I did.

"What if nobody knew?"

"I don't care … that's not the most important thing."

"What is the most important thing?"

"I don't want to have anything to do with it! It makes me sick to my stomach to even think about it!"

He stood up and sighed deeply. "I thought you would be like this," he said. Taking the magazine, he walked down the hall and into their bedroom.

Donna sat there for a moment, stunned. Then she shook her head in disbelief and went down the basement stairs to move the laundry from the washer to the dryer.

Chapter Two

It was just past ten o'clock on Christmas morning. Donna was on her knees in front of the tree she had decorated in their living room, surrounded by discarded paper and ribbons. It was late because she and Stanley had spent Christmas Eve in the happy chaos at Stanley's parents' house, surrounded by his extended family, with his two brothers, his sister, and their spouses and children all in attendance. As usual, Stanley's parents had overbought for their grandchildren, and it was past eleven when all the Porters had loaded gifts and overtired children into cars and departed.

Today was wonderfully peaceful. It was a crisp, sunny, cold day outside, and they had slept late. Donna had made the two of them pancakes and sausages for breakfast, and they had carried their coffee mugs into the living room to open the gifts under their tree. Donna's parents had sent them what turned out to be a nice check apiece from their retirement home in Florida.

Stanley had already opened her gifts to him—an expensive tool set and a soft pullover sweater. Stanley had given her a nice terry cloth robe, and now he reached under the tree for the final brightly wrapped package. He handed it to her with a big smile.

"Oh, you got me something else?" she exclaimed.

He nodded, watching as she ripped off the candy cane patterned paper.

"What's this?" Donna said. She pulled up the top of the box and looked at the object inside, which was surrounded by a lot of Styrofoam packing.

"It's a Polaroid camera," Stanley said, helping her lift it out of its packing. "Now we can take pictures without having to get them developed. See? You just load in the film, shoot, and the picture comes out of that slot at the bottom of the camera. In just a couple of minutes, the picture appears."

"Oh, my! How clever." Donna pulled out the owner's manual and flipped through the pages. "But why would we need a camera like this? We already have a camera."

"I know," Stanley replied. "But we have to take the film to the drugstore, and they have to send it off to a lab to be developed. You don't have to do that with this one."

"OK," Donna said. She reached up and kissed him on the cheek. "Thank you, Stanley. I know you love to have all the latest gadgets. I guess we'll find a use for this one." She smiled at him.

"Oh, I know we will," he said smugly. "Merry Christmas, Donna."

"Merry Christmas to you, too, Stanley," she replied.

A short time later, Donna gathered up the discarded wrapping paper and ribbons and crammed them into a big trash bag. She put away the new clothing.

Stanley had taken his new tools out into the garage, and he was still out there.

She put the new camera on the kitchen counter and busied herself around the house for a time.

Stanley came in and switched on the TV, and Donna picked

up a book she had just started reading and curled up at one end of the sofa.

Midafternoon, she fixed them some sandwiches. Stanley went back to the TV after they had eaten.

"You know what?" Donna said. "It's such a nice, lazy day. I think I'm going to try out that new bubble bath that your sister gave me for Christmas. I'm going to have a nice, long solitary soak in the tub."

"OK," Stanley responded.

Donna did just that. She lay back and relaxed. When the water cooled, she ran more hot water into the tub, but when the temperature fell a second time, she decided that was enough, and she unplugged the stopper. Stepping out of the tub, she reached for a towel—and was startled by a sudden flash of light. She whipped her head around to see Stanley standing in the doorway of the bathroom, a big grin on his face, holding her new camera.

"Stanley! You scared the life out of me! What are you doing?" she cried.

"Oh, I was just trying out your new camera," he said with a smirk.

"What? You took a picture of me without any clothes on?" She wrapped the towel tightly around herself and lunged toward him.

He stepped back out of her reach, holding the camera high. "I was just testing it." He laughed, holding the ejected picture out of her reach.

"Let me have that!"

"Uh-uh! Wait until it develops. I want to see how it comes out." He walked quickly toward the kitchen.

Donna followed him, but when she reached toward him, he evaded her easily.

After two or three minutes, he sat down on his bar stool, and looked at the photo. "Wow," he said.

"Let me see that!"

He looked at her with a frown. "Only if you don't try to tear it up."

"All right! Let me see."

Holding the photo where she couldn't grab it, he let her come closer.

Donna peered at it. She was in half profile, her extended arm reaching for the towel covering the view of her breast, but the photo showed the back of her body from mid-thigh up, and her bare buttocks were in plain view.

Stanley grinned. "See how cute you look?"

"You ambushed me!" she said angrily.

"I sure did. I wanted to see how your new camera would work."

"Well, now you know. Now give me my picture."

"Not on your life! This is mine." He held it out of reach.

"Stanley!"

"If I promise not to take any more pictures of you that you don't know about, can I keep it?"

"What are you going to do with it?"

"I won't show it to anybody. I just want to keep it. All right?"

"Well … I guess so. If you promise that you won't show it to anyone."

"Deal," Stanley said.

Reluctantly, Donna padded down the hall to get dressed, leaving Stanley sitting at the bar, still looking at the photo.

Stanley was scheduled to work the next day since the day after Christmas was a prime sales day at the used car lot. Donna, on the other hand, did not have to return to school until the day after the New Year.

In the morning, she made sure that the offending photo was still sitting on top of Stanley's dresser when he left for work. *It's not that I don't trust him to keep his word*, she told herself.

Between Christmas and New Year's, she spent an entire day giving her house a thorough cleaning, and she made some dinners that took longer to prepare than she usually had time for.

Stanley enjoyed her pot roast one night and her slowly simmered homemade soup on another evening, and the house smelled wonderful all week from the cooking aromas.

Donna was lonely, and even though she knew Stanley would not approve, she called Pennie White. Pennie had been her best friend all through their school days in Phillips, but they had not talked for weeks.

Pennie was surprised and delighted to hear from Donna, and they made plans to spend Saturday on a shopping trip to Winston-Salem. Donna could hardly wait; she hadn't looked forward to something like this in what seemed like forever.

Donna picked Pennie up at her house, and they made their way to the city, laughing and chattering like schoolgirls. It felt like no time had passed since they had been together, and Donna felt warmth spreading through her, easing the tension she hadn't even been aware of.

They made their way through several stores, and Pennie found a dress she liked, while Donna found a pair of shoes on after-Christmas sale. Finally, they made their way to a small restaurant and slid into a booth for lunch and to rest their feet.

"Oh, this has been so much fun," Pennie said as the waitress departed with their order.

"It has. I've missed this so much."

"Not my fault," Pennie replied. "You're the one who just disappeared on us."

"No, I haven't," Donna said.

"Oh, yeah? How long has it been since we've got together, you and me?"

"I don't know," replied Donna. She stopped smiling as she thought. "I guess … a few weeks?"

"Try last summer!"

Donna's heart sank. "Really?"

"Yeah!" Pennie leaned forward. "I thought you were mad at me about something."

"No! Of course not."

"What's wrong, Donna? Where have you been?"

"I don't know … I guess just busy with school … and everything."

"And you haven't been to church either."

"Well, Stanley works so hard all week, and he likes to sleep in on Sundays."

Pennie raised her eyebrows.

"I know. But I didn't used to go every Sunday."

"Now you don't go at all. And we used to go places and do things together. Now we never do."

Donna could not raise her eyes from her place mat.

"What's wrong, Donna?" Pennie asked softly.

"Nothing's wrong. Stanley just … doesn't like it when I'm not there when he gets home." Her voice trailed off.

"He doesn't abuse you, does he?" Pennie asked sharply.

"No, no! Of course not!"

"Are you sure?"

Donna forced a smile she did not feel. "Of course, I'm sure. Oh, he likes to run his mouth and gripe at me sometimes, and he wants his meals cooked for him and on the table, but that's all. He just doesn't like for me to socialize a lot, I guess."

"And you put up with it?"

Donna forced a little laugh. "It's not all that bad. I'm going to do better. We'll get together a lot more. I promise. Oh, look! Here comes our food."

"How's your mom and dad?" asked Pennie after a few bites.

"They're good," replied Donna, happy to change the subject.

"They still in that retirement village in Florida?"

"Uh-huh. Patty and Ben came down to see them over Christmas."

"Patty's the middle sister, right?" Pennie said. "She's the one who got the civil service job after high school, moved to Washington, and ended up marrying her boss?"

"Right." Donna laughed. "She always was the adventurous one of the three of us. They've got two babies now. Donnie's five, and Shelby is two. I know Mom and Dad were happy to see them."

"What about Joan? Where is she now?"

Donna said, "Oh, she and Larry are in Germany. The air force sent him there about three years ago. They both like it over there. They're having a great time sightseeing all over Europe when he has time off."

"So, you were here for Christmas—without family."

"I had Stanley!" Donna replied defensively. "And he has a big family. We went over there and spent Christmas Eve with them."

"OK," Pennie said, finishing her sandwich. "Was it fun?"

Donna smiled and gave a little shrug. "Yeah. It was good."

"You hadn't been dating him very long when the two of you got married, had you?" Pennie asked. "The wedding was just after you graduated and your folks moved to Florida, wasn't it?"

"It was," Donna nodded and gave a little laugh. "Everything happened so fast."

Pennie raised an eyebrow. "Tell me."

"When I was a senior in college, I knew that my parents really wanted to move to that retirement village in Florida. Two other couples they knew had moved down there and simply loved it! Mom and Dad even went down there to visit, and I could tell that they had their hearts set on going down there. Stanley and I had had a few dates off and on for about a year and a half, but neither of us was ready to talk about getting married. Then, when I was doing my student teaching, I heard about the opening here for the first-grade position, and I applied. It sounded perfect, and I could hardly believe it when I got the job! I came home just bursting with my news." She laughed ruefully.

"What did they say?"

"I was going to break my news at dinner, but before I could tell them, they announced that they had sold the house and were going to move away now that I was through school. I couldn't throw cold water on their plans. I didn't even tell them right then—even though I was shocked."

"What happened then?"

"Well, I had a date with Stanley the next night, and he asked me what was wrong, why I was so down in the dumps. I told him the news about my job and how my parents were leaving. I was the baby in the family, and I'd never had to do anything on my own. I'd never even had a checking account, looked after myself, or lived alone. College didn't count, because, well, because—"

"Momma and Daddy were still right there for you?"

"Right."

"So, then what happened?"

Donna looked straight at her friend. "Stanley showed up for our next date with a dozen roses! He took me out and told me how much he loved me!"

"Uh-huh," Pennie said.

"I know, I know. But he did and said all the right things, and a week later, he proposed. I was surprised. It wasn't like we were madly in love or anything like that." Donna shook her head, lost in her memories.

"But you married him."

"I did." Dona looked up, her eyes glittering with unshed tears. "He made it seem like a perfectly logical solution. I wouldn't have any other family here after they left. My sisters had been gone for years. Stanley insisted that we buy that house, way out there in the country, and I began teaching." She shrugged. "Stanley doesn't like us to socialize with the people here, and I sorta lost touch with the people I used to be friends with while I was in college. Except for you, of course."

Pennie patted Donna's hand. "I'm here for you. Always have been. You know that."

"I do."

Their eyes locked, and then Pennie broke the emotional moment. "So, what do you want to do next?"

They shopped a bit more, but Donna had lost her lighthearted mood. Soon, they headed back to Phillips. Donna hugged her friend goodbye and hurried home. She stashed her purchases in the back of the closet and started supper.

☙❧

As Donna was cleaning up the kitchen after supper a few nights later, Stanley came back in and sat down at the bar. He started reading something in front of him.

"What are you doing?" she asked.

He looked up. "Come here and sit down," he said. "I want you to look at this with me."

"OK." She came around the end of the bar, sat down, and saw what he had in front of him. "Oh, Stanley! Are you looking at that couples magazine again? I thought you threw that thing away."

"No," he said. "I kept it. I think it's interesting. I wish you would just take a look at it with an open mind. You made up your mind that it was something dirty without even looking at it."

Donna grimaced. "I'm just not interested in looking at it, Stanley. I don't know why you're so … so fascinated by that stuff."

"I just didn't close my mind before I even took a look—like you did."

She sighed. "I don't want to argue with you, Stanley."

"I don't want us to argue, either. Do me a favor, will you? Just read two or three of these."

"Why?"

He looked at her imploringly. "Just read them. Will you do that just because I ask you to?"

"Oh, all right." She took the magazine from him.

"Read the ad out loud, OK? Just a couple of them."

"Oh, all right." In a monotone, Donna read one of the ads aloud.

"So?" Stanley said. "Tell me what kind of person wrote it. You took psychology in college. Describe the person to me. Make it a game, OK?"

Donna raised her eyebrows. "All right. Hmm, let's see. Little, short words, not too much imagination." She read for a moment. "Stanley, they all sound a whole lot alike."

"Yeah, well, they're *ads*. The magazine charges by the word. But some of them are better than others. Read a few of them. You'll see."

Donna read three more ads. "OK," she said. "I see what you mean." She pointed. "That one there picked their words more carefully; it's better written."

He moved his head closer to hers and read the ad she pointed to. "Hey, you're right." He smiled. "See what I'm saying? It's pretty interesting, reading them and trying to picture the person who wrote them."

Donna pushed the magazine back to him. "Not that interesting to me," she said.

"Aren't you at all curious about the people who wrote them?" he asked.

"No, Stanley. I can't say I am."

"Well, I am. I'd like to meet some of them, talk to them, and get to know them."

"You've got to be kidding!"

"No. I'm dead serious."

"Stanley, there's a million reasons why that's impossible!"

"Name three! Tell me three reasons it's impossible!"

Donna held up her hands and pointed at the fingers of one with the other, as she enumerated. "One," she said, "It's just plain wrong! It goes against everything we've ever been taught. In church, by our parents, everything! Not only is it wrong, but we also couldn't have anybody know that we were fooling around with something like this. I'd lose my job if I did! Stanley, you know how religious and conservative this town is. I would lose my job—and we'd be ostracized for life!"

"How would anybody know?" Stanley smiled dismissively. "Who would tell anybody about it? It's our private business, and we'd certainly keep it to ourselves. You got anything else?"

"Yes, I do!" Donna replied heatedly. She held up another finger. "Number two, I do *not* want to do the kinky things those people in that magazine are talking about, and three," she finished triumphantly, "we don't have any way to meet with them to talk to them in the first place!"

Stanley held up his hand like a traffic cop. "I've been giving this a lot of thought," he began.

"I just bet you have," Donna muttered darkly.

He grinned. "I have! What if I told you I've figured out how we could meet one of those couples, and no one would ever know about it? What if we could just meet them? I promise you that we'd never do anything you objected to. I promise you that! I just want to meet a few of them, that's all. Would you be willing to do that?"

"I doubt it. But what is it that you've figured out?" she asked.

He leaned back, his eyes gleaming. "This is what I'm thinking," he said. "We could rent a post office box down in Winston-Salem, where nobody would pay any attention to the mail or know who we are. All we have to do is answer one of the ads. We pick out one that's from somebody from someplace far from here, and we travel to see them there. What do you think?"

Donna closed her mouth; she realized she had been gaping at him. "I think you're nuts!"

"Oh, c'mon, Donna! Where's your sense of adventure? It would be a real kick to actually meet some of these people! I just want to talk to them and see what makes them tick! We don't have to do anything that we don't want to do. I promise you that! Will you let us answer an ad? Please!"

Donna stared at him.

"C'mon, honey. Please? All I'm asking is that we answer an ad and see if they answer us back. Will you do that? Please?"

"I … I don't know."

"I give you my word that's all I want to do. Will you at least think about it?"

Donna sighed deeply. "I'll think about it."

Stanley did not mention the subject again for a few days.

However, in the ensuing time, Donna felt like she was being courted, and he certainly was not very subtle about it. When she got home from school the following day, Stanley's car was already in the driveway. When she entered the kitchen, there was a big bag on the center of the bar. She walked over and opened it, and the delicious aroma of barbecue filled the air. Inside were several boxes of meat and sides from the Barbeque Barn in the adjourning town.

Stanley walked into the room and said, "Hi, honey. I left work early today, and I thought I would pick up something so you wouldn't have to cook."

"I see," Donna said.

"I know how much you like the food from the Barbeque Barn."

"Yes, I do. How did you get off early enough to drive over there—and then beat me home from work?"

He shrugged, smiling. "Oh, I had some time coming to me. You go change, and I'll set the table."

Donna walked past him, and he put out his arm and stopped her when she was even with him. He gave her a big kiss and grinned at her.

"Thank you," Donna said.

"You're welcome," he said as she continued toward the bedroom.

The next evening, Donna had the meal ready and was setting the table when he came in the back door with a small potted plant in his hands. "I wanted to get you one of those African violets you like so much," he said as he handed the plant to her, "but Mrs. Reeves over at the florist said they didn't have any in the middle of January. I got you this little green garden instead."

"Thank you, Stanley," Donna said. "What's the occasion?"

"Oh, nothing," he said airily. "I just felt like getting a present for my best girl."

She watched him suspiciously as he nonchalantly walked away.

It was Friday evening before he got around to addressing what was on his mind. Donna had finished her nightly regimen and was getting into bed when he reached over and pulled her against him.

"Have you given any thought to our little talk the other day?" he asked.

"What little talk?" She stiffened.

He nuzzled her neck. "When we were talking about renting a post office box in Winston-Salem and answering one of the ads in that magazine," he said. "Have you given it any thought?"

"Not much," Donna said warily.

"Well, I thought we could work on our letter this weekend," Stanley said. "You know, our answer to the couple—"

"I haven't said I wanted to answer an ad," Donna said.

"I know, I know," he said. "I was just wondering if you'd thought about it. You go on to sleep now. Don't worry about it."

"I wasn't going to," she said, turning away from him and pulling the covers up around her shoulders.

He did not say anything about it next day, but late in the afternoon, he told her he wanted them to drive down to Winston-Salem for dinner and a movie.

Donna enjoyed both very much. The movie was a cute comedy, and she enjoyed their meal.

Stanley was charming, and they had a nice conversation as they sat in the restaurant. When they got home and went to bed, he reached for her—and they made love without any mention of the subject that Donna felt constantly hovering over them these days.

On Sunday afternoon, Donna was working on a lesson plan that involved getting her students to draw pictures of their favorite activities.

Stanley walked over and sat down beside her at the kitchen bar. "Donna, honey, I really want us to talk."

She pushed her papers to the side. "OK. What do you want to talk about?"

"I want you to agree that we'll answer one of the ads in my magazine," he said. "You know that I love you, don't you?"

"I guess so. You tell me that you do," she replied.

"Donna, you know that I do. And you know that this does not have anything to do with the fact that I love you. This is just something that I want us to do to add to what we have—not take anything away."

She looked down, refusing to meet his eyes.

He took her limp hand in his and began stroking it. "Will you let us answer one of the ads? I told you before, and I'll say it again. I promise you I won't make you do anything you don't want to do. I just want to meet some of these people. I feel like it'll be exciting to talk to them and see how they feel about … things. Nobody here in town will ever know anything about it. It'll be a secret—our exciting secret life! Don't you see how much fun it'll be? Will you do it with me?"

"What would we have to do?" she asked softly.

His face lit up. "Well, first we'll have to go rent us a post office box, so we'll have a return address. Then we'll write a letter, answering them. And I'll take a picture of you to send to them."

Donna turned pale. "What picture?"

"Oh, it says in the instructions in the magazine that we need to send your picture to the couple and tell them what I look like too so they can decide if they want to meet us."

"You mean, take a naked picture of me, like those of the girls in the ads in the magazine?"

"No, no!" he said. "I can take one of you that doesn't really show anything—with your new camera."

"How can you do that?" Donna clasped her hands together so tightly that her knuckles went white.

He rubbed her shoulder reassuringly. "I can take one of you from behind you, with you looking backward over your shoulder. All they will see is your bare back. That'll work."

Donna swayed. "I don't think I can do this," she whispered.

"Sure, you can, honey! Trust me! You'll see it and approve of it—or I won't send it. I promise." He jumped up from the stool. "Let's do it right now. We'll have it ready to go with the letter. We'll write the letter together. Won't that be fun? Maybe we can get it in the mail this week."

Donna bent over, and her stomach churned. What had she just agreed to do? She thought she was going to throw up. From the look in Stanley's eyes, she knew she was in for hours of cold harassment if she did not comply. She gave him a little nod.

They ended up taking Donna's picture in front of the bathroom mirror. She wrapped a towel over her breasts, and he took the picture from behind her, showing off her smooth, slim back while she held a hairbrush up to her short, dark hair. It was actually pretty artistic, Donna thought, as she looked at their third attempt, which they agreed would be the one they sent. She made sure she ripped up the first two, which she had rejected.

ॐ

On Monday, Stanley slipped away from work, drove to the post office in Winston-Salem, and rented a box. He came home from work, triumphantly holding up the little key for her to see.

Donna felt sick all over again when she saw it. She knew that they were on the verge of making a huge mistake.

That night, Stanley insisted that they compose their letter. The ad Stanley decided to respond to was for a couple who said they lived in Charlotte.

On Saturday, Stanley drove back to the city and checked the post office box. It was empty.

Donna assured him that it was much too early to expect a reply. Their letter would have to go to the magazine, be forwarded to the couple, and then they would have to answer and mail the answer to them. Stanley reluctantly agreed that she was right. There had not been enough time for all that to happen yet.

*C*hapter *T*hree

It took three weeks, but on his fourth trip to the post office box, Stanley returned home, burst through the kitchen door, and waved an envelope in the air.

Donna looked up, startled.

"Look!" he cried. "We got a letter." He put the fat, pale blue envelope down on the kitchen bar.

Donna stared at it as she circled nearer. "What does it say?"

Stanley took off his coat and put it over a stool. "I don't know. I didn't open it. I waited until I got home so we could read it together."

Donna extended her hand, touched the corner of the letter, and drew back.

"Well, why don't you open it?" asked Stanley. "Let's see what it says."

She eyed the envelope warily. Taking a deep breath, Donna took a knife out of the drawer, picked up the letter, and carefully slit the top of the envelope.

Stanley crowded in beside her.

She slowly drew out two sheets of matching blue stationery. She pulled them open, and three photos fell onto the bar.

Stanley grabbed them and fanned them out in his hand. "Look. Oh, wow! She looks good!" He held them down to where Donna could see them.

The picture showed a nice, average-looking young woman in a very small bikini on a sandy beach. Another one showed the same woman, but the photo had been taken indoors. She was sitting on a sofa, nude, smiling tentatively; her genital area was hidden by the placement of her legs, but her breasts were fully exposed. The third shot was of her from the waist up, again showing her outthrust nude breasts. Donna felt her cheeks redden as she looked at the photos, unable to take her eyes off them.

"Go on!" Stanley said, nudging her. "Read the letter out loud!"

Dear Stanley and Donna,

Thank you for answering our ad. We are Diane and Jimmy from Charlotte, and we would like very much to meet you to get to know you and see how things click between us. We, too, are pretty new at this, but we want to meet couples who share our likes and dislikes for friendship and good times. We live in an apartment here in Charlotte and love to entertain. We are happy to hear that you can travel here to meet us, and we look forward to seeing you very soon. We are listing our telephone number at the end of this letter, along with our address. Please call us, and we will arrange the best time for us to get together. We liked the picture of Donna very much. Enclosed are some pics of Diane, and we would love to receive some more of Donna as well. Saturdays are the best time for us to meet. Please call us.

Love,
Diane and Jimmy

Stanley was gazing raptly at the pages in Donna's hand. He looked up at her. "Let's call them!"

"You mean *now*?" Donna stammered.

"Yeah! Why not?"

"Well … we need to think about this," she replied. "We need to think about what we're going to say."

"What's to think about?" Stanley moved over toward the phone. "Let's call them and see when we can go meet them."

Donna followed him over to the telephone. She felt sick.

"What's the number?" Stanley asked.

Donna read off the digits, and he dialed. She could hear the phone ringing on the other end as Stanley held the receiver. Someone said hello.

"Hello," Stanley said smoothly in his best sales voice. "Is this Jimmy?" He paused. "Yes. Well, this is Stanley—Stanley and Donna. We just got your letter today. Is this a good time for us to talk?" He smiled broadly. "Yes, that's right. Stanley and Donna. We liked your letter very much; what would be a good time for us to meet?"

Donna sat down on the floor beside the telephone table, her heart pounding as Stanley continued the conversation. "Next Saturday?" Donna shook her head negatively, but he ignored her. "Yes, I think that would be good. Let me ask Donna. Do you want to say hello to her? She's right here." He held the telephone receiver out to her, gesturing at her, and she reluctantly took it.

"Hello," she said softly, raising the phone to her ear. "Yes, this is Donna. It's nice to hear your voice, too." She listened. "Oh, Diane's not there right now? I'm sorry we missed her too. You want to get together next weekend? Are you sure that will be all right with Diane?" Donna saw Stanley's frown at her question. "Oh, you're sure it will? OK, let me put Stanley back on so you can give him directions to your apartment." She handed the receiver back to

Stanley, and he began writing on the telephone pad. Her palms were sweaty, and she felt ill.

"OK!" Stanley said. "Me too! We'll see you guys next Saturday afternoon, around four o'clock." He hung up the phone and grinned broadly. "All right! We're going to Charlotte next weekend!" He looked like he was ready to dance around the room. "Isn't that great?"

Donna looked up at him with a sinking heart. "Just great," she said flatly. Her heart felt like a stone inside her.

To Donna's dismay, the following days seemed to fly by. On Friday evening, as they were eating dinner, Stanley looked at her with a frown. "You won't believe what happened today," he said.

"What?" Donna paused with a forkful of food halfway to her mouth.

"Sam Jordan called in sick, said he knew he was going to be out today and tomorrow. So, Bill Carson came over and said I need to work tomorrow." Bill Carson was the owner of the dealership, including the used car part of the business, which had been founded by his father more than twenty years ago. The older Carson had retired five years ago and left the business to his son.

Donna's heart leaped. "Really? Then we won't get to go to Charlotte?" She concentrated on hiding the jolt of happiness she felt.

"Not on your life! I'm scheduled to be off, and I'm going to be. I told him that I already had plans to be out of town that couldn't be postponed." He frowned.

Her heart dropped again. "What did he say?" Donna asked, holding her breath.

"Well, he wasn't happy, to say the least, but they managed to schedule around both of us." Stanley took her hand and squeezed it. "No way was I going to let anything happen so that we couldn't make our trip tomorrow."

Donna gave him a weak smile.

§⊚

On Saturday morning, Stanley was underfoot all morning. Donna knew he was nervous about going to meet the couple in Charlotte, and she was filled with dread, wishing with all her heart that she had not agreed to do this.

By lunchtime, she was ready to scream.

He asked her—for the third time—what she planned to wear.

"I don't know!" she cried. "Maybe I'll just stay here and let you go by yourself!"

He held up his hands. "I'm sorry. I just want us to make a good impression, that's all."

"So, what do you think I should wear?"

"Something sexy," he said.

"Don't worry about it," Donna said wearily. "I'll do my best to look nice."

"I know you will," Stanley said.

§⊚

At Stanley's urging, they began making preparations to leave shortly after noon.

Donna went into the hall bathroom and showered, leaving Stanley the use of their small bath off the master bedroom. She toweled off, applied deodorant, and brushed her short, straight hair, quickly blowing it dry. She had spent some time thinking about what she would wear since Stanley was so anxious about their appearances. All the things she had been wearing to teach in seemed too dowdy; she had chosen them for that very reason. She wanted to appear older and more mature to belie her natural youthful appearance. At only five feet two inches, her petite figure made her look younger anyway, and she had gravitated toward more matronly clothing. She had discovered, hanging in the back of her closet, one of her all-time favorite dresses. It was a black and royal blue print polyester knit dress with a fitted bodice, a full A-line skirt, and big balloon sleeves that ended in tight cuffs at the wrists. She'd always loved its silky fabric that clung and caressed her and the short flirty skirt that ended about two inches above her knees. She pulled on her pantyhose and slipped on a pair of black pumps with medium-high heels. Looking at herself in the full-length mirror on the inside of the bathroom door, she smiled with satisfaction. She always felt pretty when she wore this dress.

She walked back to their bedroom to find that Stanley was having a hard time deciding what he would wear. On the bed, there were three shirts that he had obviously tried on and discarded. He was dressed, standing in front of the mirror over the sink, messing with his hair. Stanley's light brown hair was beginning to recede, much to his dismay, making him look older than his years, and he spent a lot of time trying to comb it in a way to disguise its thinning. He was not really a handsome man, only about five ten, and on the bony side of slim. His average-looking face was long and thin. *He could be quite charming,* Donna thought, *if only he'd smile more.* He was beginning to get frown lines, and creases were beginning to form beside his mouth. He looked at her through the open doorway as she came into the bedroom. "How do I look?" he asked. "Is this outfit all right?"

"Of course, it is. You look very nice," Donna replied.

He put down his hairbrush. "Well, I guess we ought to get going. We don't want to be late."

"Oh, we have plenty of time," she said. "It only takes a little over an hour to drive down there, and it's not even one o'clock yet. Do you have the directions?"

He patted his pants pocket. "Right here. I just want us to have plenty of time in case we get lost or something."

"We'll be fine."

ॐ

A few minutes later, Stanley insisted that they put on their coats and get into the car, and they were on their way toward the interstate.

As Donna had predicted, they reached Charlotte in just over an hour. Following the directions that Jimmy had provided, they drove to the apartment complex with no trouble at all. Because they were almost two hours early, Donna suggested that they drive back over toward the interstate and stop at a fast-food place to kill some time. They ordered sodas and settled into a booth, and the time passed very slowly as they waited.

Finally, Stanley decided that it was time to drive back to the apartment complex. He stood up, and Donna followed as he headed out to the car. They got in and made the short drive. Although it was still a quarter to four, they walked from the parking area and made their way to find the apartment number written on their directions. Stanley took a deep breath and rapped on the door.

Donna's eyes traveled quickly over the smiling man who opened the door. He was a few inches taller than Stanley, and he had broad shoulders and brown hair. "Hello. Are you the Porters?"

"Yes," Stanley said, moving aside slightly. "I'm Stanley, and this is Donna, my wife."

Donna saw the man's eyes go from Stanley to her, and his eyes lit up as he looked at her. "Hello. I'm Jimmy. Y'all come on in." He stepped backward, swinging the door open for them to enter. "Diana will be out in just a minute. Let me take your coats." He closed the door behind them.

Jimmy took their coats, slipped them neatly onto empty hangers, and led them into the living room. "Diane? Our guests are here."

Donna recognized the woman from her picture in the magazine. She was about a head taller than Donna, with shoulder-length light brown hair and wide blue eyes, and although she was attractive enough, there was nothing spectacular about her, Donna decided.

Everybody exchanged hellos, and they got settled on the sofa and matching side chair. The men quickly found a mutual topic of conversation in college basketball, and Donna and Diane simply sat, listening, as they discussed who would take the title this year. When the conversation moved on to work, Stanley told them that he worked at a car dealership, and Donna said that she was a secretary. She and Stanley had discussed this earlier, and they had agreed it might be safer if no one associated with their new interest knew she was a teacher. Diane said that she did bookkeeping work, and Jimmy said he worked at a savings and loan.

Diane said, "Um ... I hope it won't hurt your feelings if we don't ask you to spend the night. Our little boy is spending the night with his grandparents, but they're bringing him back early in the morning. I'm sorry."

"Oh, no! That's fine with us," Donna said quickly. "We planned to drive back tonight anyway. Isn't that right, Stanley?"

"Oh, yes, sure," Stanley said.

Diane visibly relaxed. "Oh, good. I'm sorry."

"No, that's quite all right," Donna said.

Stanley said, "Oh, by the way, we're just getting started at this. We were wondering if you know any good couples we should meet in our area."

Jimmy said, "Yeah. We don't know a whole lot of people, but I've got two couples in mind who we met. They are really great people. I think you'd like them. You didn't happen to bring the magazine with you, did you? I'll point out their ads to you."

"As a matter of fact, I did," Stanley said. "It's out in the car. I'll get it." He left and returned in five minutes, carrying his copy of *Choice*.

Jimmy took it and began turning pages. "Here," he said, pointing. "This is Eric and Jennie. They live in a town east of Winston-Salem. What is the name of it, Diane? I think it starts with a K."

"Kernersville," said Diane.

"Yes, that's right. Kernersville. Do you know where that is?"

Stanley nodded, marking the ad.

Jimmy turned the page. "And here. This one. This couple is David and Pam. We really liked them, didn't we, Diane? They're from down close to Chapel Hill. You'll want to meet them too."

"That's great!" Stanley said. "Thank you so much."

"Oh, you're welcome. When you write to them, tell them that you met us. I'm not supposed to give you their address or phone numbers. You'll need to get in touch with them through the magazine. That's the rules, and that's how it needs to work."

"I understand," Stanley said. "Thanks again for your help."

Jimmy cleared his throat. "Well, Diane and I talked before you all got here. We thought we could all go out for dinner. Maybe we could make it a real early dinner someplace so we can come back here and have a lot of time together to, uh, get better acquainted after we eat."

Stanley brightened. "Yeah, that sounds great."

Donna saw Jimmy looking at her avidly. She shifted uncomfortably and glanced at Diane, who was staring down at her folded hands in her lap.

"Why don't we go find us a restaurant right now?" said Jimmy.

"OK!" Stanley said, getting to his feet. "That all right with you, honey?"

"Um, sure. I guess so," Donna mumbled.

They all got to their feet and retrieved their coats.

Jimmy drove them all to a nearby Friday's, a popular, moderately priced chain restaurant, a few blocks from the apartment. When they were seated, the waitress asked for their drink orders.

Jimmy and Stanley asked for beers.

"Donna will probably want a soda, right, Donna?" Stanley said.

"No," Donna said. "I want a whiskey sour."

Stanley looked at her with surprise on his face.

Donna kept her eyes downcast. *I really need a drink*, she thought.

"I want a drink too," said Diane. "I want a daiquiri."

"Coming right up," the waitress said, moving away.

The drinks arrived, and they chatted as they decided on their food orders.

Donna drained her small glass, and the whiskey tasted strong as it went down her throat.

"Do you want another one?" asked the waitress.

Donna nodded, and she moved away to get it.

The men were soon talking sports again.

Donna finished her new drink and saw that Diane was sipping slowly on her first one.

When the food arrived, Donna nervously pushed it around her plate, unable to force it down. No one seemed to notice; Stanley and Jimmy were heartily enjoying theirs, and Diane was steadily eating.

The waitress took her empty drink glass away and thoughtfully brought her another. She picked it up, and the liquid slid smoothly down her throat.

Diane slid her chair back from the table. "Do you want to go with me to find the ladies' room?"

Donna nodded, took her napkin from her lap, and put it on the table. She walked carefully, following Diane as she threaded her way between the tables toward the corner of the restaurant. She was definitely feeling the effects of the unaccustomed drinks.

They each took a stall and then met back at the sink. No one else was in the bathroom.

Washing her hands, Diane met Donna's eyes in the mirror. "So, what do you think of us?"

"Wh-what do you mean?" Donna said.

Diane's expression was very serious. "Jimmy likes you a lot. I can tell. You're just the type he really goes for … so petite and pretty. Do you want to swing with him tonight?"

Donna's mind felt fuzzy from the drinks. "I … don't know …" She tried to concentrate. "Do you enjoy this? Do *you* want to do it? Do you want to have sex with my husband?"

Diane's lips trembled, and tears welled in her eyes. "I just want Jimmy to be happy," she said.

Donna tried to clear her mind as she looked sharply at the girl. "Are you doing this for him? Because Jimmy wants you to?"

Diane nodded miserably. "It's OK. I mean, your husband seems real nice. And I think *he* wants to—"

"Look, Diane," Donna interrupted. "It's OK if you don't want to. It really is! I'm not too crazy about this whole idea, to tell you the truth."

"No! Jimmy really wants to be with you. I know he does! And I do like Stanley. So, it's OK. I'm good with it."

Donna shook her head emphatically, fighting to think clearly.

"No. We'll just go back to your place and tell them we don't want to do this—and Stanley and I will drive back home."

Diane drew back. "No. Please. I really want us to swing with you guys. Please, Donna. Please do it."

Donna stared at her. "Why?" she asked quietly.

Diane hung her head.

"Is Jimmy making you do this?"

"No!"

"Then why?"

"I just love him so much," Diane's voice was so low that Donna could barely hear her. "I want us to be together, but he wants to have sex with other women—as well as with me. If I don't go along with it, he'll leave me." Tears spilled out of her eyes. "And if he does that, I'll just die!"

Donna felt a rush of sympathy. "He won't do that," she said.

"Yes, he will! He told me so. 'Swing—or I'll divorce you!' That's what he said!"

Donna put her arms around Diane. She didn't know what to say.

"But we do it in separate rooms," said Diane. "That's the only way I can handle it. I know that some couples like to be in the same room, but I don't want to see Jimmy with another woman. He's OK with that." She gave a small laugh. "He still gets what he wants."

After a moment, Diane pulled out of Donna's embrace and straightened up. She dabbed at her eyes with a paper towel. "I'm sorry. I didn't mean to say all that."

"I'm glad you did," Donna said. "What are we going to do?"

Diane's lips curved upward in an obviously fake smile. "Why, we're going to swing tonight! We're going to have a wonderful time. Isn't that right, Donna? Oh, please do this … it's nothing, really. Please say you'll do it."

Nothing? How can she say it's nothing? Donna took in a deep breath and watched as Diane took out her compact and repaired where her tears had messed up her makeup.

Diane gave her a rueful smile, and they left the ladies' room and walked back to their table.

The men were smiling broadly as they joined them. "We bought you girls some fresh drinks," Jimmy said happily.

Donna sat down and picked up her new whiskey sour.

"Let's make a toast," Stanley said, picking up his glass.

Everyone clinked their glasses together across the table.

"Here's to new friends and a wonderful evening," Stanley said.

Donna finished off her drink. She felt it hit her almost empty stomach, and the warmth begin to spread out through her.

"Are we ready to go back to the apartment?" Jimmy asked shortly afterward. He and Stanley put money on the table, and they all got up and pulled on their coats.

Donna stumbled slightly as they walked away from the table. Jimmy put his arm around her, steadying her, and Stanley moved to Diane's side, walking beside her.

Stanley got into the back seat and pulled Diane in close beside him. Donna hesitated, and then she sat down in the passenger seat beside Jimmy. As Jimmy started the car and pulled away, she breathed deeply, fighting the dizziness, now regretting the drinks she had consumed without eating. She glanced toward the back seat. Stanley had his arms around Diane and was kissing her. His hands were moving over her body under her coat. Quickly, she averted her eyes, and Jimmy's hand fell on her leg, his fingers gently squeezing. She closed her eyes, and then they were pulling into the parking slot at the apartment.

They went inside, and coats were removed and hung in the closet. The four of them walked into the living room. Stanley was beside Diane, his hands roving over her body, and she was passively letting it happen.

Jimmy took her arm and led her over to the sofa. "Diane," he said over his shoulder, "why don't you show Stanley our bedroom? Donna and I'll stay out here."

Diane took Stanley by the hand and led him out of the room.

Donna opened her mouth to speak, but Jimmy bent his head down, and his mouth was on hers, kissing her deeply. He put his arms around her and gathered her up against his body, urging her down onto the sofa. She felt his hand fumbling with the zipper at the back of her dress, pulling it down. She brought her arms up against him, feebly pushing at him, but her back was against the seat of the sofa. Her head was spinning, and her arms felt like they were made of lead. She felt Jimmy peel her dress down her body and over her legs, discarding it. His body was on top of her, and his hands were moving over her. She was drifting; everything felt strange and unreal.

She heard him whisper "You are so beautiful." She felt his hands caressing the small mounds of her naked breasts. *Naked? How could they be naked?* She drifted off again. Later, she felt something hard and hot between her legs, and then his fingers were parting her. "God! You are so tight. So little and tight! This K-Y will help." He was rubbing something cold on her, and then she felt him pushing into her; she hovered on the edge of consciousness, realizing what was happening, but unable to do anything about it.

The next thing that she knew, she heard Stanley's voice calling her name. "Donna, wake up!" He was shaking her gently. She tried to raise her head, but it lolled back down against the pillows on the sofa.

Someone was lifting her body. "She's really out of it," she heard someone say.

"I guess she had too much to drink," she heard Stanley say. "Here, help me get her dressed."

She was being tugged at, and she felt the whisper of fabric against her skin. "Don't bother with her pantyhose," someone said. "You'll never get them on her. Just put them in your pocket."

Donna slitted one eye and peered out. She felt like a rag doll. Stanley was holding her upright, and her coat was being pulled up her arms. The next thing she knew, she was in a car, and it was moving. The heater was blowing out the most delicious warm air, and Donna drifted back to sleep.

$\mathcal{E}\mathcal{O}$

The next thing she knew, she cracked her eyes open, and the light hurt her eyes. Her head felt like someone was beating on it with sledgehammers. She peered through slitted eyes and discovered that she was in her own bed at home. Her stomach roiled, and her head hurt so bad. She closed her eyes again, hoping the sickness would go away.

Later, she moved experimentally. To her dismay, she realized, as her body moved against the sheets, that she was in bed, naked. She moved her head again and groaned out loud.

"Well, are you finally awake?" Stanley asked.

She slitted her eyes again and saw him standing in the doorway with a mug of steaming coffee in his hand. "What happened?" she croaked; her voice raspy.

He laughed. "You got really drunk last night. You must have passed out after you and Jimmy had sex. We got you into your clothes, and I brought you home and put you to bed."

I what? Her head pounded as she struggled to put the pieces of memory together. Her hand flew up to cover her mouth in dismay as horror washed over her.

He sat down on the edge of the bed beside her. "Don't worry

about it," he said. "We all had a good time. Everything was cool. Maybe we'll get together and swing with them again."

Donna stared at him. "What?"

"Jimmy said you were great. And I know I sure had a good time with Diane. When we finished, we came back out into the living room, and you were sound asleep on the sofa. I couldn't get you awake enough to dress and leave, so we all helped you into your clothes, and I drove us home. When I got here, I carried you into the house, and then I took off your clothes and put you into bed."

Donna covered her face with her hands. She felt the heat of her mortified blush all the way from her face to her chest. "What time is it?" she whispered.

Stanley looked at the alarm clock. "It's a little past one o'clock in the afternoon."

"Oh, God!"

"Don't worry about it. Do you want something to eat?"

Her stomach roiled at the very thought of food. "No!"

"I've never seen you get drunk before."

"I've never *been* drunk before!"

He grinned. "Well, you have now."

"And … and are you telling me that I had sex with … with that man? With that Jimmy person? I just don't remember!" She clutched her head and moaned.

Stanley raised his eyebrows. "Evidently, he liked it. He said you were good."

"Oh, God! Oh, God! I never got drunk before in my life! And I never had sex with anybody but you!"

Stanley stood up. "Well, you had a couple of firsts last night then, didn't you?" He patted her shoulder. "Don't worry about it. Everything turned out just great. Everybody had a great time! And we got some leads on some more couples—we'll have to answer their ads this week. I can't wait to do this again. Just don't drink so much next time, OK?" He walked out of the room.

Donna closed her eyes, her head pounding, about to throw up as the enormity of the situation began to soak in. *How could this have happened?*

⬥

Donna pulled into her usual parking spot at school on Monday morning and walked to her classroom. Noisy conversations, punctuated by the occasional shriek, filled the air as the children made their way into the school. She still felt sluggish and headachy. Her physical hangover was gone, but she still couldn't believe what had happened. She still didn't have a clear memory of all the details, but everything inside her shrank from what she did remember. How could she have let that man touch her like that? Use her like that?

And Stanley! She wanted to scream every time she pictured him with Diane: stroking her, kissing her, and having sex with her! It wasn't jealousy, she told herself. It was beyond jealousy. It was shame and outrage and … what? She tried to put it out of her mind. She couldn't think about it anymore. Not now. This was what was real, this was sanity, this was work. She had to concentrate and take care of her students. She took a deep breath and told herself to relax. She was in her favorite place in the whole world, and she felt she had come home after a long journey.

The bell rang as she stowed her purse in her desk drawer, and her first graders began settling into their assigned seats.

She bestowed what she hoped was a bright and happy smile upon them. "Good morning, class!"

"Good morning, Mrs. Porter," they chorused in response, just as she had taught them.

I have to do this, she thought, trying to concentrate. *This is my life, my real life. I have to forget about that other stuff. I have to.*

Chapter Four

When Stanley got home from work that evening, as soon as they finished eating, he insisted upon taking more Polaroid shots similar of Donna. He sat down and composed letters in response to the two ads that Jimmy and Diane had pointed out in the magazine.

Donna didn't know what to do. She was still trying to get her mind around what had happened.

For a change, Stanley was in a great mood. He wasn't harassing her and yelling incessantly.

She wanted to talk to him and tell him how upset she truly was. Several times, she opened her mouth to say something, but she did not speak. It was so good not to be railed at, and she really needed the time to figure this out. She just went along with him, letting him take her picture and write the letters.

Two weeks passed, then three, and there was no response. Donna knew that Stanley had made several trips to Winston-Salem to check his post office box, with increasing frequency in the past few days, and she was beginning to hope that they would not receive any answers to his letters this time. *Maybe he will give up on this crazy idea of his.*

As the days passed, she let the matter fade from her thoughts, pushing it back into her mind and concentrating on projects for her class. Her first graders were coloring Easter eggs and bunnies, and she set up a bulletin board with pictures of spring flowers to teach them the names of each: tulips, daffodils, hyacinths, and daisies.

One evening, Stanley came hurrying into the kitchen from his car. He was grinning like a maniac, and he reached into his coat pocket and triumphantly pulled out an envelope.

When he held it aloft and waved it in the air, Donna knew immediately what it was. Her heart sank.

"One of the couples answered us," he said eagerly. "Let's see which one it was."

Donna stood mutely beside him as he sat down at the counter and ripped the envelope open, pulling out a sheet of paper with three photos inside the fold. He spread out the Polaroid shots in front of him.

Donna looked down and saw that two of the photos were of a very pretty, slender blonde. She gasped when she realized that the woman was unabashedly nude in one of them, smiling toward the camera, and the third was a full-frontal view of a well-built young man who was also naked, happily grinning as he displayed himself to the camera.

She heard the hiss of Stanley's intake of breath. "Whoa!" he exclaimed softly. His eyes were gleaming as he picked up the hand-written note. Reading quickly, he put it down and picked up the woman's nude photo and studied it. "They want to meet us! They say that they prefer to drive here." He picked up the other photo of the woman, a nice headshot, her head thrown back, laughing, and he gingerly moved the man's photo with the tip of his finger. "Do you think we should take a nude picture of me to send to them?"

"No!" cried Donna, aghast.

He looked searchingly at her. "Maybe you're right," he said quietly. "I don't look as good as he does."

"It isn't that," Donna said quickly. "I just don't think it's a good idea, period, to be sending naked photos through the mail."

"Maybe you're right." His expression brightened. "Let's call them up right now and see when they can come up here!"

"Wait ... wait," Donna stammered.

"What for? Let's call them tonight!"

"At least wait until after dinner," she said, glancing uneasily at the photos.

"OK. We can plan what we're going to say while we're eating. Look at her! Isn't she pretty? They both look like nice folks. Maybe we can get together with them this weekend!"

"Well, let's see what they say first. Maybe they already have plans." Donna licked her lips nervously.

"I hope not. I can't wait to meet them." Stanley picked up the woman's nude photo again.

Donna went to get plates for the table. "Which one of the couples was that?"

Stanley looked at the note. "Pam and David. They're the ones from down near Chapel Hill."

Donna scarcely had time to start the dishwasher after dinner before Stanley was dialing the number from the note. She walked slowly from the kitchen to the living room.

Stanley was sitting with the phone receiver to his ear. He was talking and smiling happily. He waved her to sit near him as he continued his conversation. "Yes," he said finally. "OK, David, I'll put her on. She's right here." He covered the mouthpiece with his hand. "David's putting Pam on the line—she wants to talk to you," he said in a stage whisper, handing her the phone.

"Hello?" Donna said softly.

"Hi," a warm, female voice said. "I'm Pam! Is this Donna? It's so good to meet you."

"Yes, I'm Donna. It's nice to meet you too."

They exchanged pleasantries, and Donna was surprised at the amiability and quick humor she found as she and Pam continued to talk. In spite of herself, she felt like she was beginning to relax. Pam seemed so warm and likeable.

"So, Stanley says you guys might be OK with our getting together this weekend," Pam said.

Donna's stomach knotted again. "Uh, yes," Donna replied. "That is, if you don't have something planned." She mentally crossed her fingers.

"No! We'd love to drive up there and meet you!" Pam said.

"Let me put Stanley on," Donna said. "He can give you details." She quickly passed the receiver back to him and closed her eyes as Stanley began giving directions to their house.

When Stanley hung up the phone, he was beaming. "All right!" he cried. "They're driving up here on Saturday afternoon. I told David we'd grill some steaks."

Donna nodded mutely.

Stanley retrieved the letter and studied the photos some more.

Donna mercilessly cleaned her house every evening that week, using her nervous energy to mop, dust, and shine. Somehow, Stanley had pulled strings at work and did not have to be there on Saturday. She did not ask him how he had managed to do that since Saturdays were normally the busiest days at the car lot.

Saturday morning arrived, a crisp, sunny day. After breakfast, Donna went around rechecking everything she could think of:

straightening the freshly laundered towels hanging in the bathroom and fluffing the pillows on the bed in the guest room since the couple had let them know that they would be staying overnight.

Stanley went to a convenience store to buy a twelve-pack of beer. When he returned and stowed the beverages in the refrigerator, he suggested that she go ahead and shower and get dressed. The nervous tension in his voice told her that he was as keyed up as she was.

When she finished in the shower, he took it over, and she took her time dressing and applying her minimal makeup. A quick application of mascara and lipstick was all she ever used; her short, pixie haircut required only running a hairbrush through it, and she was finished. She wandered back into the living room, yearning for something to do to pass the time. She could always work on paperwork or planning for her classes, but she dared not get any of that out since they had agreed to conceal the fact that she was a teacher. She picked up a magazine and leafed through it, trying to find something to occupy her mind.

A while later, Stanley came out of the bedroom, dressed and ready. He sat down in the side chair, and they waited. Neither of them initiated a conversation.

Finally, they heard a car coming up the driveway. They both got to their feet and went out the front door as the car stopped in front of the garage.

A tall, youthful young man and a slim blonde woman approached, smiling happily.

"Hi," the man said.

"Hello," Stanley said, extending his hand. "I'm Stanley. You must be David and Pam."

"Sure are!"

They shook hands.

Pam put her arms around Stanley in a hug, and then she turned to Donna and embraced her warmly. David was right behind, and he hugged her as well. Both were grinning happily, their blue eyes guileless and friendly.

"Well, welcome to our house. Come on in," Stanley said.

"Can I get you something to drink?" Donna asked as they entered the living room.

"A glass of water would be great," said Pam, taking off her coat.

Stanley took their coats. "I've got some beer in the refrigerator," he said to David. "Want a beer?"

"Sure! Sounds good."

Donna put the drinks on a tray in the kitchen while Stanley hung up the coats in the hall closet. Everyone was seated when she carried the tray into the room and handed the drinks around.

"This is a pretty house," said Pam, taking her glass of water and looking around the room.

"Thank you," replied Donna, taking a seat beside her on the sofa.

Everyone began making light conversation, and Donna was surprised to find much of her tension disappearing as they continued to talk. Pam and David seemed very laid-back and friendly, laughing easily and totally relaxed. Pam was pretty, radiating an unreserved attitude, and David's big build and aw-shucks demeanor made Donna think of a good-natured farmer. *I actually like them,* Donna thought in surprise.

In what seemed like no time at all, they were talking easily.

When the men started talking sports, Donna caught Pam's eye. "Would you like something else to drink?" Donna asked.

Pam nodded. "Sure. Let me help you get it." They got up and went into the kitchen.

"I really do like your house," Pam said, looking around as they got beers and sodas out of the refrigerator.

Donna smiled. "Thanks."

Pam hesitated, standing next to Donna, and put her hand on Donna's arm and looked at her kindly. "You guys haven't been swinging very long, have you?"

Donna bit her lip, shaking her head.

Pam smiled. "I didn't think so. I noticed that you seemed sorta nervous, and I was pretty sure that was why."

Donna turned her big, brown eyes up to Pam. "You're only the second couple we've met. Please don't think that—"

"I understand perfectly!" Pam said quietly. "I felt the same way when we first started." She smiled warmly. "Don't worry about it. We aren't going to pressure you in any way. Let's just relax and enjoy getting to know each other, OK?"

Donna expelled a big sigh. "OK," she said, and they carried the drinks into the living room.

After a while, Stanley suggested that they start the charcoal in the grill. He and David went out onto the small patio, and Donna and Pam went into the kitchen to assemble the rest of the meal. It was too chilly to eat outside, so they began setting the table and making the salad.

Stanley came in and got the steaks out of the refrigerator where they had been marinating.

When the men carried in the platter of still-sizzling steaks, they all took seats and began eating.

About halfway through the meal, Stanley paused, his fork halfway to his mouth. "Say, David, can I ask you and Pam a question about something you said in your ad?"

"Sure." David raised an eyebrow. "What do you want to ask?"

"Well," Stanley paused, and waited until he had the attention of all three of them. "Exactly what does it mean when you say in the ad, talking about Pam, 'can be bi'?"

David grinned, and Pam giggled. "It means Pam can be bisexual—you know, do a scene with the girl—if she feels compatible with her," David said.

"Do a scene? What does that mean?" asked Donna.

"It means they make love to each other," David said, smiling.

Donna felt her mouth open in astonishment.

Stanley grinned and finished taking his bite of steak. "I thought so," he said. "I thought that's what you meant."

David looked at Donna slyly. "Yeah. Donna, I've been watching you sneaking those looks at Pam!"

"But … I haven't …" Donna said.

"How about it, hon?" David said to Pam. "Are you in the mood to get with Donna?"

She smiled at him. "Maybe," she said teasingly, giving him a flirtatious look.

David clapped his hands together. "Oh, man! Stanley! We are in for such a hot night! You haven't lived until you've seen two beautiful, hot chicks like Pam and Donna going at it! Oh, wow!"

Donna was stunned. She looked from the grinning David to Stanley. His eyes were shining, and he looked like he was about to lick his lips in anticipation.

Pam was sitting quietly with a smile curving her full lips. When their eyes met, Pam raised a finger and winked at Donna.

Donna stifled the protest that was about to pour out of her as Pam looked hard at her, as though trying to send a message through her big blue eyes. After a few frozen seconds, Donna put down her fork. Her throat felt closed, and she was unable to take another bite.

Everyone else resumed eating.

After what seemed like hours, they had all finished the meal.

The men put their napkins on the table and stood.

"Come on, David," Stanley said. "Let's go make sure the fire's out in the grill, and I'll show you what I've done out in the garage while the girls clean up in here."

Donna took a deep breath and stood. Pam hurried to her side as the men went out the kitchen door. She put a hand on her arm and captured Donna's eyes with her wide blue ones. "Hey," she said in a low voice. "I saw that look you had earlier. Let me explain to you how this works!"

Donna stared up at her mutely.

"Don't look so scared!" Pam smiled reassuringly. "It's like a game. It's fun … really, it is! We just act like we're making love to each other, and it turns the guys on like you wouldn't believe! Have you ever kissed another girl?"

Donna stared up at her in frightened silence and shook her head.

Pam laughed softly. "It's kinda nice … and as a woman, I know exactly what feels good and what doesn't! Because I know what feels good *to me*. And if you don't really come, then all you have to do is moan and pretend that you do. Just act like you're really coming. The guys are so worked up by then that they're so ready that they're about to burst! They have the most wonderful time that they've ever had in their whole lives. I'll take the lead on this, and you just relax and play along. Are you game for this?"

Donna took a deep breath and opened her mouth, but no words came out. She was torn between her guilt and the easy camaraderie that was so rare and precious in her life.

Pam gave her a hug. "It'll be fun, Donna. Let's do it. Let's do it for the guys. Come on! Let me help you get this mess cleaned up, and we can go into the living room and get things ready. Do you think we could make a fire in the fireplace? David and I always insist on swinging together in the same room, and it would be so much fun if we could all be together on the floor in front of a fire. Can we do that?"

Donna gave a small nod. "I guess so," she said in a small voice.

"Good!" Pam said. "Let's get the dishes cleared up." She began gathering up the plates.

When the men came back in, Donna and Pam had the kitchen cleaned up and had carried several blankets into the living room.

Pam said, "Stanley, will you be a love and build us a fire in the fireplace?"

He looked around, saw what they were doing, and smiled happily. "I sure will! David, want to help me carry in some wood?"

"You bet!" David followed him back outside.

When the fire was blazing and crackling, Pam began spreading out the blankets on the floor.

Stanley and David moved the sofa back, creating a large open area by the hearth. Stanley switched off all the lights except for one lamp on a table in the corner, and the room became dim, the firelight creating a soft glow in the room.

Pam kneeled beside the hearth and reached up to Donna, taking both of her hands and pulling her gently downward. "Come here," she said softly.

Donna sank to her knees, facing Pam, and Pam placed her hands on either side of Donna's face. She bent her head forward, and Donna felt Pam's lips on hers, strangely soft, as Pam embraced her and pulled her closer, the kiss deepening.

David and Stanley dropped down to sit side by side on the pushed-back sofa, their eyes glued to what was happening in front of them.

Pam ended the kiss, and her eyes gripped Donna's hypnotically as her hands moved to unzip Donna's dress. The zipper parted, and without shifting her gaze, Pam pushed the garment off Donna's shoulders to puddle on the floor. She reached around Donna's back and opened the clasp on her bra, pulling it forward and down her arms.

Donna unresistingly and obediently let Pam remove the bra, exposing her small, perky breasts. There was an audible intake of breath from both men as Pam bent forward and kissed Donna again. When she ended the kiss, she lowered her head to gently kiss each exposed breast in turn. She gently sucked on the second one, and Donna closed her eyes and arched her neck backward. Pam's lips moved up to place a line of kisses over and up Donna's neck, and then she claimed her lips once more.

This time, when the kiss ended, Pam urged Donna to her feet. Moving quickly, she removed her own clothes down to where she wore only a pair of lacy black bikini panties. Then she placed her hands on Donna's waist and urged her to step free of her dress, then sink back down to the floor. Her hands moved in gentle caresses over Donna's body, followed by her lips. She urged Donna to her back, hovering over her, again caressing her breasts, and kissing them.

Pam sat up, hooked her thumbs into the sides of her own panties, slid them down her legs, and discarded them. She positioned herself between Donna's legs and tugged Donna's panties off. As she did so, there came a wordless sound from the sofa, and a flurry of movement as the men began undressing. Pam spread Donna's legs wide and brought her face down to her exposed crotch. With a tiny moan of pleasure, she spread the intimate folds wide and lowered her face, her tongue penetrating them.

Donna's eyes flew open as a wave of sensation curled in her lower abdomen. Pam's tongue was insistently probing and suddenly found its target, nuzzling and stroking the tiny button of nerves inside her. Feelings Donna had never before experienced radiated outward from where Pam's tongue unrelentingly attacked her pleasure spot. Stanley had certainly never done anything like this, and Donna had come to him inexperienced and innocent. She realized that her body was moving instinctively in counterpoint as Pam's mouth claimed her. Frightened by the overwhelming sensations she was starting to feel, Donna moaned and thrust her pelvis upward, interrupting contact, as she pretended to come.

Immediately, Stanley was beside them on the floor, pulling Pam away, his hands and mouth claiming her, and Donna felt David's harder mouth come down on hers, as he positioned his body over her, fingers invading between her legs, his erect penis pressing against her stomach. She craned her head sideways and saw her husband situated between Pam's legs, his body moving rhythmically, his face a mask of sexual desire. David was entering her, as well, and he was pushing deep, invading, taking every inch of her. She brought her legs up, scissoring around his waist as he buffeted against her, enthusiastically pillaging her.

When he eased himself down beside her, spent, he smiled boyishly. "Whoa, Donna. That was great," he said happily. He reached over and took Pam's hand. "Was it good for you too, sweetheart?"

"Oh, yeah," she heard Pam's voice. "It was really, really good."

Later, they all got up, piled up the discarded clothing on the sofa, and gathered up the blankets. They spread one over the sofa and sat down, naked.

Stanley hurried out to the kitchen, coming back with beers for the men and sodas for the women.

"Wow," Stanley said, passing around the cold beverages. "That was unbelievable!"

"Next time will be even better," Pam said and took a swallow of her drink.

"Don't see how it could be," Stanley said.

David just smiled.

They made conversation for a while, and someone suggested that they should get a shower.

Donna led them back to the main bathroom off the hall, and she and Stanley went to the master bath off their bedroom. She made sure that soap and towels were at hand, and when Stanley finished in their shower, she stepped in, letting the hot water wash over her as she leaned back against the tile wall. When she got her towel and stepped out, she found everyone in their bedroom.

"Glad you've got a king-size bed in here," David said with his big grin. "Pam and I like to be together, as we told you before. We can all fit on the bed."

Donna's eyes widened with surprise. She hadn't expected this. There was some confusion as they sorted out the positions. She took the left-hand side edge, David got next to her, Pam positioned herself between David and Stanley, who was on the outside right-hand side of the bed. They all stretched out, and everyone had enough room, even though it was somewhat restricted. Stanley snapped off the lamp beside him, and Donna turned on her side, facing outward, and when everyone settled down, she drifted off to sleep.

Sometime later, she was awakened by muted voices and movement of the bed. Lying still, she stared into the darkness, trying to comprehend what was taking place. David was semi-upright beside her, and she realized that he was having sex with Pam. Suddenly, however, as his body moved backward toward her, and the bed rocked as the squishy sound of intercourse reached her ears, she realized, with shock, that David was kissing Pam, while her hand enclosed and masturbated him and that Stanley was positioned between Pam's spread legs, pounding into her again.

She held her body absolutely still, not wanting them to know she was awake. A pang of jealousy shot through her, and she was overwhelmed by a feeling of sheer isolation. She neither wanted to be a part of this—nor for them to know she was aware of what they were doing. Scalding tears ran out of her eyes to be absorbed by the soft pillow as the sex went on and on, seemingly endlessly. Never had she felt so alone; jealousy and a terrible sorrow formed a hard black knot inside her as she held her body rigid and struggled not to make the slightest movement. Her husband, the man she had pledged her whole life to, was so freely giving what she longed for with her whole being to another woman—and one he had met only hours before.

Finally, after what seemed like hours, the moans and wordless cries ceased, and they stretched out on the bed and grew quiet. Their peaceful breathing soon signaled that once more they slept, but it was a long time before Donna joined them.

But sleep she did, and she was awakened by the sounds of people getting out of bed.

David stirred beside her and grinned down at her. "Morning, beautiful."

"Good morning." She managed a smile.

"They've got the shower in here," he said. "Let's you and me go hop in the other one, down the hall."

She looked at him, seeing no way to get out of this. "Sure," she said, sliding her legs off the side of the bed.

He hooked an arm around her as they went down the hall to the other bathroom. Donna got another set of towels out of the linen closet and turned.

David had started the water spraying down into the tub, and he was standing inches away. He tilted her head back, bent down, and kissed her, his big hands sliding down her body to cup her bare buttocks and lift her up against him. With a laugh, he stepped into the tub, carrying her with him. The water covered them, and David grabbed the bar of soap, rubbing it over their bodies playfully. He pressed it between her legs, rubbing it back and forth. "Here," he said, pressing it into her hand. "You do me." He stood there expectantly, hands to his sides, waiting for her to do what he'd asked.

Donna took a washcloth and lathered it thoroughly. She ran it over David's chest as he stood passively, obviously enjoying himself thoroughly.

He captured her hand that was holding the soap and moved it down to his crotch. "Go ahead, wash me," he said softly.

She moved the soap against him as he began to harden. Donna felt totally disconnected, moving reflexively, almost detached.

Abruptly he lifted her up in the air and pushed her back against the tile wall of the shower. With his arms around her, he pushed his body between her legs, bringing them around him on either side of his waist. Positioning himself, he pushed himself inside her, his strong arms lifting her up and down as she clung to him helplessly. "You are such a tiny little thing," he said next to her ear as the water poured over his shoulders. "My God, you are so tight! Oh! This is so good! I can't hold back any longer." With a shudder, he emptied into her, and then he slowly lowered her to her feet. He reached down and retrieved the soap and washcloth, which had fallen to the floor of the tub, and tenderly bathed her. Then he dropped a kiss to her shoulder and set her out of the tub and onto the floor of the bathroom.

Donna picked up a towel and silently handed one to him as he turned off the water. She began to dry off as he stepped out and started running the towel over his muscular body. "Don't you think we should get some clothes?" she asked as he moved out of the room.

"Nah!" David grinned.

Stanley and Pam were already in the kitchen, starting the coffee.

"See?" David said. "Looks like we're going to have us a naked breakfast."

He was right. Stanley and Pam were filling the coffeemaker, unselfconsciously standing in the kitchen in the nude.

David walked up to Pam and gave her a long, passionate kiss.

Donna hesitated and then moved to the stove and pulled out her favorite frying pan. "Everyone OK with bacon and eggs?"

Stanley nodded.

"Sounds good to me," said Pam. "I'm famished. Where's your bread? I'll make the toast."

As they ate, Stanley said, "I hear you guys are members of some kind of club that meets in Chapel Hill."

"Oh, yeah." David nodded. "You mean Choice—like the magazine."

Stanley looked at him inquiringly.

"You guys wanna join?" asked David.

Stanley nodded. "I think so. We at least want to look into it, but I hear that someone who's already a member has to recommend us."

Pam said, "That's right, but we'll be happy to recommend you-all, if you want us to."

The grin almost split Stanley's face. "We wish you would," he replied.

"OK, no problem," said David. "I'll contact them this week and give them your names and address."

They finished eating, and David and Pam went to get dressed and get their things together.

Donna began clearing the table and starting the dishwasher.

"We had *such* a good time," Pam said as they came back into the kitchen.

"We sure did," David said, shaking Stanley's hand. "We have to do this again."

"Oh, yes! We sure do," Stanley said.

Pam giggled. "I don't know if we'll make it back home or not before we have to stop. After one of these get-togethers, we can't get enough of each other."

David looked at her and grinned. "That's right. Let's go home, sexy! I wanna take you straight to bed."

There was a flurry of hugs and kisses, and the couple went out to their car and drove away.

Stanley turned to Donna and looked her up and down.

Donna suddenly felt her body flush with embarrassment as she realized she was uncharacteristically standing in the middle of her kitchen totally naked.

"Come on. Let's you and I go back to bed," he said hoarsely.

Donna looked at him. "You want us to have sex now?" she asked.

"You bet I do! I don't think I've ever seen you standing here in the house, naked, in the middle of the morning." He grabbed her hand and pulled her down the hallway to their tousled bed, which smelled musty with the odor of sex. Stanley pushed her down on the bed and began kissing her.

As his hands moved over her body, Donna could think only of the picture in her mind of him and Pam having sex—of him pounding into a woman he had known for only a few hours. She closed her eyes, telling herself that this was her *husband*. This was the man she loved and had married. And the casual sex they had shared with others this weekend meant nothing in the life they were building together.

But it didn't work. Donna closed her eyes and felt absolutely nothing except the physical pressure as Stanley parted her legs and enthusiastically entered her.

Chapter Five

On Monday morning, Donna drove into the school parking lot, feeling strangely numb and detached. She scarcely remembered navigating the road from home; it was almost as though she were an observer outside her body, watching herself make the familiar trip.

She parked, gathered up her tote bag and purse, and entered the building. As she made her way down the tiled hallway toward her room, the familiar sights and sounds of small bodies scurrying about and high-pitched voices raised with laughter and squeals washed over her like slipping into a warm, soothing bath. She felt herself smiling as she entered her classroom. Here was safety. Here was normalcy.

Seating herself behind her desk, she stowed away her things and simply sat and drank in the mild hubbub as her students came in and found their way to their assigned seats amid the usual distracting conversations and interactions. As the strident sound of the warning bell filled the air, they settled, and Donna raised her head, directing a loving smile across the room. "Good morning, class."

"Good morning, Miss Porter," they replied.

A warm feeling of contentment enveloped her as she rose to her feet to begin her day.

Donna's stress began to fade as Monday morphed into Tuesday, Tuesday into Wednesday, and Wednesday into Thursday. Amid scraped knees at recess, young voices raised into song, vocabulary lessons, pictures colored, and laughter and tears, her world was once again familiar and cherished. She felt almost normal again as she moved about her kitchen on Friday evening, preparing their supper.

The plates were set on the bar, and the food was simmering on the stove. Donna was frowning at her watch when she heard the garage door clatter open.

Stanley's car drove inside, the kitchen door flew open, and he came in with a happy grin on his lean face.

A feeling of dismay swept over her as he kissed her cheek, waving envelopes in the air. "Look at this! I drove down and checked out the mailbox. Look what came!"

"What?" Donna's voice went flat, lifeless.

Stanley did not notice. "We got a letter from that other couple, Eric and Jennie—the ones from Kernersville—*and* we got our invitation to the monthly party down in Chapel Hill that David and Pam were going to recommend us for!"

Donna took a deep breath. "Great," she managed to murmur.

Stanley slipped out of his jacket and deposited the mail on the bar. He looked as though he could barely keep his rangy body from dancing as he moved around, full of nervous energy. "This is so great, Donna. I went ahead and opened them up as soon as I got back to my car. I couldn't wait!" He picked up one of the envelopes, pulled out the single sheet of paper, and looked down at it. "The party is on a Saturday night, two weeks from tomorrow. I'll put in for the day off so we can have plenty of time to drive down there. This tells us the address of the motel where it's being held. We need to call and get a reservation for a room for the night, and we have to send in our money for an admission ticket to the couple who's in charge of it. Dinner is on our own. We don't eat at the motel. The party starts at eight o'clock. There is a live band for dancing, and drinks are available at our cost." He looked at her, eyes shining.

Donna managed to lift the corners of her mouth into a smile.

Stanley grabbed her waist and twirled her around. "This is so great!"

"What's in the other envelope?" Donna asked when he came to a stop.

He grabbed it. "Oh! That's an answer from the Kernersville couple that we wrote to. They say that we should call them, and maybe we can get together." He frowned. "I guess it's too late to call them and ask if we can get together this weekend."

"Yes," Donna said firmly. "It certainly is."

"Well, I guess we can still call them tonight. Maybe we can see if we can get together next weekend."

"No," Donna said. "We can't do that."

"Why not?" Stanley shot her a sharp look.

Donna felt her face grow hot. "We just can't."

Stanley stood very still, his eyes flinty. "Why not?"

Donna winced and met his cold stare "Because ... well, we'd be meeting them to ... maybe have sex, right?"

Stanley gave a terse nod.

"Well, I'm not having sex with anybody next weekend," Donna said defensively. "I'll be having my period."

"Oh," Stanley said.

Donna felt a tiny tweak of satisfaction.

"Well," Stanley said, seating himself at the bar. "We can still call them tonight, right? We don't want them to think we're not interested. Here." He pushed the second envelope over toward her. "Go ahead and read their letter."

"I will," she said, turning toward the stove. "But right now, I'm going to get the food on the table."

After they had eaten, and the dishes were in the humming

dishwasher, Stanley looked pointedly at her and then back to the letter.

Donna reluctantly picked it up and began to read. Eric and Jennie wrote that they would, indeed, be interested in meeting them. When she finished reading the letter, she nodded.

Stanley took the letter back from her, moved to the phone, and began dialing.

After exchanging a few sentences, Stanley handed the receiver to Donna. "This is Jennie," he whispered. "You talk to her."

Donna said hello, and a warm voice responded, "Hello, your-self, Donna. It's nice to hear your voice. We liked your picture."

"Thanks," Donna said. "Uh, we're looking forward to meeting you in person."

"So are we! I'd let you speak to Eric, but he's not here right now."

"Oh, that's OK," replied Donna quickly.

"When do you guys think you'd like to get together? I know we don't live that far apart, so it won't be a long drive."

"Well, next weekend is a bad time," Donna said. "And we have plans for the following weekend as well."

"Oh, actually, so do we."

Donna hesitated. "You wouldn't happen to be going down to Chapel Hill weekend after next, would you?"

"Yes!" cried Jennie. "Are you guys going to the party at the Holiday Inn in Chapel Hill?"

Donna made herself laugh. "That's exactly where we're going! Is that where you're going, too?"

"It is! Oh, how funny! Have you gone to one of these before?"

"No, it's our first time," Donna said.

"Oh, you're going to have so much fun! I can't wait to see you there! We'll introduce ourselves there. Who put in for you to attend?"

"David and Pam. Do you know them?"

"We sure do! We're good friends with David and Pam. Don't you just love them to death? Are they going to be there?"

"I think so," Donna said.

"Oh, how fun! Well, I guess we'll see you in two weeks. I can't wait to meet you, Donna."

"You too." Donna hung up the phone pensively.

"Well?" Stanley said. "What's going on? What did she say?"

Donna looked up at him. "We're going to meet them at the party in Chapel Hill."

Stanley frowned and then brightened. "OK! Good. I'll call tomorrow and make us a reservation at the motel. I'll also put our money in the mail for our tickets." He patted Donna on the shoulder. "Good job, honey."

Donna did not reply.

꿍

Two weeks later, on Saturday morning, Donna packed an overnight bag for them and hung Stanley's good suit, along with a freshly laundered dress shirt and tie, and her favorite dress in the car.

The drive to Chapel Hill was fairly quiet. Stanley sat stiffly behind the wheel, occasionally fiddling with the radio dial, switching between FM stations, uncharacteristically silent for the most part.

Donna watched the scenery through her window. As the miles passed, she glanced at her husband out of the corner of her eye. *Stanley's spent his whole life in the world of cars, he sells them for a living, and he prides himself on his expertise in driving. Today, his relaxed mastery of the vehicle is nowhere to be seen.* He sat stiffly upright, and while he was still in total control of the car, his posture gave away his nervous tension. Donna tried break the tension. "It turned out to be a pretty day for our trip."

"Yep, it did."

"How many people do you think will be at this thing?"

He glanced sideways at her. "I have no idea."

"Well, at least we'll know David and Pam. It won't be a crowd of complete strangers."

Stanley finally gave a small smile. He reached over and patted her hand. "We're going to have a good time, Donna. Don't worry."

"I'm not." She turned her face back to the window and watched the miles go by.

When they reached the outskirts of Chapel Hill, Stanley pulled a paper out of his shirt pocket and glanced at the address.

A few blocks later, Donna saw the motel sign.

Stanley was smiling slightly as he pulled up to the entrance. He shut off the engine and started to open the car door. "Why don't you wait here? I'll go check on our room."

Donna nodded and watched him walk up to the office door and disappear inside.

Moments later, he reappeared and got back into the car. "This is it," he said. He showed her the door keys. "I'm going to pull around to our room." He started the car and pulled slowly down the side of the building, watching the signs indicating room numbers, and pulled into an empty parking slot.

They got out of the car, retrieved their clothing and bag, and walked to a doorway. It led to a hallway with several rooms on either side.

Stanley turned left, stopped by a door, and inserted the key.

The cool, pleasant room was dominated by a king-size bed. It was dimly lit, and the curtains were drawn over the window opposite the bed. There was a sink at the far end with a closet on one side and a bathroom on the other. Stanley flipped on the lights, illuminating the oranges, browns, and beiges of the bed covers and the chairs.

"Pretty nice." Stanley dropped their bag on the bed.

Donna carried their clothes over to the closet and hung them on the rod. "So, what are we going to do now? It's only half past two."

Stanley shrugged. "I dunno. I asked the desk clerk where there was a good place to eat, and he said the nicest place anywhere in the area is the Angus Barn. He said it's about a half hour from here. He gave me directions."

"But it isn't time to eat yet," Donna said. "It's a long time until eight o'clock when we need to be here."

"Yeah, I know. Let's go eat at six. The clerk said we want to go over there early. There's always a huge crowd—and a long wait if we don't."

"Did you see anybody you thought might be here for the party?" asked Donna.

Stanley shook his head. "I guess we're too early. What do you think we should do?"

Donna had an idea. "Let's drive over and look at the college. You know that the University of North Carolina at Chapel Hill is here. We could go look at the campus. I've never seen it."

"OK," Stanley said. "I guess we could do that. We should shower and change into what we're going to wear tonight before we leave so we'll be dressed for dinner. The Angus Barn is pretty pricey, according to the desk clerk. We don't want to go there dressed like we are now."

"All right," Donna said. "Do you want to shower first—or shall I?"

"You go ahead," Stanley said, switching on the TV.

They showered, dressed, and drove around the Chapel Hill campus for a while, looking at the stately old buildings and the smattering of students walking, bicycling, or otherwise wandering around, intent on their daily pastimes. Donna felt nostalgic and a little sad. They were so intent, so carefree, and so caught up in their cloistered spheres, feeling so adult and so unaware of what might lay just ahead. She almost started when Stanley spoke.

"Ready to go?"

Donna came back to the present. "Sure," she said.

Stanley turned the car back to the interstate, and after a thirty-minute drive, they found the restaurant. At just before six o'clock, a lot of people were already being seated for an early dinner. They were seated, and they had a really great meal.

When they arrived back at the motel, the parking spaces were nearly all occupied.

"Wow," Stanley said. "Do you think all these people are here for the party? The motel looks like it's almost full."

"I don't know." Donna felt a surge of nervousness as she looked at the almost-full parking area. Fortunately, the parking space for their room was empty.

Stanley pulled in, and they walked back to their room. As Stanley was unlocking the door, two couples, laughing and talking loudly, appeared at the other end of the hallway and then disappeared into a room.

"Do you think they're with our group?" asked Stanley.

Donna shrugged and shook her head. "I don't know."

They freshened up, and Donna applied her lip gloss.

At precisely eight o'clock, Stanley sprang to his feet. "Let's go!"

Donna slipped her feet into her unfamiliar high-heeled pumps, and they walked down to the ballroom. A large sign, "Private Party," stood outside the double-doored entry, and a security guard with muscular arms crossed over his chest watched the arriving people. They walked over to a folding table where a woman in a floor-length dress with long, grayish hair sat; a rotund man with a suit and a thick black beard stood behind her chair.

Stanley pulled their invitation out of his suit pocket.

The woman looked up at him, and the man's gaze swept over Donna—head to toe.

Stanley said, "We're Stanley and Donna Porter."

The woman looked down at a list, checked something off, and smiled brightly. "Welcome to Choice. We're your hosts, Frederick and Olga Tessler. This is your first time joining us, yes?"

"Yes," Stanley said, accepting the outstretched hand that Frederick thrust toward him.

"Welcome, welcome." Frederick's deep bass voice matched his appearance exactly.

Donna smiled at Olga. "Thank you," she said.

Frederick said, "Please go on in and find a seat at any table you choose. There is a cash bar. Do not hesitate to introduce yourselves to everyone, dance, and have a good time."

In the dimly lit ballroom, another couple came up to the table behind them. The band area was empty, but music was coming from the speakers. It was a slow, syrupy number, and several couples were locked closely on the dance floor, swaying to the music. People were standing three deep in front of the portable bar, which was just to the right of the band area, and two bartenders were working swiftly and smoothly, pouring drinks. About a third of small, round tables for four were occupied. Donna counted quickly. *There must be fifty tables or more. Do they expect two hundred people?*

Stanley took her hand, pulled her toward the middle section of tables, and stopped at one next to the dance floor. "This one OK?"

She nodded and sank into one of the chairs.

"I'm getting a drink," Stanley said. "What do you want me to bring you?"

"Something alcoholic," Donna said.

Stanley shot her a questioning look before heading toward the bar.

Donna watched the entrance as couple after couple arrived and checked in. As they entered the room, many were either greeted by another couple rushing up to hug them or hurrying across the room to exchange hugs and kisses. All the women looked glowingly beautiful, and the men were attractive and smiling. She felt like she had entered a strange Hollywood world.

"Donna!" Her head whipped around, and she came to her feet just as Pam and David reached her. She was enveloped in Pam and then David's exuberant embrace.

"Where's Stanley?" asked David.

"He went over to the bar. He's getting us a drink."

"That's a good idea," said Pam. "David, why don't you go get something for us too?"

He grinned his boyish grin and headed across the room.

Pam took Donna's hands in hers as they sat down. "Oh, I'm so glad you came!" she said. "It's so good to see you again."

"It's good to see you too," Donna said warmly, and she realized that she really meant it.

Pam opened her mouth, but before she could say anything, they were interrupted by the arrival of two couples at the table. One of the women put her hand on Pam's shoulder, and both of them greeted her with happy cries as she turned her head toward them. Pam rose from the chair and was immediately enveloped in hugs from all four of them. Turning back to the table, she introduced Donna to the new arrivals, her arms still loosely wrapped around the women.

"Donna, these are my friends Janice and Fred." With her chin, she indicated the big-busted redhead and a slightly built man with light brown hair and a pleasant expression. "And this is Tina and her husband, Claude."

Tina, a short woman with straight brown hair, was smiling broadly. Her husband was several inches over six feet and very slim with dark, curly hair. He met Donna's eyes and grinned approvingly.

"This is my new friend, Donna," Pam said. "Her hubby and my David are getting drinks. Why don't we pull two of these tables together, and you-all sit down with us?"

There was a flurry of activity as chairs were moved around and tables were pushed into place. Stanley and David appeared as they were settling around the tables, and the introductions were repeated.

The room was getting noisier as more people arrived, and many of them were cheerfully greeting each other. Members of the band appeared and were setting up in the area beside the dance floor. Someone switched off the recorded music.

Donna sipped the citrusy drink that Stanley handed her and listened as her tablemates chatted, adding her occasional comment to the conversation. Two couples stopped to greet Pam and David—and were introduced all around—and another couple came up to say hello to Janice and Fred. Donna had already lost track of the names of all these new people by the time Stanley, David, and Claude got up to make another drink run.

The band began to play, and a few couples drifted out onto the dance floor.

An attractive blonde woman, who was almost as short as Donna, and a dark, handsome man hurried over, and Pam rose to embrace them warmly. "Does everybody know Jennie and Eric? Donna, have you-all met in person yet?"

"No." Donna stood, and Jennie's eyes met hers warmly.

Smiling, Jennie released Pam and embraced Donna.

"It's so good to finally meet you, Donna." Jennie's voice was low, melodious, and slightly breathy in Donna's ear as she gave her a hug.

"You too." Donna felt shy at her warm intimacy.

The man stepped forward, and his lips upturned in a cool smile as his eyes took in Donna, top to toe. He took her hand. "Hello. I'm Eric," he said softly.

"I'm Donna." Her heart stuttered as she met his predatory gaze.

Pam put her hand on his forearm. "You two sit down here with us. We'll get some more chairs. They're playing a good song. Eric, come dance with me."

Another chair appeared from somewhere, and Jennie pushed it into the tiny space between Janice and Donna as Eric and Pam moved away.

"It's so good to see you again, Jennie," Janice said. "We've missed seeing you two lately."

Jennie flashed her a quick smile. "I know. We've missed coming for the past couple of months. There have been some … things come up."

"How are your girls?" asked Janice.

Jennie's face brightened happily. "Oh, they're just wonderful! They're growing up so fast!"

Janice looked over at Donna. "Jennie and Eric have two beautiful little girls."

"They're the love of my life!" said Jennie.

"Oh, how nice," Donna said.

"Do you and Stanley have children?" asked Jennie.

"No." Donna took a deep breath. "How old are yours?"

"They're five and three," said Jennie. "Well, Josie, the oldest, isn't really mine. She's Eric's by his first wife, but she's mine, nevertheless. I adore her as much as I do Lannie. Lannie's the three-year-old, and she's mine and Eric's."

"Jennie's the most doting mother I've ever met." Janice laughed.

"That's probably true," Jennie said with a smile.

The men came back from the bar with the fresh drinks, and

Stanley met Jennie. Before they could all sit back down, the dance ended.

Pam and Eric reappeared, and he and Stanley shook hands. Eric touched Jennie's arm. "We need to go back to the table with Carol and Ben."

"You're right," she said. "We agreed to be with them tonight. I excused us to come over and say hello when I saw you-all."

"Oh," Stanley said. "I'm sorry to hear that."

Jennie touched his arm lightly. "Come over and dance with me later," she said with a smile. "Eric and I definitely want to get with you and Donna another time. But come over and get me for a dance, OK?"

"Yeah, I'll do that," Stanley said.

Eric gave Donna a smoldering look as they departed, making their way across the room to another table where a couple was already seated.

Stanley was standing just behind Donna's chair as some of the others at the table got up and began to mingle, and the dance floor filled as the band launched into a slow, syrupy love song. Stanley bent over, his mouth close to her ear, and said, "I'm going to ask someone to dance. You need to smile—get somebody interested in you! Look for an attractive couple and flirt with the man! We don't want to be left out tonight." He frowned at her as he backed away from the table.

Donna realized that she was the only woman left at their pushed-together tables. She looked around, and her mouth felt stiff with smiling. As her gaze swept over the dancing couples, her eyes widened as she took in the indecorous poses and lewdness of the wandering hands of the swaying couples.

Fred, the quietly unremarkable husband of the busty Janice, was the only other person still sitting at their tables. He walked around the empty chairs and held out his hand. "Would you like to dance?"

She nodded, rose, and took his hand.

They maneuvered themselves into a spot on the crowded dance floor, and he held her lightly, but his hand on the small of her back guided her efficiently in their limited space. She smiled gratefully at him, and his eyes warmed understandingly as he pulled her slightly closer.

The song ended, but the band morphed seamlessly into another.

Donna relaxed slightly as Fred continued to simply hold her and move to the music reassuringly. When that number ended, he guided her back to the table.

Pam and Tina both returned with their partners, but Pam was claimed immediately by another partner as the music began on the next number.

"Hi, I'm Troy," said a man beside Donna's chair. "Want to dance with me?" She found herself swept back onto the dance floor, his tight grip pressing her against his body. "What's your name?"

"I'm Donna," she said against his chest as his hands cupped her buttocks, mashing her hips against his, moving her against him, and she felt his semi-hardness through their clothes.

"Mm-mm. I noticed you all the way across the room," he said, his hands roving over her. "Have you made any plans for later on yet?"

"I ... I don't know," she managed to say. "We'll have to check with my husband."

"Where is he?"

"He's here somewhere, dancing with somebody." She tried to push him away to get a little bit of space between them as Troy's roving hands explored what seemed like every inch of her.

"Hey," he said, when she turned her head as his lips lowered, trying to capture hers in a kiss, and his mouth found her cheek instead. "What's the matter? Don't you like me?"

Donna looked up at him, still trying to push backward. "It's not that," she said. "I just think … I mean, don't we need for your wife and Stanley to meet, or something, first?"

"That's no biggie," he said. "C'mon, honey." He lowered his mouth toward her again, but again, Donna avoided the kiss.

"OK, OK!" He released her and raised his hands in surrender. "I get it, baby! See ya!" He turned and left her alone among the dancing couples.

Chagrined and confused, Donna made her way back to her chair and sat down.

Knowing what Stanley had told her that he expected of her, Donna sat and smiled inanely as two or three numbers played. Finally, someone did come over to claim her, and she gratefully moved back with him to join the undulating couples. But he returned her, without comment, to her table when the music paused, and Donna wondered what she was doing wrong.

Stanley appeared beside her, pulling along a lanky blonde who he introduced as Amy.

Donna obediently got up to cross the room with them and was introduced to Jack, Amy's husband. Although she smiled gaily when presented, Jack barely spared her a glance, and he left them abruptly, heading off to approach someone else.

Stanley glared at her like a thundercloud as he escorted her back to their table. "Put yourself out there a little bit, will you?" he hissed as pulled out her chair and seated her.

"But I don't know what I'm doing wrong!" Donna practically wailed under cover of the music.

Stanley just glared at her and headed away again, plastering on his big salesman smile.

The evening dragged past, and Donna was feeling more and more miserable as the minutes crept by. Pam, David, Tina, Claude, Janice, and Fred all came back at intervals to alight for a minute and then disappeared again.

Finally, Stanley came back alone when Pam and David both happened to be sitting at the table, sipping drinks.

Stanley smiled as he sat down beside Pam. "So, what are you guys doing later? Can Donna and I get with y'all later?" he asked as Janice and Fred returned to the table.

Janice sat down beside Donna.

Pam grimaced. "I'm sorry, Stanley, not tonight. We're already committed to be with another couple." She patted him on the hand. "We'll do it another time, OK?"

David made a small gesture, and they both excused themselves and melted back into the crowd.

Stanley gave Donna another hard look. He sat motionless for a few seconds, and then he abruptly shoved back his chair without saying a word and threaded his way across the room.

Donna dropped her head, staring down at her hands clasped in her lap.

Janice leaned over toward her. "So, you haven't made any connections for the night yet?"

Donna shook her head, feeling the sting of tears threatening.

"Well, Fred and I are going to join in a group thing with three other couples. They're all real nice folks. Would you like to be with all of us?"

Donna raised her eyes to see Janice looking at her with obvious sympathy in her eyes. "Stanley … I don't know what he wants to do," she said.

Janice grinned wickedly. "Oh, don't you worry your little head about Stanley." She cupped her hands under the mounds of her large bust and lifted them slightly. "See these babies? I know how to use them the way diners use a knife and fork! You leave Stanley to me … I'll go find him right now, and he'll be more than happy to come and play with us! If that's all right with you, of course."

Donna looked at her gratefully. "Yes. Thank you so much, Janice."

"All righty!" Janice stood and looked around at the thinning crowd. "Now where did that Stanley go? Oh, I see him. Be back shortly," she said cheerfully.

True to her word, just after the next dance number ended, Janice and Stanley came back to the table, arm in arm. Janice was pressing against Stanley, and he was smiling down at her.

"Janice says that she and Fred are partying with some other couples—and that we're invited," Stanley announced as they stopped at the table.

Janice winked at Donna.

Fred got to his feet. "Are we ready to go down to the room?"

"Yep!" said Janice. "It's room 106. Are you ready, Donna?"

Donna rose and nodded, and Fred took her arm. They followed Stanley and Janice down the corridor that led to the rooms. They halted about halfway down the hallway, and Fred rapped firmly on the door. It opened a crack, and someone peeked out. It closed enough so that they heard the rattle as the chain disengaged, and then the door opened just wide enough to admit them into the dimly lit room.

Donna could not suppress a gasp as she entered the room. A naked man closed the door firmly behind them, relocking it. On the middle of the king-size bed lay a woman, nude and spread-eagled, a man with a huge erection kneeling between her widely spread legs, and next to another naked woman. She raised her head from where she had been curled up near the headboard, sucking on the prone woman's breast.

"Hey, y'all," the voice of the man who had admitted them came from behind them. "We started without you. Take off your clothes and join in."

Stanley was already unfastening the buttons on his shirt, gazing raptly at the spread crotch of the woman on the bed.

Janice unzipped her dress and pulled it over her head.

Donna stood frozen. She took a deep breath and inhaled the acidy odor of sex. Fred took her arm gently as Stanley and Janice finished discarding their clothes and climbed atop the bed. She watched Stanley's hand as it went to the woman's crotch, fondling it, and the man who had let them in walked over, embraced Janice, and began kissing her, his hands busy on her large breasts.

Fred urged Donna toward the side of the room, turning her slightly away from the orgy atop the bed. "Come on," he whispered. "Let's just go over here and take our clothes off. I promise you won't have to do anything you don't want to. Just let's get naked, like everybody else is, and sit down over here. Nothing will happen unless you want it to, OK?"

Donna moved like an automaton. She let him guide her by the elbow over to the small, round table flanked by two chairs by the drawn drapes at the window.

Fred smiled at her reassuringly. "May I?" he asked, his hand moving to the top of the zipper at the back of her dress.

She stood passively as he drew it down, and her dress opened at the back. Standing so that he shielded her view of the bed, he slid the dress down her arms, and it fell in a puddle around her feet as he used both hands to unhook her bra. That followed the dress to the floor as he gently turned her to face the drawn drapes and hooked his thumbs in her lacy panties, drawing them down her legs. His warm hand lifted first one foot, then the other, as she stepped out of the clothes. Unhurriedly, he straightened and began removing his clothes, and she stood, unresisting, facing the drapes. He bent down, gathered all the clothing, placed it on a chair, and turned her to face him.

The comforter, sheets, and pillows were in a pile on the floor beside the chair. Fred guided Donna down to sit on them, fanned the fingers of one hand behind her head, and drew her face toward

his. Gently, his lips captured hers as they sank down into the softness of the piled bedclothes.

Donna made a small whimpering sound, and he ended the kiss,
pulling her head into the crook of his neck above his shoulder. They
lay like that as murmurs of bodies moving and the wet sounds of
sex came from the bed above them.

After a while, Donna felt his erection grow against her.

Fred's hands moved slowly and soothingly over her, caressed her
small breasts, and started moving lower. One of his hands moved
between her thighs, working its way upward until it halted at the
junction where her legs met. He was kissing her gently, and she slowly
relaxed her body enough that he parted her legs, his fingers touching,
and then parting her wide enough for his fingers to enter her.

With a sighing, wordless sound of surrender, Donna shifted,
opening her legs enough for his hand to freely explore. He shifted
his body, moving between her legs, and she felt the heat of his
erection at her opening. She was too dry for him to penetrate, so
Fred spat onto his fingers and rubbed the saliva over her vulva
before pushing himself into her. He let out an involuntary cry as
he entered her fully, then began ever-quickening strokes as she lay
beneath him, absorbing his pistoning movements. His body stiffened as he made a final, deep penetration and climaxed, sinking
down beside her, replete.

One of the men above them on the bed peered over the edge of
the mattress and extended his arm, his fingertips grazing Donna's
nipple.

Fred pulled her protectively out of reach, and the man, dis-
tracted by something up on his level, turned back away and disappeared from view.

Donna lay still as the tangle of limbs just above her and out
of sight continued to move and shift, seemingly endlessly, punctuated by the occasional cry or groan. Someone—one of the

men—climbed off the bed, walked into the adjoining bathroom, and turned on the shower. He was followed by a woman—not Janice, one of the other two—and the water ran for some time. It stopped, and the couple came back into the dimly lit room, backlit by the bright lights through the bathroom door, wrapped in towels.

The other couple, neither of whose names Donna knew, got off the bed and walked past the first two. The shower ran again for a while. When they came back into the bedroom, Janice and Stanley got off the bed and walked over to the bright bathroom doorway.

As they reentered the bedroom after what must have been a long shower, Fred gently nudged Donna and gestured for her to follow him. They silently threaded their way through the group and went into the humid bathroom. Fred turned on the shower, and Donna stepped over into the tub beside him under the falling water. They bathed, shared the last clammy towel, and joined the other people who were talking quietly, sitting on the bed or in the side chairs.

One couple dressed, and they walked the short distance toward the door.

Hugs were exchanged, and Janice walked over to Fred, her body spectacular in the dim light. She kissed him. "Have a good time, sweetie?" she asked.

"I sure did." Fred reached out and drew Donna into a three-way hug with them. "This little girl was wonderful," he said.

Janice grinned at Donna.

The man Donna did not know frowned. "I didn't get my turn," he said. "Y'all stayed down there on the floor and didn't come up on the bed to get in on the action with us."

"Wasn't enough room for us up there," Fred said. "Next time."

Stanley was sorting through a pile of clothes, picking out his, as he turned to Donna. "Are you about ready to go to the room?"

"Yes," she replied, moving toward the chair where her clothes were in a wrinkled pile.

"Let me get mine, too," said Fred.

Janice was already donning her things.

The four of them left the room together, and Fred turned to Stanley in the hallway. "Meet us for breakfast?"

"Sure thing! What time?"

"Oh, about eight o'clock. See you in the motel restaurant," Fred replied.

"You got it, buddy," Stanley said, turning to walk toward their room. Donna walked with him, and they got into bed a few minutes later. Donna was grateful that Stanley fell asleep almost as soon as he lay down.

ॐ

When Stanley and Donna walked into the almost-full restaurant in the morning, they were greeted warmly as they passed by the booths occupied by people they had met the night before. Everyone was eating and happily conversing, acting like classmates who had spent years together.

Janice and Fred were in a booth near the back, and they waved.

Pam and David called out to them from where they were seated with another couple, and Jennie and Eric waved from the back of the restaurant.

The waitress wasted no time before setting steaming cups of coffee in front of them. The service was excellent, and the food was pretty good—a couple of notches above so-so.

As people finished and left, there were jovial goodbyes and see-you-next-months flying.

Donna and Stanley checked out after breakfast, and Donna was happy to see that he was in a very good mood as they drove back toward Phillips.

Chapter Six

Stanley was happy; that was the only thing that made it possible for Donna to hold it together. The respite from his overbearing demands and caustic tongue kept her stress level just low enough to keep her from dissolving into a screaming fit. She had almost convinced herself that this swinging thing was no big deal—and that it was having no effect on her life between sessions. Until now, that is.

In the days that followed their weekend "party" in Chapel Hill, Stanley went around with a pleasant expression on his face. He was almost smiling. She had actually heard him whistling as he messed with his spring maintenance on the lawn mower, preparing it for use in the near future. And a careless word on her part had not sent him into one of his long, loud monologues of an argument over something trivial since they had gotten home on Sunday.

But whenever her thoughts crept toward the events of their weekend in Chapel Hill, and what they had done there, she went into panic-attack mode. Her chest compressed, and she felt like she could not get sufficient air into her lungs. Her stomach roiled with nausea, and perspiration dewed her body. She would vigorously pull her thoughts away to something else, exerting every ounce of self-control to avoid any reminder. She shuddered. No way did she ever again want some strange man running his fingers over her naked body, spreading her legs, and pushing himself into her!

At that moment, she wasn't even too crazy about the thought of Stanley doing it! But he had been more active than usual since the party, his hands seeking her body almost every night.

Try as she might, she could not imagine what drove these people to so avidly pursue this. *Sex?* Sex was no big deal to her. When she and Stanley had first married, she had felt all pleasantly warm and happy that her body seemed to be giving him so much pleasure, but that had not lasted all that long. As the months passed, his bad moods and temper had killed all her efforts toward him in that area, and she soon began walking the tightrope of avoidance of any triggers that would set him off. She drew in a shuddering breath. Her skin crawled at the thought of going through another of those events. She had no desire for him, but if she refused his overtures, she knew she would pay for it through Stanley's bad temper and tirades over her slightest misstep.

Automatically, she made the final turn toward home, dashing away her sudden rush of tears with one hand as she drove. It was as if a dark cloud hovered over her, and she could see no way out of her dilemma.

She was surprised to see a car in their driveway. Not sure who it was, she pulled alongside it in the double drive, and her lips turned up involuntarily when she saw her friend Pennie sitting behind the wheel, calmly reading a magazine as she waited.

As Donna put the car into park and scrambled to open the door and get out, Pennie calmly laid her magazine aside and got out of her vehicle. Smiling, she opened her arms as Donna reached her, and they embraced.

"Where have you been keeping yourself, girl?" Pennie asked, stepping back from their embrace. "I haven't talked to you in *weeks*. So, I said to myself, 'Get over there and ambush her.' So here I am!"

"Oh, I'm so glad to see you," Donna said, lowering her arms. "Come on in the house and let me fix you something to drink."

"Can't stay," Pennie said. "I just wanted to come by and make sure you're OK." She peered closely at her friend. "God, you look awful! What's with the dark circles under your eyes?" Her eyes narrowed. "What's Stanley doing to you? Is he being an even worse jerk than usual? He hasn't hit you or anything, has he?"

"No, no!" Donna lowered her eyes to avoiding Pennie's scrutiny. "Not ... no, of course not. He hasn't hit me."

Pennie simply continued to stare at her skeptically.

Donna forced a smile. "I'm fine," she said.

"Well, the other reason I came over is to see if you'd like to go somewhere tomorrow. Maybe down to Hanes Mall for some shopping, and we could get a nice lunch somewhere. I haven't seen you in *way* too long."

Donna thought for a moment. "All right. Yes!" She smiled. "Tomorrow is Saturday, and Stanley has to work all day to make up for being off last weekend. I can go."

"Great! I'll pick you up in the morning then. About ten?"

"Sure! Maybe we can have lunch at that little place where they serve those wonderful crepes. What's the name of it? You know, that little restaurant across from Thruway Shopping Center?"

"You mean Berries? Yes, I love their food. I can never decide whether to have those wonderful chicken crepes with the mushroom sauce or a strawberry and whipped cream dessert crepe! Let's do it! I'll see you in the morning."

"See you!" Donna smiled and waved as her friend climbed back into her car and backed down the driveway.

Donna was waiting eagerly when Pennie drove up the next morning. Stanley had already left to go to the dealership. She climbed into Pennie's car, and they made their way down the interstate, chatting lightly. They found a parking place near the Belk's entrance and happily entered the big mall.

Donna found herself relaxing as they made their way through several stores, browsing and exclaiming over the merchandise. Pennie found a pair of shoes, and Donna bought a scarf that they agreed would brighten up a couple of her neutral tops.

At one o'clock, they decided it was time for lunch. They drove the mile or so to Berries, and the waiter quickly brought drinks and took their orders.

Donna took a sip of her ice water and glanced up to see Pennie scrutinizing her from across the table. "What?" she said with a smile.

Pennie continued to regard her seriously. She leaned forward. "Are you sure that you're all right?"

Donna took another sip of water. "I'm fine. Why?" she responded, her smile fading.

"I'm worried about you," Pennie responded. "You seem like you're under such a strain lately. Are you sure that you and Stanley aren't having problems?"

"We're fine!" Donna said.

"Look, Donna, we both know that he can be hard to get along with. I don't know why you stay with him with the way he treats you sometimes! I just want you to know that I'm here for you if you ever need me—to listen or anything else you need."

"I know that, Pennie. You're a good friend, and I really do appreciate your concern, but I'm fine. Really. Oh, look! Here comes our food. Mm, doesn't it look wonderful?"

The waiter put their plates on the table.

Pennie gave Donna another look, but she dropped the subject—and they dug into their crepes.

Chapter Seven

As the days passed, Stanley twice tried to telephone Jennie and Eric, the couple from Kernersville, but their phone rang and rang each time he tried to call them. "Wonder why they aren't answering?"

"Dunno," Donna replied. "Maybe they're out of town or something."

"They must be," Stanley answered. "They seemed like they really did want to get together with us."

"Yes, they did." Donna was secretly thrilled each time they failed to make contact.

Stanley brightened. "Well, maybe we can get together with them at the next Choice party."

Donna's heart sank. "What date is that again?" she asked.

"Weekend after next. I'm going to ask off tomorrow. We need to send in our money and make a reservation at the Holiday Inn."

⁊⑤

Stanley came home from work the next day scowling.

"What's wrong?" Donna asked.

"You won't believe this! Bill Carson said that I've taken off too many Saturdays lately, and he won't give me the day off Saturday after next. I've gotta work every Saturday this month until six o'clock. Looks like we won't be able to go down to Chapel Hill after all. Can you believe this shit?"

"Oh, really?" Donna tried to sound disappointed, but her heart was racing with joy.

"Yeah! You know, there's times when I can push it, but I could tell he really meant business this time." Stanley slammed his open palm down on the kitchen bar, making Donna jump. "I'm sorry, hon. I just can't miss work this time, but I went ahead and put in to get off for the one next month."

Donna turned her back on him and went over to the stove, where dinner was cooking, to hide her expression. "That's OK, Stanley," she said.

"We'll just keep on trying to get in touch with Jennie and Eric," Stanley said. "Maybe we can get with them between now and next month's Choice party."

"OK."

However, that was a futile effort as well. Donna was thrilled at her respite, but Stanley's mood became darker and darker as the days passed. All in all, she decided, she preferred her husband's bad temper to the way their new lifestyle made her feel. Maybe. Either way, she decided, she simply did not know how she could live like this.

He began scanning the Choice magazine again and talking about choosing another ad for them to answer.

꒰ᔕ꒱

Easter came and went. Donna's first graders colored pictures of bunnies, and they had an egg-decorating day with varied artistic successes, but all her little ones were delighted, nonetheless. Their reading classes toughened, and they were introduced to simple mathematics. The end of the school year was fast approaching, but Donna knew that another date was approaching that she could not avoid: the upcoming Choice party.

They drove down to Chapel Hill early in the afternoon. Stanley's mood was pleasant, and he was almost jovial as they stopped for a very early dinner on their way. They checked into the motel, and Donna looked around to see if she could spot anyone they knew as they made their way to their room.

Promptly at eight o'clock, they made their way down to the event room.

Just as before, Olga Tessler was sitting at the small registration table. She looked up with a smile of recognition as Stanley gave her their names.

"Welcome back," she said with a smile.

"Thanks." Stanley's gaze swept the room. "Looks like you don't have quite as many tables set up tonight as you did two months ago."

Olga's glance followed his. "Oh, not quite as many. Our attendance does fall off somewhat in the summer."

"So, not as many people signed up for tonight then?" asked Stanley.

Olga shrugged. "Not quite. But we still have a big number. You will have a good time. You will see."

"Oh, I don't doubt that!" Stanley put his hand on Donna's arm, urging her inside, toward the tables.

They walked in and selected a table, looking around at the early arrivals.

Donna did not see anyone she recognized.

"Want a drink?" asked Stanley.

She nodded, and he headed toward the bar.

The band had already begun to play before Donna saw a familiar face. She felt a surge of relief when she saw Fred, Janice,

Tina, and Claude walk past the registration table. She stood up and waved.

Janice spotted her, and a big smile lit up her face. She pointed, and the foursome changed direction and headed toward their table.

Donna saw Stanley coming back with their drinks.

A flurry of greetings ensued; the men shook Stanley's hand, and hugs were exchanged by the women. Chairs were pulled into place, and they sat down.

"How have you guys been?" Janice asked. "We missed you-all last month."

"I had to be at work." Stanley grimaced.

Fred nodded understandingly. "Happens," he said. He headed to the bar and quickly returned with drinks for his group.

Stanley looked around. "Doesn't look like as many people are here this time."

Janice nodded. "Yeah, you're right. Well, I don't think Pam and David will be here tonight. And I guess you know what happened with Jennie and Eric."

Donna looked at her sharply, and Stanley's attention was captured as well. "No, we don't. What happened?" Donna said.

Janice leaned forward confidingly and spoke under the sound of the music. "They've separated. They had been going through a rough spot in their marriage for quite a while, but Jennie just found out that Eric was having an affair with a real young girl at his job. When she confronted him, he literally kicked her out of the house. He's filed for divorce and full custody of both the little girls."

"No!" exclaimed Donna. "How can he do that?"

"He owns the house they were living in. He bought it while he was married to his first wife, and Jennie's name isn't on it. And you know that the oldest little girl is his from his first marriage—she's not Jennie's. And that's not the worst of it!" Janice paused dramatically and took a sip of her drink.

Stanley and Donna were staring at her, taking in every word.

"What?" Donna asked.

"Eric's mother moved into the house to look after the little girls, and he's sued for full custody. He claims that Jennie's an unfit mother."

Donna gasped. "Jennie? She seemed to be totally wrapped up in those children."

"She is." Janice nodded. "She absolutely adores them! She's always been a perfect mother."

"Then how can he claim that she's an unfit mother?" asked Donna.

"He has a video," Janice said. "You know how she's into the bi thing? Well, he made a video of her and another girl making love, and he's using it against her in court!"

"You're kidding! Wasn't Eric there while the girls were together?" asked Stanley.

Janice nodded. "Sure, he was. He and the other guy were in the room, watching, and Eric is the one who shot the video."

Donna took in a shaky breath. "That's evil!"

"It really is," Janice said.

"Poor Jennie," Donna said.

Janice nodded. "She's totally embarrassed. It's all gone public, and worst of all, she may lose her children. I hear that the judge is one of those old-school conservatives—he's an old guy who's real religious and all that."

"No wonder we couldn't get ahold of them when we called," Stanley said softly.

They all were silent for a long moment, thinking about it.

Stanley said, "Do you think this had anything to do with there being fewer people here tonight?"

"No, no," said Janice. "There are only a few of us who know what's happening with Jennie and Eric. Pam and David know, of course. They're real good friends with Jennie. I know that's why they aren't here, but hardly anybody else knows."

Claude said, "Well, we're here to party, right? Let's not let this good music go to waste." He stood and took Tina's elbow. "Let's go circulate, right, honey?"

Tina stood, and they made their way across the room.

Any partying mood Donna had was gone. She and Janice exchanged a look, and Janice gave a small shake of her head.

"Say!" Janice exclaimed. "We didn't exchange phone numbers last time, did we?"

"No," Donna said.

Janice scrambled in her small evening bag, pulled out a card, and handed it to Donna "That's our home phone number."

Donna tucked the card into her own bag. "Thanks."

"You can call me anytime," said Janice, getting to her feet. "I want us to be friends—you know, away from here as well. I'd like you to be my friend."

Donna smiled. "I'd like that too."

"Let's dance," Stanley said to Donna. "We can scope out the crowd and see if we spot anybody we'd like to meet."

"See you later, Janice," Donna said over her shoulder as Stanley pulled her out to the dance floor.

Later in the evening, they met another couple who were attending for the first time.

Stanley put on his best charm, showering the wife with compliments and dancing with her.

Donna made small talk with the husband at the table since he did not dance. When Stanley invited them to come back to their room after the party, they agreed. Donna did her best to play her role, and Stanley seemed satisfied with their evening. He displayed a positive attitude at breakfast as they talked with others in the restaurant before they checked out and drove home.

֍

Donna leaned back, pressed against the hard back of the booth, and took a deep breath. "That was so good, Pennie. I'm stuffed. I don't eat out much these days," she added with a little grimace.

"I know." Pennie gave her a stony look.

"Stanley likes me to make him a home-cooked meal every night," Donna said weakly, hating the apology she heard in her voice.

"So, how'd you escape tonight?" Pennie asked.

"Oh, Stanley had to go help deliver some vehicles. One of Mr. Carson's biggest clients ordered two of those big ol' pickups for his business, and they got here today. Stanley and one of the mechanics had to drive them all the way up to Mt. Airy, and another guy is following in one of the cars off the lot to bring them home after they make the delivery. Since they're going to get something to eat on the way back, I decided to call and see if you could eat with me tonight."

Pennie smiled. "I'm glad you did."

"Me too."

"So what else is going on with you?" Pennie asked. "I haven't talked to you in ages."

"Not much," Donna said. "I just go back and forth to work. It seems like that's about all I do these days."

"I know Stanley keeps you cut off from all of us—"

"Now, Pennie, don't start! Please?" Donna sighed. "Tonight's been such a nice break for me. Don't let's spoil it."

Pennie spread her hands. "You're right. Let's just enjoy our time together."

After a little silence between them, Donna said, "I'm in charge of organizing the little fall festival at school when we go back next year."

Pennie's brows rose. "Really? That's good. You mean they're thinking about next year's fall festival already? Before school is out this year?"

"There's a lot of work involved. We have to plan it out ahead."

"I guess so."

"There really is. I'm thinking of asking Agnes Purdue to be in charge of the food. She's taught for more than twenty years, and she knows everybody in town."

Pennie nodded thoughtfully. "Good choice."

"And I thought I'd ask that new teacher, Aaron Woods, to be in charge of the games and activities."

Pennie frowned. "Maybe you shouldn't do that."

Donna looked up at her. "Why not? He's young and athletic, and all the kids seem to like him."

Pennie cleared her throat. "Uh, I'd still hold off on that."

"Why?" Donna leaned forward, and her eyes narrowed. "What is it, Pennie? Tell me."

Pennie glanced around, ducked her head, and whispered, "I don't think Aaron Woods will be coming back to teach next year."

"Why not?"

"I don't think his contract is going to be renewed," Pennie said softly.

Donna's eyes widened. "Where did you hear that?"

Pennie shook her head.

"But … everybody likes him. He's popular with the students, friendly with the parents …"

"Maybe a little *too* friendly," Pennie whispered.

"What do you mean?"

Pennie sighed. "Do you know Betsy Green?"

"Ben Green's wife? Yeah, I do. Why?" Donna leaned forward.

"Well, the way I heard it, there was a parent-teacher thing at the school a couple of weeks ago …"

Donna nodded.

Pennie lowered her voice even more. "Well, it seems like your Mr. Woods made a pass at Betsy Green. They were caught in a compromising situation in an empty classroom with the lights out—and by none other than her husband, Ben."

Donna gasped. "Oh, no!"

Pennie nodded.

"And Ben Green's on the school board." The full implications hit Donna, and she felt her face turn pale.

Pennie smiled. "Betsy claimed that he lured her in there—and she *innocently* followed him into the room. And since they were caught with his hands where his hands ought not to have been … and with some of their clothes undone …"

"Oh, no! I can't believe that Betsy Green was all that innocent. You know how she was back when we were in school."

"Exactly," Pennie said. "But Ben believed her."

Goose bumps rose on Donna's arms as the significance hit her. "And they're *firing* him?"

"No," Pennie said. "They're letting him finish out the year, but he won't be back. You know how it is around here. Any hint of improper behavior by a teacher." Pennie wriggled her eyebrows.

Donna nodded. The dinner she'd so enjoyed was now a hard lump in her stomach. She swallowed the bile that rose in her throat.

"Bunch of self-righteous hypocrites, we all know," Pennie said.

Donna grimaced, swallowed again, and rubbed the chill bumps on her forearms.

"So you'd better think of somebody else for your games chairman."

Donna whispered, "Yeah. I will."

Chapter Eight

The next Choice party was scheduled for late May. Donna tried to avoid going to it by telling Stanley that she was almost snowed under with the end-of-school paperwork, which was true. However, he had managed to finagle having the day off again, and he insisted that they had to go. Taking the path of least resistance, Donna caved.

As soon as they checked in, Donna noticed that attendance was down—even from the previous month. She saw Janice and Fred sitting at a table. "Hi, guys!"

"Hi," Janice said without smiling. "Sit down for a minute. We have something to tell you."

"What is it?" Donna asked as they pulled out chairs.

Janice reached over and took her hand. "We aren't staying tonight. We just came in to tell people who hadn't heard about what happened."

Donna's free hand flew to her face, and alarm shot through her. "What?"

"Jennie Jordan committed suicide the day before yesterday."

Donna felt the blood leave her face. "Really? How? What happened?"

"Eric's unfit mother custody case went before the judge this week. The judge ruled in Eric's favor. He was awarded full custody of both girls—and he took out a restraining order against Jennie so she couldn't visit the girls or even see them at all." Janice's gaze hardened. "Jennie hung herself."

Donna gasped. "Oh my God!"

"I know! It's just so awful! The only reason we came here tonight was to tell those who knew her and might not have heard about it. We're not staying."

Donna took in a deep breath.

Stanley said, "Well, we really didn't know them *that* well—"

"But she was so warm and sweet," Donna said.

Janice glared at Stanley and then looked back at Donna. "I know. She was one of the nicest people I've ever met. We'll all miss her so much."

"What about Eric?" Donna asked.

"What about him?" Fred's lip curled into a sneer. "There's no law against being a total … SOB. I guess he's free to cozy up with his new girlfriend now. Maybe she'll get to be wife number three."

"That's awful!" Donna said.

"Well, we thought you'd want to know," said Janice. "We're hoping to catch up with a few others here and tell them too."

Stanley nudged Donna. "Well, thanks for telling us. C'mon, Donna."

Numbly, she got up, and Stanley guided her over to the bar. He lowered his lips close to her ear. "Let's get a drink, Donna."

Donna felt her eyes filling with tears. "Oh, Stanley, isn't that the most horrible thing?"

He looked at her with puzzlement in his eyes. "Yeah, I guess so, but I don't see why you-all are taking it so hard."

Donna stopped dead in her tracks. "You don't?"

"No," he replied. "I really don't. Here. Sit down here at this table, and I'll go on over and get us our drinks. It's not like she was a lifelong friend or a relative or something."

Donna sat down. "Stanley, I can't believe you said that."

He shrugged. "I'll get us something to drink. I'll be right back. Donna, we're not going to let this spoil our evening. We're here to have some fun and find a nice, good-looking couple to swing with. I expect you to straighten up and get your mind back on doing what we came down here to do." He walked away, leaving her sitting there alone.

A bit later, when Donna looked around the room, she did not see Janet and Fred. *They must have left*, she thought.

She smiled, danced, and flirted, aware of the dark glances Stanley threw at her when she hesitated to throw herself at one of the men, going through her motions robotically. It was late in the evening when Stanley finally seemed to connect with someone who pleased him.

Donna intensified her efforts to attract the woman's husband. She smiled into his eyes, laughed at an inane comment he made, and even forced herself to lean against him, brushing her breast against his arm.

The four of them left the party as the band was playing the last number of the night, and they went back to the new couple's room.

A couple of hours later, she and Stanley entered their own room. Donna numbly showered, brushed her teeth, and slipped into bed, her back to her husband, hoping for sleep to claim her.

Chapter Nine

As Donna finished setting the table for dinner on a Friday evening a couple of weeks after their last trip to Chapel Hill, she heard the garage door clatter open. Minutes later, it rattled closed, the kitchen door opened, and Stanley came in with a sour expression.

She forced a smile. "Hey! You're running late. I hope nothing's wrong."

He pulled an envelope out of his jacket pocket. "Not really." He tossed the envelope beside her plate on the bar. "I drove down to check the post office box after work today. We got a letter from Frederick and Olga. They're suspending the parties for the summer due to decreased attendance. There won't be another one until September."

"Oh!" Donna struggled to keep from smiling. She turned toward the oven to hide her reaction.

"Yeah. I know. I'm disappointed too. But don't worry. I fixed it so that maybe we won't have to wait until fall to meet somebody new."

Donna's heart sank. "What do you mean?"

Stanley grinned and pulled a folded-over magazine from the inside pocket of his jacket. "I stopped by that adult bookstore and picked up the latest issue of *Choice*. A new one just came out. See? After dinner, we can go through it and pick out some new ads to answer. I sorta glanced through it, and there's lots of new ones." He looked at her expectantly.

She took in a deep breath. "Let's eat before the food gets cold."

"Sure thing! I'll just go wash up, and then we'll go through the magazine together, OK?" He headed down the hall to the bathroom.

Donna closed her eyes. Her appetite was gone. She turned and automatically began bringing the food to the table.

After they finished the meal, Donna cleaned up and loaded the dishwasher.

Stanley had the magazine open on the bar in front of him. He looked up and said, "Come sit down next to me, and let's go through the ads."

Donna stood still. "No. I don't want to."

His brow furrowed. "What?"

"I don't want to."

"What do you mean? Oh, I get it—you think there's something else you think you need to do now to finish cleaning up." He gave a dismissive little wave. "Let it go, hon. Come on over here, and let's look at the ads together. Let's pick out somebody we want to answer—so we can get together with them."

She did not move. "No, Stanley. I don't want to look at ads with you. I don't want to pick out somebody to answer. And I don't want to meet any of those people."

His face flushed, and he stared at her disbelievingly. "Well, I do!"

Donna shrugged and walked out of the room. She took a load of dirty laundry to the washer in the basement and loaded it into the machine. When it was going, she returned to the living room, retrieved some of her students' papers from her tote bag, and settled into her chair under the floor lamp. After she finished that task, she returned to the basement and switched the laundry to the dryer.

When she made her way back up to the main floor, she glanced toward the kitchen and saw that Stanley was still poring over the magazine at the bar. She shrugged and turned her attention back to her paperwork.

After completing her grading and making another trip downstairs to fold and bring up more laundry, Donna went back to their bedroom and went through her usual ritual to get ready for bed. She stretched out underneath the covers. She didn't know how long it was before Stanley joined her; she was asleep before he came to bed.

When the alarm woke them, Donna went to the kitchen to make breakfast.

Stanley dressed for work, came down to the kitchen, and began eating from the filled plate she put in front of him. Few words were spoken, and neither of them made any reference to the night before. The magazine was nowhere to be seen, and as soon as he had finished eating, Stanley gathered up his car keys and left for work. Donna cleaned up the kitchen with a sense of dread; she knew that a stormy encounter was inevitable.

A week went by without the expected verbal explosion on Stanley's part. Donna began to relax her guard, but she still felt like she was walking on eggshells around him. Her days were filled with cooking meals and escaping into her job at school. She watched the calendar with dismay as the days sped past. All too soon, school would be dismissed for the summer—and her world would shrink drastically. She began to realize just how cut off she had become from everything and almost everybody who used to be in her life, and it frightened her.

School had been out for a week. To help fill her empty days, Donna threw herself into a fit of housecleaning, and the house sparkled from her efforts. She cleaned up after dinner and went to take a shower.

Stanley moved in front of her in the hallway, blocking her passage. "I'm glad to see you're using your time working on the house." His eyes were flat and unreadable, and he grasped her arm.

She gave a slight shrug, her eyes falling to where his bony fingers wrapped around her forearm, and goosebumps rose on her arms.

His mouth curved in a smile that did not reach his eyes. "We've got company coming this weekend. The house needs to look nice for them."

Donna's mouth went dry. "Who?"

"I answered some ads in the new magazine. One of the couples answered, and I invited them here on Saturday night."

"Without even asking me?" Donna hated the way her voice sounded. *It's so reedy and pathetic.*

Stanley shrugged. "Since you weren't interested in talking about it, I went ahead and set it up."

"And you expect me to just go along with it?" Donna felt her face flush.

Stanley tightened his grip on her arm. "Yes. I do. You aren't much of a wife to me, and this is something I enjoy. You'll use that pretty little body of yours to entertain the man, and I'll get me some new, hot nooky! I sure don't get much of that from you."

Her shoulders slumped. "That's not fair, Stanley! I try so hard to be a good wife! I do everything you ask. I cook for you, keep the house clean, run errands for you—"

"Yeah, but you aren't much good between the sheets! A man likes to have somebody who at least acts like she wants him. You're a cold fish, Donna! You're real pretty, but you act like you're doing me a big favor every time we have sex. A man needs more than that!"

"And you think you've found it by swinging with these couples?"

He let go of her arm, and she rubbed unconsciously at where his grip had been. "Yeah, I have. These women really like what I've got to offer. They're hot, and they make me feel like a man. I do like it! And you're going to go along with it! You're going to spread your legs for their husbands and act like you mean it. If you don't …"

"What, Stanley?" She glared at him. "What are you going to do if I don't do that?"

He gave her a threatening look. "You just play along, Donna. I mean it. You'll be real sorry if you don't. I promise you that." He turned and strode down the hallway.

Trembling, Donna went to take her bath.

Chapter Ten

Donna was appropriately dressed for their evening in her new A-line minidress with the big, flowing long sleeves. She was standing by the window in the living room, when an older-model muscle car with huge tailfins and a bad paint job in almost neon aqua slowly pulled up the driveway and came to a halt in front of the garage.

"Stanley! I think our guests have arrived," she called out softly as the car doors opened.

A man and a woman climbed out of the car. The man was short—with a muscular barrel chest above too-short legs—and his dirty-blond hair was long enough to touch the collar of his shirt, framing a ruddy, rough-skinned face. On the other side of the car emerged a tall, lanky woman with a definite dry-straw bleach job. The woman towered several inches above the man, Donna observed, as they walked side by side toward the front door.

As Stanley came into the room, Donna let the curtain drop back into place and fell in beside him as he headed toward the front door.

The doorbell sounded, and Stanley pulled the door open with a big smile. "Hello, hello. You must be Mitch and Jean."

The man extended his hand, "Sure are!" His eyes lingered over Donna and finally went back to Stanley. "You have to be Stanley.

And this little gal must be Donna?" His gaze swung back to her again.

Donna kept her smile in place as Mitch let go of Stanley's hand and grasped hers, his eyes boldly traveling over her body and mentally undressing her.

The woman took Stanley's hand, bent forward, and murmured something in his ear.

"Well, come in. Come in, y'all." Stanley tugged the woman forward as she continued to hold onto him.

"Yes, do come in." Donna slipped her hand out of Mitch's grasp.

"Would you-all like something to drink?" Donna asked as they all sat down.

"Oh, yeah! That'd be good," Mitch said.

"Whaddya got?" Jean asked.

Donna stood up. "Sodas, beer, maybe a glass of wine?"

"Got any whiskey?" Jean asked. "I'd rather have that."

Stanley got to his feet and grinned at the woman. "I think maybe we can find some. How 'bout you, Mitch? Whiskey for you too?"

"Sounds good to me."

Stanley followed Donna into the kitchen and pulled a bottle of Jack Daniel's out of a high cabinet over the stove, and she began filling glasses with ice cubes. He poured generous amounts of whiskey over the ice in three of the glasses, and Donna got out her bottle of diet soda.

Drinks distributed, Donna sat down in the armchair, and Stanley squeezed in beside Jean on the sofa. Everyone settled back, and the getting-to-know-you conversation began.

"So, what do you do for a living, Mitch?" Stanley asked, taking a sip of his drink.

Mitch took a big swallow and let out a contented sigh. "I drive a truck. A big rig." His eyes narrowed. "Why don't you bring that bottle in here and set it on the table. Be more convenient for refills."

Donna got up quietly and started for the kitchen.

"This little ol' gal here goes with me on some of my cross-countries," Mitch added.

Donna picked up the Jack Daniel's bottle and turned back toward the living room.

"Works out real nice," Mitch said. "She keeps me company, an' I can score me some nooky when we stop. Ain't that right, hon?"

Jean laughed loudly. "Sure is, Mitch." She reached over and put her hand on Stanley's thigh.

"Thank you, little lady." Mitch reached up to take the bottle from Donna. He generously replenished his glass and set it down, open, on the coffee table.

Donna sat back down.

"What do you do, Stan?" Jean asked.

"I sell cars," he replied.

"Oh, really?" Mitch said. "Maybe you could score me a good deal one of these days."

"Maybe I could. How do you like driving long hauls?"

"It's pretty good. I'm pretty much my own boss, most of the time. 'Course the big man is always bitchin' an' moaning about something. Never get the job done fast enough or whatever. Never can make him happy."

"You got that right," Stanley said. "You should have heard mine when I asked for the day off today. You would've thought the world was coming to an end. I've even got to go in and work tomorrow afternoon to make up for it! Can you believe that?"

"You didn't tell me that," Donna said.

Stanley frowned. "Yeah, I gotta go in tomorrow at one." His frown faded as Jean's hand moved up his leg, and her fingers played over his crotch. "Oh, yeah, baby," he said softly.

Jean giggled.

Mitch turned his attention to Donna. "So, what do you do, pretty lady?—or do you just stay here at home and keep ol' Stan over there happy?"

"Well, actually, I'm not working this summer."

Stanley said, "Hey, Donna, why don't we all go get those steaks on the grill? Let's get supper over with! I feel like we're all going to have something better to do after we get done eating."

"Good idea!" Mitch sprang to his feet and snatched the Jack Daniel's.

Everyone got to their feet, and the men were soon busy at the grill.

Donna pulled the big bowl of cold pasta salad out of the refrigerator, put it on the table, and began warming up a side dish of green beans.

Soon, the four of them were sitting around the table with sizzling steaks in front of them.

"Tell me something, Mitch," Stanley said when they were almost finished with their meal.

"What's that, buddy?"

"Well, in your ad, you used the phrase 'enjoy light discipline.' Explain to me just what you meant by that?"

Jean giggled again.

Mitch leaned back in his chair and grinned. "Oh, we just like it a little bit rough—with some spanking, maybe using a little paddle or whip to warm things up. You ever tried that?"

"No," Stanley said.

Donna felt her eyes go wide as her breath caught, and a flicker of apprehension coursed through her.

"Oh, yeah! Jean, why don't you go out to the car and bring in our little goody bag to show them."

Jean obediently got up and started out of the house.

They sat in silence until she returned with a long, slim paper bag.

Mitch got to his feet and took it out of her hands.

Jean sat down and looked up at him expectantly.

Mitch set the bag upright beside his chair, reached into it, and pulled out a thin, flexible plastic paddle, about eighteen inches long and two inches wide. He waved it back and forth a couple of times and then struck the palm of his other hand with a sharp whack.

Donna started at the sound.

Mitch laughed. "I like the paddle, but Jean prefers the little whip." He put the paddle on the table and pulled a miniature buggy whip out of the bag. He flourished it, and then he brought it down playfully on Jean's shoulder.

Jean caught it, brought her lips to it, and kissed the leather.

Donna gasped.

"Are you serious?" Stanley said.

"Oh, yeah! Oh, we don't hurt each other—it's all in fun! It just warms her up for the main event, don't it, hon?"

Jean nodded enthusiastically. "When he paddles me, it really turns me on. My butt gets all hot, and then everything else gets hot too … if you know what I mean."

Mitch looked at Stanley. "You wanna try it? She really loves it."

Stanley did not reply.

"It's all just playacting," Jean said.

Stanley shrugged and looked at Jean. "You want me to?"

"Oh, yeah, handsome! I sure do!" Jean grabbed the whip out of Mitch's hand.

Stanley grinned. "I'm always open to trying something new."

"How about you, Donna?" Mitch looked at her, eyes glittering.

Donna tried to swallow, but her mouth was dry. "No, I don't think so."

"Oh, c'mon, Donna," Jean said. "You're Mitch's favorite type.

You look like a little schoolgirl. He loves to play like he's the big, bad daddy, punishing you for something naughty that you did."

Donna shook her head back and forth emphatically.

Stanley glowered at her. "Oh, c'mon, Donna. What will it hurt? It's just a game."

"I won't hurt you, Donna." Mitch held up his right hand. "I swear. I'll quit whenever you say to. I promise."

Jean was standing beside Stanley and running her hands all over him. "C'mon, handsome. Let's you and me go back yonder and find us a bedroom. Let's let them work it out, OK? I'm all hot just thinking about you an' me back there together."

Stanley reached out and cupped Jean's ample breasts, looking hard at Donna.

Jean scooped up the little whip and grabbed Stanley's crotch again. She put her mouth by his ear and licked him. "C'mon. Let's go."

Stanley grabbed her around the waist, and they started down the hall. He threw another dark look back over his shoulder at Donna as they walked toward the bedroom.

Mitch began stacking up the empty plates as Donna continued to sit mutely in her chair. "C'mon, pretty thing. I'll help you clear off the table—and then let's you an' me go on back in the living room and have us another drink and talk this over, OK?"

After a moment, Donna got up.

She began carrying the dirty plates and silverware into the kitchen, and Mitch helped her carry some of the things. She automatically began loading the dishwasher, and soon the dishwasher was humming. Mitch moved beside her, put a beefy arm around her, and guided Donna back toward the living room.

They sank down onto the sofa.

"I didn't scare you, did I, honey? I sure didn't mean to," Mitch said softly. "This is just a little game that Jean and I play sometimes. You aren't scared of me, are you?"

"No," Donna said. But her mouth was dry.

"Can I tell you how we play our game?"

Donna shrugged. "You can if you want to," she said.

Mitch looked at her and licked his lips. "My God, Jean was right. You are so beautiful." He reached out and touched her breast tentatively. "Well, if you were Jean, and we was playing our game, I'd ask you to take off your bra and have those pretty little round breasts of yours all naked under that dress. And I'd ask you to take off your panties too. Now that wouldn't hurt you none, would it?"

Donna shook her head. "I guess not." She attempted a smile.

"Good! Now you know that ol' Stan and my wife, Jean, are back there having themselves a good old time right now. Are we gonna let them have all the fun?"

Donna relaxed a little and gave a small laugh at herself. "All you want to do is playact a little bit? Is that what you're saying?"

"Exactly!" Mitch said. "Now will you do that for me?"

"All right," Donna said, getting to her feet. "You just want me to take off my bra and panties and leave on my dress. Do I have it right?"

"Yes! Will you do that for me while I fix me another drink?"

"Sure. I guess I can do that," Donna said with a sigh.

"You want one?"

Donna shook her head.

Mitch went back into the kitchen. She heard the refrigerator door open and the clink of ice cubes as she unfastened her bra and maneuvered it down her arms and off without taking off her dress.

As she stepped out of her panties, he came back into the living room, drink in hand. He stared at her as he drained his glass. He smiled, and his eyes began to glitter again. He set the empty glass down on the coffee table and turned to face her, his breath becoming heavier. "Young lady, you've come home late again," he said softly as he reached out toward her, grabbing her hand.

"I'm sorry, Daddy," Donna said, playing along.

He put one of his muscular arms around her shoulders and drew her to him, bringing his other hand up to graze her breast. "And have you been out running around without your bra on again?" He walked her over to the end of the sofa and turned her to face him. His free hand went up under her dress and over her bare buttock. "And you don't have your panties on either! Oh, you're such a bad, bad girl! You know you must be punished!" His breath hitched, and he began almost panting as turned her, bent her over the arm of the sofa, and pushed her dress up over her bare bottom. He ran his hand repeatedly over her bare buttocks, caressing her and murmuring, "Bad girl! Bad, bad girl. Don't you move! You stay right there!" He almost ran into the dining room to retrieve his paddle.

Donna stayed still as he returned.

He pushed her legs wide apart, caressing her buttocks and between her legs, and trailed his fingers up and down her crotch.

Donna felt the hardness of his erection against her as he leaned against her leg. Suddenly, he put an arm under her waist, scooped her up, and moved her behind the sofa. He leaned her over the back of it, her legs dangling, and hiked up her dress, leaving her bottom uncovered.

She heard the swish of the paddle through the air, and her whole body jerked as it came down on her bare buttocks with a painful whack. "Ow!" she cried in shock and surprise. "That hurt!"

The initial blow was followed by several others in quick succession.

Donna tried to roll away—her entire backside on fire—but he grabbed her and pulled her back into place.

"Stop it!" cried Donna. "That's enough. Mitch, I mean it, stop!"

He chuckled, his chest rising and falling with excitement

and exertion. "Oh, no! You've been bad! You have to have your whipping."

Donna writhed and fought in earnest now, but he held her firmly, the thin, flexible paddle landing with a steady rhythm.

It was really hurting now, and she felt like she was on fire. Twisting her head, she saw his eyes glittering madly above her. "Please, Daddy," she gasped, trying to gain his attention. "I'll be good."

He actually paused, hearing her plea, and she took the opportunity to twist and flip her body in a somersault from underneath his grasp. She heard her dress rip. She hit the floor, landing on one knee between the sofa and the coffee table, almost knocking the breath out of her. She scrambled backward as fast as she could as he came around the end of the sofa after her. Trying to gain her feet, her hand encountered something metal and cold behind her, and her fingers curled around the end of the poker on the hearth.

She swung it wildly at him, one handed, as he came at her, bent over, arms reaching for her. She felt the impact as it struck his shoulder, almost losing her grip on it, but his momentum carried him closer, even as she twisted to get out of the way. He let out a bellow of rage as she scrambled to get upright. She got both hands on the poker and swung at him again as he came at her, this time catching him on the shin, and she screamed at the top of her lungs, "Stanley, help me!"

"You little bitch! You little hellcat!" Mitch roared.

A moment later, Stanley came pounding down the hall and into the room, stark naked. "What in the world is going on?"

Jean followed him into the living room, also without any clothes on.

Donna stood at the ready, clutching the poker in front of her with both hands.

Mitch was glaring at her, and his expression said he wanted to tear her limb from limb.

"I said, what is going on in here?" Stanley repeated.

"That man was beating me. He wouldn't stop," Donna said.

Mitch glanced sideways, caught sight of Stanley, straightened up, and took a deep breath. "Easy, everybody, easy." He was breathing hard. "It's just a little misunderstanding."

Donna continued to hold her poker at the ready. "Get your things and get out of my house—both of you!" She glanced over at Stanley. "Get them out of here, right now, Stanley—or I'm going to call the sheriff and have him do it for me!"

"Donna, what is going on?" yelled Stanley.

"You heard me! You get them out of here, or I'm going to back up to the telephone and call 911," she replied, never breaking her gaze at Mitch.

Mitch held up both hands in front of him. "We're going. We're going. Jean, get your clothes on! We're getting out of here."

Jean turned and scurried off down the hall.

Donna backed up as Mitch came forward.

Stanley was still staring at them. "Will somebody tell me what is going on?"

"I told you! That man was beating me—and he wouldn't quit." Donna breathed in and out deeply, adrenaline still coursing through her.

"Is that right, Mitch?" Stanley said.

"No, no! I told you that it was a misunderstanding! Come on, Jean. Hurry up!"

Jean came down the hall, dressed, looking back and forth from one of them to the other.

"C'mon. Let's get out of here!" Mitch grabbed Jean by the arm and pulled her toward the front door. He was favoring his right leg, where she'd hit him with the poker, Donna noted with satisfaction.

"Donna, what happened?" Stanley yelled.

The car started, and lights flashed on the living room window as it backed down the driveway.

"What the hell have you done?"

Donna looked at him with disdain. "Well, while you were busy screwing your brains out in our bed, that man was beating me up in here."

Stanley's jaw dropped even more. "Are you serious?"

"Oh, you bet I am!" She crossed over to the fireplace and put down the poker.

He stood staring at her without speaking.

She brushed past him, went down the hallway to their bedroom, pulled a suitcase out of the closet, and started throwing clothes and toiletries into it.

"What are you doing?" he asked from the doorway.

"What does it look like I'm doing?" Donna shot back. "I'm leaving." She snapped the suitcase shut and picked it up, along with her purse.

"Donna, have you gone crazy? Where do you think you're going?" Stanley cried.

Donna stopped dead still and looked at him. "I don't know." She pushed past him, walked out to the garage, and threw the suitcase into her car. She opened the garage door, got into the car, and backed out.

Stanley followed her into the garage.

As she backed down the driveway, she saw him standing framed in the garage door, naked, staring after her.

Donna drove toward Winston-Salem. As her adrenaline wore off, her buttocks began to hurt more and more. She could scarcely walk when she pulled up at a motel at the outskirts of Winston-Salem and checked into a room. The sleepy desk clerk paid her little mind as she filled in the form and handed him her credit card.

After parking her car and getting her things into the room, she pulled down the covers on the bed. She whimpered as she stripped the dress from her body and threw it aside. She crawled up onto the bed on her knees and lay down. Waves of pain from her buttocks and the backs of her thighs washed over her; she hurt so badly that she could not lay any way except on her stomach. The pressure from the covers hurt so much that she finally pulled up only the sheet over her naked body. She cried into the pillow for a long time before she finally fell into a fitful sleep.

When she awoke in the morning, sunlight was coming into the room through a crack in the drapes, and she heard the slamming of car doors outside. Her whole body hurt when she moved. She almost screamed when she brought her legs underneath her to try to get out of bed. Stiffly, she walked across the carpet, and made her way to the back of the room where a big mirror covered most of the wall above the vanity and sinks. She flipped on the light and turned, looking over her shoulder at her backside. Donna gasped.

From the top of her buttocks almost to her knees, she was a massive red bruise, just starting to change color. Her body stung and throbbed; it felt as though her whole backside was emitting heat. She simply stared at the image in the mirror over her shoulder, unbelieving. "Oh my God," she murmured.

Finally, she went into the bathroom and turned on the water in the shower. It took an effort to step up into the tub. She let tepid water flow over her. After several minutes, she got out and toweled off as best she could. When she looked at the contents of her suitcase, she saw that she had at least had the presence of mind to put clean underwear and a long midi shirt and blouse into it. She picked up the torn minidress that she had worn last night and angrily threw it into the trash can. She never wanted to see it again.

Donna got the rest of her things together and walked stiffly and slowly out to her car. She got the suitcase back in with no trouble, but when it came time to sit down and start the car, that was another story. Her body simply did not want to bend into a sitting position, and by the time she maneuvered herself under the wheel, sweat had broken out on her face. She was almost in tears from the pain in her backside. "What am I going to do?" she whispered.

Slowly and carefully, she drove down the road to a restaurant and spotted a bank of pay phones by the doorway.

She parked in the lot, went inside, managed to sit down in a booth, and ordered coffee and toast. When she paid her bill, she got several dollars' worth of change from the cashier and stiffly walked out to the telephones. To her surprise, when she looked at the wall clock above the cash register, she saw that it was almost eleven o'clock.

Donna dialed a long-distance number from memory, praying for an answer. When a voice said hello, she followed the recording's instructions and fed quarters into the phone.

When the pinging of the money ceased, she almost burst into tears. "Pennie, is that you?"

"Hello, hello?" said the voice in the receiver. "Donna, is that you?"

"Oh, Pennie," Donna said weakly. "I need help!"

"Where are you?"

Donna took in a long, quivering breath. "I'm just outside Winston-Salem. I'm fixing to drive back up there, but I need your help. Can you help me?"

"Of course, I'll help you! Donna, what's the matter? Are you hurt? Tell me what's wrong?"

"I'm not hurt. At least not real bad. I'll tell you all about it when I see you. Can I come to your house?"

"You know you can! Momma and Daddy are gone to church. I happened to stay home today. You come on then—I'll be waiting for you to get here!"

"Thanks, Pennie," Donna said.

It took her more than an hour to make the drive. She had to bite her lips and force herself to continue to sit on the car seat and push her foot against the accelerator, but Donna eventually made it to Pennie's parents' house at the edge of Phillips.

Pennie evidently had been watching for her because she came running out of the house the minute Donna stopped the car.

Pennie pulled the car door open, and Donna swung her legs sidewise with a grimace and prepared to get out.

"Oh my God, girl! You're as pale as ashes! What's wrong with you? You *are* hurt!"

Donna forced her feet to the ground, righted herself, and slowly straightened up.

"No, well, yes. Sort of. Pennie, I've left Stanley," Donna said.

"Thank God!" Pennie threw her arms around Donna. "Tell me what happened! He finally hurt you, didn't he?"

"It's a long story, but will you help me think? I've got to figure out where I can go. I've got to find a place to stay."

"Well, you could always come here. Momma and Daddy wouldn't care if you stayed here for a while."

"No, no! That won't work. I have to find a place I can go where Stanley won't be looking for me. I need a place of my own."

"Have you thought about Mrs. Adams?"

"Who?"

"You know! Mrs. Adams! The white-headed widow with the big old house beside the library. She takes in boarders!"

Donna's face lit up. "She does, doesn't she? Do you think she'd have a room?"

"Well, we can call and ask her."

"Let's do that!" Donna started to take a step forward and winced.

"You *are* hurt!"

"It's nothing! I'm just walking slow today. Let's go make that call."

Pennie frowned and led the way into the house.

It took three attempts to reach Mrs. Adams. The widow had been at church and had just walked into her house as they made their third call. She sounded skeptical, but she told Donna to come on over to her house to talk about renting a room.

They got into Donna's car, rode over into the main part of Phillips, and pulled down the shady driveway beside Mrs. Adams's house.

The spry, white-haired woman was waiting for them on the wraparound porch. She got right to the point. "Which one of you girls is looking to rent a room?" She opened the door, which was off her kitchen.

"I am," Donna said.

Mrs. Adams cocked her head sidewise and peered at Donna. "And you are who?"

"I'm Donna Porter. I teach first grade down at the elementary school."

"And who are you?" Mrs. Adams asked Pennie.

"I'm her friend Pennie White. I'm just helping her today."

"Pennie White? Marion and Jeb's Pennie?"

"Yes, ma'am."

"Yes! I know you from church." Mrs. Adams peered at Donna. "And how do I know you?"

"Well, my parents lived all their lives here—until they moved to Florida a few years back. Jack and Stella Glenn."

Mrs. Adams's expression cleared. "Yes! I knew Jack and Stella. How are they doing? How are they liking Florida?"

"Just fine," Donna said, relaxing a little.

"And what happened to your two sisters? They got married and moved out of state, didn't they?"

"They did. I'm the only one left here."

Mrs. Adams's eyes narrowed. "Porter, you said? You married a Porter?"

"Yes, ma'am. Stanley Porter."

"The Stanley Porter who works down at the Carsons' Ford dealership?"

"Yes, ma'am, but you see—"

"Humph! So why are looking to rent yourself a room?"

"She's left him," Pennie said.

Donna shot her friend a look.

Mrs. Adams's eyes narrowed. "I don't need no domestic trouble here."

"There won't be," Donna said forcefully.

"She really needs a place to stay," Pennie said. "Please, Mrs. Adams, do you have a room that she can rent?"

Mrs. Adams was silent for a long moment, looking back and forth at them. "I don't know," she said.

Tears sprang to Donna's eyes. Her body was throbbing, and she could think of no other option. "There won't be any problems ... I promise. Please Mrs. Adams."

Mrs. Adams took a deep breath, staring at her. "Well, I do have one room. It's on the ground floor, but I have very strict rules. I have two gentlemen renting rooms upstairs, and the same rules apply to everybody. No visitors of the opposite sex in my house. You can use the kitchen and put your food in my refrigerator or cabinets, labeled with your name. No loud music, no disturbances of any kind. You keep your room clean and clean up after yourself in the bathroom. I won't stand for any violations whatsoever. You want to look at the room?"

"Oh, yes. I sure do." Donna exchanged a relieved look with Pennie.

"Well, come on in." Mrs. Adams led them across the kitchen and into the central hallway. On the other side of a stairway, there was an old-fashioned parlor, and just beyond that, another short hallway led to toward the back of the house. Mrs. Adams stopped at the first door, and the girls followed her into a medium-sized room, furnished with a double bed, a dresser, and two armchairs flanking a small rectangular table. A reading lamp was on a tiny table beside the bed. The walls were papered with an old-fashioned yellow cabbage rose print, and the chenille bedspread on the bed was white. The floor was covered with worn beige linoleum.

"The bathroom next door is mine, and my bedroom is just past that. I'll share the bath with you ... if you see fit to rent from me. It's got a tub with a shower, a lavatory, and a commode, of course."

"It looks fine," Donna said. "How much do you charge?"

Mrs. Adams told her.

"Can I move in today?" asked Donna.

"I guess so." Mrs. Adams frowned slightly.

"Now, if I could just find someplace to put my car out of sight from the street," Donna said.

Pennie nodded.

Mrs. Adams said. "I've got a shed out back. I used to keep my old Caddy in it, but it's been empty since I sold it to my nephew. I'll let you use that—for another twenty dollars a month—as long as you ain't driving in and out two or three times a day."

Donna smiled for the first time all day. "It's a deal!" She pulled her billfold out of her purse and started counting out money.

"I'll write you a receipt and leave it on your table," Mrs. Adams said.

"Good!" Donna said. "Come on, Pennie. Will you come and help me get my clothes? Stanley is working today until six."

"Let's go!" Pennie said. "Are you sure he won't be home?"

"I'm sure. Bill Carson laid down the law. He has to be at work today."

"We'll swing back by my house and get my car too. We can move more of your stuff that way."

"OK. We'll do that," Donna said.

They picked up Pennie's car and drove to Donna and Stanley's house. Donna quickly unlocked the door, and they hurried inside. Donna set Pennie to pulling her clothes out of the closet, and she gathered the framed photos of her family and a few books. She found a cardboard box in the garage and dumped her toiletries into it. When all her clothes were stowed in Pennie's trunk, they walked back inside.

"What about the rest of your stuff?" Pennie asked.

Donna shook her head. "This is all I'm taking. It's all I want."

Pennie said, "Are you sure?"

"I'm sure," Donna said. "Oh, no, wait a minute." She opened a cabinet and began taking out pieces of a very fragile-looking tea service. "This belonged to my grandma. I want this." She ran a caressing hand over the teapot.

"Let's see if we can find another box," Pennie said. "You can wrap up the cups and saucers in dish towels. That way, they won't break."

They couldn't find another box, but Pennie grabbed a laundry basket from the basement. "Let's line it with towels," Pennie said. When Donna hesitated, Pennie glared at her. "You at least deserve to take a couple of good towels with you—after putting up with that man all this time! Now, go get you a couple of those big, fluffy towels that I saw in the bathroom."

Donna meekly went down the hall and came back with the towels.

They put the tea set, photo albums, framed photos, and books in Donna's car.

Donna spotted the Polaroid camera on the closet shelf, and on an impulse, she added it to her cache.

"Are you sure that's all you want?" Pennie asked.

Donna nodded. "I'm sure."

"Well, let's get out of here then." Pennie got into her car.

Donna carefully locked up the house. Giving it a last look, she maneuvered, wincing, behind the wheel of her car, and they drove back to Mrs. Adams's house.

It was almost dark when Donna pulled the door of Mrs. Adams's shed closed and made her way back into her new lodging. Pennie had helped her settle her things in her room, and then they had driven over to the Burger Chef for take-out sandwiches for dinner. They had eaten at Mrs. Adams's kitchen table, and then Pennie gave her a hug and prepared to leave.

"Wait!" Donna said. "There's one more favor I'm going to ask of you before you go home."

"Sure. What is it?"

"Come on back to my room. There's something I need you to do for me."

Pennie followed her to her new room.

Donna picked up the Polaroid camera and handed it to her friend.

Pennie looked at her inquiringly.

"I'm going to take off my clothes, and I need you to take a picture of me," Donna said.

"What?"

"Wait. You'll see in a minute." Donna quickly took off her skirt, stepped out of it, and turned her back to Pennie.

Pennie gasped. "Oh my God! Did Stanley do that to you?"

"No, but he let somebody else do it to me—and he didn't keep him from doing it."

"What happened?" Pennie asked.

Donna grimaced and took off the rest of her clothes. "I can't tell you right now. Please just trust me—and don't tell a soul about this. Please, Pennie. I need you to take a picture of my bruises. Will you do that?"

"Of course, I will. Oh, Donna, that looks awful. Are you sure you don't need to see a doctor? Does it hurt a lot?"

"It does, Pennie. It really does. But no doctor, OK?" Donna slipped off her panties, stood beside her bed, and leaned over slightly. The bottom half of her body was naked, and her legs were together, and Pennie took several shots of her discolored derriere. The red welts were beginning to darken into ugly shades of purple. The two of them studied the photos and decided the bruises had been documented clearly.

Donna got back into her clothes, and the two of them walked outside. Pennie headed home, and Donna stashed her car in Mrs. Adams's shed.

Donna made her way back to her new room, exhausted and throbbing. She visited the bathroom, undressed in her room, pulled on a roomy nightgown, and lay down on her stomach, trying to find some measure of comfort. All her moving and carrying had actually kept her from stiffening up that afternoon. She opened the medicine cabinet while she brushed her teeth and helped herself to some aspirin from a big bottle on the shelf. After a while, lying on her stomach in her new bed, Donna fell asleep.

ॐ

Donna hid out the next day. After work, Pennie brought her a plate of food from the diner. "Stanley's looking all over the place for you," Pennie said. "He called my parents' house twice to see if I'd seen you."

Donna shrugged.

"Are you going to call him?" asked Pennie.

"No! I don't know," Donna said.

"You know you can't hide from him forever."

"I know," Donna said.

Pennie looked at her. "Well? What then?"

Donna took a deep breath. "I'm going to go talk to a lawyer."

Pennie nodded. "That's a great idea."

Chapter Eleven

Tired of hiding out in the four walls of her new room, Donna pulled her car out of the shed, drove out of Phillips, and headed to the neighboring town of Madiera. She had an appointment at two o'clock with Marshall Owens, a young lawyer who split his practice between his office in the county seat and as a member of a firm in Winston-Salem.

Donna's bruises were getting better, if more colorful now, having gone through several shades of purple and green. They were now mostly an ugly grayish purple and mustard yellow. More importantly, she could finally walk normally and sit in her car without too much pain. It was the second time she had ventured out. Yesterday, she had walked down the block to have a late breakfast at the diner. She been chagrined when heads turned her way and conversations stopped when she walked in.

Head held high, she nonchalantly made her way to an empty booth.

The buzz of conversation slowly resumed.

Clara Smith, her usual waitress, hurried over with a coffeepot, a mug, and a laminated menu.

Donna smiled at her. "Hey, Clara."

"Hey!" Clara filled a mug and set it down in front of Donna. "How you doin'? Haven't seen you around for a few days."

"Yeah, I guess not," Donna said with a smile. "Can I get some bacon and eggs?"

"Sure can." Clara scribbled on her pad. "Toast? Grits with that?"

"No grits. Just some wheat toast," Donna said, aware of nearby ears listening.

"You … been out of town?" asked Clara.

"No." Donna handed over the menu.

"Stanley's been in here a few times," Clara said. "He's been asking everybody if anybody's seen you."

"Is that right?" Donna said.

Clara nodded. "Yeah. What's going on, girl? Have you left him? Don't he know where you are?"

Donna beckoned her nearer and lowered her voice almost to a whisper.

Clara leaned in closer.

"I guess he doesn't," Donna said. "Do me a favor, will you? Let me eat my breakfast before you call him and tell him I'm here. OK?"

"Well, sure." Clara glanced around. "But, Donna, I got no reason to call and tell him anything. Of course, I can't speak for these other folks in here."

Donna sighed. "I know. Just hurry up with my breakfast, will you?"

"You got it!" Clara scurried back to the kitchen.

Donna wasted no time when her steaming plate arrived. She ate quickly, drained her coffee mug, and threw a bill on the table. Most of the same people were still sitting there as she hurried out of the diner and back toward the library. She cut through the pretty library grounds so she would not be exposed any longer than necessary to the street traffic. She made it back to her new house, slightly out of breath and seething with frustration and anger. Pausing in the hallway by the stairs, she picked up the telephone directory by Mrs. Adams's telephone, sat down on the bottom stairs, and scanned the yellow pages. She picked up the telephone receiver and dialed. Minutes later, she had her appointment with Marshall Owens.

ॐ

Arriving a few minutes early, Donna took a seat in the rather humdrum waiting room area at the direction of the girl behind a scarred desk who returned to typing furiously and popping her gum as she concentrated on her work.

Promptly at her assigned time, the door beside the reception desk opened. "Mrs. Porter?" Marshall Owens said and beckoned to her.

Donna tried to size him up as she walked into his office and took the proffered chair across from him. *Quite ordinary looking,* she thought as she sat down. Medium height, light brown hair, dressed in suit pants and shirt and tie. Then she met his sharp, piercing eyes, and her estimate of him jumped considerably.

She shook her head at his offer of something to drink, and he began asking questions, making an occasional note on the writing pad in front of him on his desk. Donna began to relax slightly as she filled him in on the basics of her situation, warily careful about what she said.

"This sounds fairly simple," the lawyer said.

Donna sat ramrod-straight in her chair with her hands clasped in her lap.

"You say that you have moved out of the home and want to file separation papers?"

"Yes," Donna said.

Marshall Owens leaned forward. "Donna, is there anything else I should know?"

Donna frowned. "What do you mean?"

"What precipitated this? I know you didn't just get up one morning and—out of the blue—decide that you didn't want to stay with your husband anymore. Was there some particular incident that triggered your move?"

Donna inwardly cringed. *Oh, God*, she thought. *This man is my attorney … surely, I can trust my attorney. No! I can't trust anyone—not with this mess. Not when it means I could lose everything if it becomes known what Stanley and I did. This town is so conservative that I would be crucified if it came out. I can't take a chance.*

Donna stared down at her hands. "I told you that Stanley and I don't have anything in common anymore. We don't like the same things, and we don't talk to each other. I'm just a convenient servant to wash his clothes and cook his meals and pay the bills. I'm tired of it—that's all."

He frowned thoughtfully. "Pay the bills?"

"Well, yes," she replied.

"Tell me about that."

"Well, I don't pay them all … just most of them. See, I'm a teacher, and I get a regular monthly paycheck, ten months out of the year. Stanley is on commission; since he sells cars, his income is never the same. When we got married, we set up a joint checking account. I put my check in there, and we pay the household bills out of it."

"And what does he do? Do his commission checks go into that account as well?"

"Oh, no. He saves them in another account—for when we use up mine."

"And is your name on that account?"

"No," Donna said. "Just his. That's the account he had before we got married." Her eyes widened as she realized what she had just said.

"I suggest that you open another account, just in your name, and put no more money in this joint account of yours."

"I will. I'm going to do that as soon as I leave here."

"All right, Donna. I'll begin the process and start drawing up the papers. If you decide that there's something more that I should know, please don't hesitate to let me know at once." He leaned back and looked at her. "I don't like being broadsided by something my client should have told me, coming out of left field from the other side. I'm your lawyer. You can tell me anything, and it's absolutely confidential. Understand? I've heard just about everything. I doubt if you could surprise me. And I do need to know the whole picture, so I can protect you. Now, Stanley's not been abusing you, has he?"

"No," Donna said. "He hasn't hit me."

Her attorney took a deep breath. "There's more than one kind of abuse, you know? I know it may be hard to talk about, but you can trust me, Donna."

"I know that." Donna looked down at her hands. "I just want out—that's all. I don't want to be married to him anymore."

"All right, Donna." He stood and offered his hand. "I'll begin the paperwork. I'm going to send a certified letter to your husband today. Remember that I'll be right here for you if you need me, OK?"

Donna's smile wavered. "Thank you, Mr. Owens. I'll remember that."

Three days later, Stanley found her. Donna had taken her car out of the shed and driven to the grocery store for bread, eggs, sandwich meats, and a few other things she could prepare for herself in Mrs.

Adams's kitchen. She had just placed the bags inside her car and was straightening up when she sensed someone standing behind her. She whirled around and felt the blood drain from her face.

"Hello, Donna," Stanley said.

She caught the side of the car for balance, taking an involuntary step backward.

"I've been looking all over the place for you, Donna," he said in a low voice. "I can't believe you treated me this way. I've been worried sick."

"I can't imagine why," she managed to say through suddenly dry lips. Her eyes darted around frantically. The parking lot was busy, people were going in and out of the store, but no one was paying any attention to them.

Stanley smiled a mirthless smile, his eyes fixed hypnotically on her. "I don't understand why you would say that." He extended a hand toward her.

Donna flinched, moving back from him.

"But that's all right. Come on, sweetheart. Let's go on home."

Donna shook her head. "No."

"But it's all right. I forgive you."

"Forgive *me*?" Her head jerked up. "*You* forgive *me*?"

His hand dropped. "Donna, I don't understand you. Why are you acting like this? Come on. Let's go home. We can talk about whatever it is that's bothering you. You know that you belong at home with me. Just get in the car, and I'll follow you. We'll go home."

"I'm not going anywhere with you, Stanley."

"C'mon, honey. Tell you what … let's go over to the Burger Chef and get a cup of coffee. We can sit and talk this out." He spread his arms out entreatingly. "You know how I feel about you. I need my sweet little wife at home with me. And you know that's what you want too. Let's sit down and talk about this." His eyes were fastened coldly on her.

"Didn't you get the letter from my lawyer?"

He shook his head dismissively. "Oh, yeah. I got it. Don't worry about it. We'll just put that stuff aside. Come on now. Let's get you moved back in—and we'll forget all about that foolishness." He took a step closer.

"Get away from me, Stanley," Donna said. "I told you I'm not going anywhere with you. Our marriage is over. If you don't get away from me, I'm going to lean on my car horn until I get somebody to come help me!"

His lips curved up in a persuasive smile. "Come on, Donna. You know how much I love you. You need me! We can work this out."

Donna looked into his cold eyes, which certainly did not match his entreating smile. "Not this time, Stanley. You can't charm me again! Now go on! Leave me alone."

His smile turned ugly. "All right, Donna. I'm leaving, but you'll be sorry. You can trust me on that. I gave you a chance to straighten up." He strode over to his car, which was parked a short distance away, gave her another dark look, and drove away.

Donna sank into her car seat, and her knees turned to liquid. After several minutes, her heartbeat slowed to normal. Watching the cars around her, she drove back to Mrs. Adams's place.

She called Pennie, and the two of them drove down to Winston-Salem on Saturday. Over lunch, Donna related her encounter with Stanley.

"So, what are you going to do?" asked Pennie.

"Well, I'm certainly not going back to him," Donna said with a little shudder. "I won't fall for that persuasive line of his a second time. I know the real Stanley too well now."

Pennie raised her eyebrows.

"You know, Pennie, I can't imagine why I was in such a hurry to marry him ..."

"Donna—"

"No! You know what? I was just scared. My parents were getting ready to move to Florida, and I just took the path of least resistance. You know what? I would have been just fine. I would have made it on my own—right here—but I let Stanley convince me that I couldn't and that I needed him to take care of me." She made a snorting sound. "I could have done just fine by myself."

"Of course, you could have."

"I know that ... now. I was so dumb. Stupid and dumb!"

"No, you weren't."

"Well, I know better now. It was such a mistake, marrying him. I thought I'd be all alone without him."

"You know you would not be all alone. You had us ... all your friends."

"I know that now, but Stanley made me think I wouldn't. He made me think I would be all alone without him—and that I couldn't cope."

Pennie frowned. "That's so not true, Donna. How did he get you so beaten down and so dependent on him?"

Donna wrinkled her forehead as she thought. "He just wouldn't shut up. I know that sounds silly, but he would just talk and talk—for hours on end. He wouldn't stop talking, and he wouldn't even let me go to sleep until I agreed with him or agreed to do something. He would tell me over and over how stupid I was. He didn't want me to have friends or go anywhere—not even his family. It got to where it was easier just to go along with what he wanted and agree with him on whatever opinion he had."

"You were brainwashed," muttered Pennie.

"I guess I was."

"Well, it's going to be better for you now."

"Maybe. Oh, Pennie, these past few days have been hell! I've been hiding out in that little room until I was ready to have a screaming fit! I'm so glad we could do this today."

"You have to get out and be around people again," Pennie said.

"How am I going to do that? School's out, and I've lost touch with everybody I used to know."

"Come back to church. You and your folks used to be there every Sunday. Come with me—and my parents—tomorrow."

Donna looked at her strangely. "I don't know."

"Oh, come on! You know that we're like a family there. You'll be with a whole community of people who care about you, and everybody will be so glad to have you back with us. Me and my mom and dad will swing by and pick you up in the morning on our way."

Donna sighed. "Oh, all right. What time?"

Donna was dressed and ready when the car pulled up in the morning. She walked out and climbed into the back seat with Pennie and exchanged warm greetings with her parents. Mr. White was dapper in his Sunday suit and tie, and Mrs. White was pretty in her dress, smelling softly of flowers.

Pennie squeezed her hand. "I'm so glad you decided to come with us."

"I am too," Donna said.

Minutes later, they pulled into a parking place in front of the small, familiar brick and white trim church. It took a few minutes for them to get into the building since several people stopped them to express their pleasure at seeing Donna again.

Donna and Pennie made their way to one of the classrooms in

the basement for the Sunday school lesson and then merged with the other congregants. Rejoining Pennie's parents, they slid into a long pew near the back of the church.

Donna took a deep breath, and an unexpected feeling of pleasure and peace washed over her as she looked around at the familiar sanctuary. She had attended the little church when she was a small girl, and most of the people filling the pews were familiar—even if she could not put the proper names to all of their faces. Many of them smiled at her and nodded as she gazed around.

The minister walked out to the pulpit, the pianist began to play a familiar hymn, and the choir stood.

"Turn in your hymnals to page 84," the minister said.

Donna reached in the rack on the back of the pew in front of her and took a hymnal as the congregation rose and began to sing. Her eyes filled with tears as she realized just how much she had missed being there. Why had she given in so easily to Stanley and stopped coming to church?

More people greeted Donna at the end of the service.

When they climbed into the car, Mr. White said, "Why don't we head over to Madiera and get some barbecue for lunch?"

"Oh, that's a fine idea," said Mrs. White. "Is that all right with you, Donna?"

"Oh, yes! It surely is," she replied.

Chapter Twelve

Donna continued to keep a low profile, staying in her rented room much of the time and doing a lot of reading. She began attending church with the Whites on a regular basis; they simply drove by and picked her up on Sunday mornings thereafter.

The Fourth of July was coming up, and the town of Phillips planned its usual celebration with fireworks on the grounds of the elementary school.

Pennie wheedled Donna until she agreed to go and watch the fireworks with her. Pennie parked her car at Mrs. Adams's house, and they walked the few blocks to the school.

Most of the parking places were filled along the street near the school, and people were gathering in the bleachers by the ball field to watch the display.

They paused at the end of a set of bleachers.

Pennie said, "It looks like they're selling cold sodas over there. I'll go get us one, and then we'll pick out seats."

"OK." Donna watched as her friend began walking toward the concession stand.

Suddenly, someone grabbed her legs and hugged her. "Hey, Mrs. Porter!" a small voice cried happily.

She looked down at the grinning boy. "Why, hey, yourself,

Benjie." She kneeled down to his level and gave him a hug. "Are you enjoying being out of school for the summer?"

"Yes!" he said.

"Did your daddy bring you to watch the fireworks?"

Benjie nodded happily.

Donna smiled back. "Where is your daddy?"

"He's over there." Benjie pointed. "See him?"

Donna caught sight of Quinn Cavanaugh, and she felt her heart give an unexpected jolt. He was seated on the second tier of the next set of bleachers, and his long legs were stretched straight out on the seat in front of him. Just as she spotted him, he leaned backward, and she saw the woman sitting next to him. His arm was resting across her back, and his hand cupped her shoulder possessively. The woman threw back her head and laughed at something he said. Her tall, slender body had miles of tanned legs beneath skimpy white shorts, and her shirt was tied in a knot just under an impressive bust, revealing a taut midriff.

A sharp pang ran through Donna's stomach. "Who's that with your dad?"

Benjie grimaced. "Oh, that's Jerri."

"Is she his girlfriend?" The words slipped out of her mouth before she could stop them.

"I guess." Benjie's face brightened, and he caught her hand, tugging at her. "Do you want to come and say hello to my dad?"

"Not this time." Donna quickly freed her hand, stood up, and smiled. "I'll say hello to him some other time, OK? I need to wait here for my friend. She's going to bring us something to drink."

"OK." Benjie turned and scampered away.

Pennie appeared with their sodas. "Ready to go find a seat before they're all taken?"

Donna nodded and accepted her soda. She was careful not to

look toward the couple again as they scanned the bleachers for a good seat. But her festive mood had disappeared.

They climbed up to a high perch on another set of bleachers, just as the first of the fireworks screamed its path up into the dark velvet sky and burst in a multicolor spray, accompanied by the oohs of the crowd.

Donna's eyes returned to Quinn and his lady friend. Benjie was sitting next to them, and all three had their attention focused skyward. She took a sip of her soda. *What business is it of mine who Quinn Cavanaugh has with him?* Annoyed by her own reaction, she turned her head back around and forced herself to watch the colorful sky.

૪ⓢ

Donna slid into their usual pew near the back of the church. Their Sunday school class had ended, but Pennie had stayed behind in the classroom to chat with another student. Donna reached forward and picked up the hymnal, not really paying attention as someone slid in beside her.

A male voice said, "Hello. You're Donna Glenn, aren't you?"

She looked over quickly to see an older gentleman, nattily dressed in a summer-weight suit and coordinating shirt and tie. He was smiling at her.

"Why, yes, uh, actually I'm Donna Porter now, but my name used to be Donna Glenn when my family and I used to come to church here."

"I thought so." He extended his hand. "My name is Harry Collins. I thought I remembered you." He smiled cordially. "Donna Porter. So, you're married now?"

"Well, not exactly," Donna said. "Actually, I'm separated."

"I see. Well, I wanted to welcome you back to our church."

"Thank you." Donna took his proffered hand. "I'm sorry, Mr. Collins. I'm afraid that I don't remember you."

"I didn't expect you to, but I've been noticing you coming to church with the Whites for the past few Sundays. I just wanted to come over and introduce myself."

Donna smiled. She realized that he still had hold of her hand, and she slipped it out of his grasp. "I'm glad you did, Mr. Collins," she said.

"It's Harry. Please call me Harry," he said.

"Harry," she repeated, still smiling.

Mr. White appeared at the end of the pew. "Hello, Harry," he said.

"Hello, Jack." Harry scrambled to his feet. "I was just introducing myself to Donna."

"I see." Mr. White shook hands with Harry.

Harry said, "Uh, I was just wondering, Donna, if maybe you'd like to get a cup of coffee with me after the service."

Donna's eyes widened. "Uh, no, but thank you for the offer. I already made plans to have Sunday dinner with the Whites."

"Oh, well, perhaps another time then." Harry eased past Mr. White. "Nice to have made your acquaintance, Donna. Nice to see you too, Jack." He walked up the aisle and took a seat in a pew on the other side of the church.

As Mr. White sat down beside Donna, Pennie squeezed past her father's knees. Donna slid over, and Mrs. White walked up.

The churchgoers settled in for the service. Minutes later, the pastor took his place up front, and everyone stood for the opening hymn.

After the service, they all made their way out to the car.

As Mr. White was pulling out to the street, he turned to his wife with a grin. "Well, Thelma, it's started."

"What's started?" she asked.

"They've found out our Donna may be available, and the men have started sniffing around her."

Donna felt her face grow hot.

"What are you talking about, Daddy?" asked Pennie.

He chuckled. "Harry Collins just made his move. When I came up, he was trying to get Donna to go have coffee with him. Word's getting around that she's available."

"Harry Collins?" Pennie said. "But he's *old!*"

"Oh, he's not *that* old," said Mrs. White. "He's a widower. Maybe he's lonesome."

Pennie stared at Donna. "Did he really ask you out?"

"He sure did!" Mr. White chuckled again. "Maybe I shouldn't have interrupted, huh, Donna?"

Donna's face was burning. "No! I'm glad you did," she said. She felt a little embarrassed, but she was also thrilled—not at being asked out, but by the warmth surrounding her. Being teased like this felt so good. It felt like she was part of a family again—and she loved it.

Chapter Thirteen

At last, it was time for school to start again. Donna felt a tingle of excitement when she received notice of her first teachers' meeting. Earlier in the summer, she had opened a box at the little post office on Center Street and directed the postmistress to put anything addressed to her at her former residence into her new box. Phillips being Phillips, her written notice of change of address was redundant; the postmistress and her mail carriers were fully aware that she was no longer living with Stanley in their house.

She stood for a moment, smiling down at the postcard, reading again the announcement of the day and time of the first faculty meeting of the year, before turning her attention to the other items in her hand. The remaining pieces of mail that she had pulled out of the small box were an advertising flyer for the grocery store and a long, fat, business-sized envelope, addressed to her in hand-printed block letters, much like what her students would be capable of writing near the end of the school year.

Donna sighed as she stared at the envelope. It looked just like the first four or five she had received since she had left Stanley. She walked slowly back out to her car, sat down behind the wheel, and tore open the envelope. She pulled out four sheets of white typing paper, all written in that childish block printing. She did not have to look at the signature; it was from Stanley. She scanned the pages.

It was an impassioned plea for her to come back to him, professing his love for her. Phrases like "breaking up our happy home" and "joined by God" leaped up at her.

She closed her eyes, remembering the first one, which she had received about two weeks after she had left. She had read it, hope and yearning welling up in her as she absorbed his words—until she got to the very last page: "Please come back home to me, and I will forgive you for what you have done to me." His words ran through her like a shock.

You'll forgive me for what I have done to you! Donna had been outraged. *Who got beaten black and blue to the point of being unable to sit properly for nearly a week? Who was so busy screwing some skanky woman that he was unaware that his wife was in trouble with the woman's low-life, sadistic husband?* Donna had torn the letter into tiny pieces before flushing them down the toilet.

When the second and third letters had arrived, her first impulse had been to throw them away unread, but curiosity got the better of her. She had read them impassively. They were essentially carbon copies of the first, mixing declarations of love with manipulations of guilt. This one did not move her, and it simply made her feel sad.

Donna started her car and made her way down to the grocery store. She tossed Stanley's letter into the big trash can by the entrance. Her thoughts turned back to the beginning of the new school year, and she smiled happily, thinking about how much she looked forward to having a classroom filled with little ones again, eager little faces looking up at her for guidance and learning. Donna gave a little skip as she walked down the aisle. She could hardly wait.

As Donna was making her way from her Sunday school class up to her usual place in the sanctuary, Harry Collins was standing at the end of the pew.

"Good morning, Miss Donna," he said with a friendly smile.

Donna halted. "Good morning, Mr. Collins. How are you doing today?"

"Just fine. And please call me Harry," he said, his smile gentle and his eyes guileless.

"Harry," she repeated, returning his smile.

He moved aside for her to enter the pew. "Um, I was wondering if you had given any thought to what I asked you last Sunday," he said.

"You mean, our getting together to have coffee?"

He looked directly into her eyes, and she saw the underlying sadness there. "Doesn't have to be coffee. I'd be proud to take you out to have supper one night—if you're of a mind."

Donna hesitated. Her mind went to her own empty evenings, alone in her little room.

"Whenever you say," he said.

Donna made a quick decision. "All right, Harry." She saw the quick flash of hope in his gray eyes.

"When?"

People milled around them, finding their seats for the Sunday sermon, and some of them were casting curious looks at Donna and Harry.

"Tuesday night?" Donna said softly. "Do you know where I live?"

He gave a quick negative shake of his head, glancing at their audience.

"Do you know where Mrs. Adams's house is … by the library?"

"I sure do," he said quietly. "Would seven o'clock be all right for you?"

Donna nodded. She gave him a final small smile as she slid over.

He gave her a wink and a small nod, and he moved casually toward his usual place as Pennie slid onto the pew beside Donna.

Pennie gave her a sharp look. "Was that Harry Collins you were talking to?"

Donna gave her an innocent look. "Yes. He just stopped to say good morning."

Harry Collins arrived at seven o'clock on the dot on Tuesday evening, and Donna was waiting for him. She dressed as she would for school—in a loose, mid-calf skirt and a long-sleeved blouse—and his eyes swept over her approvingly when she opened the front door.

Harry was dressed in sharply pressed pants and a dress shirt, carefully tucked in and buttoned up all the way to his neck. His shoes were carefully shined. He looked like he did at church, minus his necktie.

As she stepped out of the house, Donna could not help but notice how the shirt pulled tight over the little bulge of his stomach and the crepey skin on the backs of his hands.

"Good evening." He offered her his arm with a smile.

Amused, Donna slipped her hand inside his elbow as he turned back toward the walkway. "Good evening to you, Harry. How are you today?"

"I'm just great, now that I've seen you, my dear," he responded. "Where would you like to go to have our supper?"

"I don't know," Donna said as he opened the car door for her. "What did you have in mind?"

"Do you like barbecue?" Harry asked. "I thought maybe the Barbeque Barn, over by Madiera."

"The Barbeque Barn sounds good to me," Donna replied.

Harry closed her door and walked around the car, and they drove off on their date.

Donna enjoyed the evening. Harry was a perfect gentleman, opening doors and making sure she was seated comfortably. They talked easily, and he proved to be knowledgeable about a wide range of current topics. He even made her laugh with a witty comeback. She relaxed as the evening progressed, enjoying his company. After they lingered over their meal, he drove her back to Mrs. Adams's and walked her to the door.

She turned to face him with an easy smile.

He took her hand, raised it to his lips, and planted a soft kiss on her knuckles. He looked at her over her upraised hand, and his eyes glowed in the ambient light of the streetlight. "I really enjoyed our evening."

"I did too, Harry."

"Do you think we could do this again?"

"I don't see why not."

He smiled happily. "I look forward to it, my dear. How shall I get in touch to arrange it?"

"I guess you can call me on Mrs. Adams's phone, but my school meetings start this week. I'll be gone some of the time."

"Then why don't we just set up another time right now. On Tuesday of next week? At the same time?"

"All right." Donna turned and inserted her key in the lock.

Harry held open the screen door as she got the door open and then gave her another smile as he turned. "Until next week then. Good night, Donna."

"Good night, Harry." She stood in the doorway and watched him return to his car. He gave her a small wave as he got in. Donna closed the door and went down the hallway to her room. She was smiling.

Chapter Fourteen

School had been in session for almost a month, and Donna had learned the names and many of the personalities of her new class of eighteen youngsters. They ranged in variation from quiet, shy little Ruby, who was from the trailer park on the north side of town, to the outgoing Rory, the athletic and boisterous son of Dr. Hanes, who practiced dentistry over in Madiera. There was the spectacled Sammy, nerdy and highly intelligent, and pretty little Alicia, who spent the first three days of class sobbing for her mother to come back and take her home.

They were coming together as a unit. Donna was in her true element, devising activities and games to bring them together and forge teamwork and friendships without anyone realizing they were actually learning. The hardest part was bridging the gap between those who had spent their short lives around music, books, and activities and those to whom a box of crayons and a picture to color was something new and foreign.

So, on an evening in early October, Donna had just cleared the school grounds and turned down the sidewalk toward home, deep in thought, when her reverie was abruptly broken.

A man walked quickly up beside her, grasped her arm, and pulled her around.

Her heart gave a lurch as she looked up. "Stanley!" She yanked her arm in a vain attempt to free herself. "What are you doing? What do you want?" She gave a hasty look up and down the deserted sidewalk. *No one in sight. This is not good.*

"What do I want? I want to talk to my wife—that's what I want."

Donna gave a final pull, trying to dislodge his grasp, but she could not. She looked up and down the empty sidewalk again, her heart pounding. What could she do? There was no one around to hear her if she screamed. There was no one to help her. She would have to handle him all by herself. She stopped stock-still and looked up into his face, his eyes glittering, lips tightened. "What do you want, Stanley?"

"I told you! We need to talk," he said.

"What's there to talk about?"

"Plenty!"

Her arm hurt under the grip of his fingers. She needed a safe place to go. "Fine. Let's walk down to the diner. We can sit and talk there." It was the only thing she could think of. There would be people there.

He considered it a moment, and she could see him weighing the situation. Finally, he gave a brisk nod, hanging on to her arm and almost pulling her along as they walked the block and a half down the street. They entered the almost-empty diner, and he finally let go of her as they reached the first set of booths.

She rubbed her arm as she sank down on the seat. *Thank God! There are witnesses in here, and I am somewhere safer.*

He sat across from her, glowering at her.

When waitress approached, Stanley frowned and shook his head.

Donna looked at her and said, "Two coffees please, Clara."

Clara gave her a long look, nodded, and hurried away.

"What do you want, Stanley," Donna asked.

"You know what I want. I want you to come home."

Donna's mouth curved up in a mirthless smile. "You know that's not going to happen."

He spread his hands on the tabletop. "Why not, Donna? You know how much I want you to. I've told you how much I love you. I don't understand why you're acting like this."

Clara came and set two steaming cups of coffee in front of them, which they ignored, and she left.

Donna leaned forward. "I can't believe you, Stanley. You know exactly why I have no plans to *ever* go back there again."

"Oh, yeah? Well, you might just be changing your mind!"

She shook her head. "I don't think so!"

"Not even if it meant you would keep your job?"

"What are you talking about, Stanley?"

He grinned again. "I don't think you'll be holding on to that precious job of yours once the school board sees *this*." He pulled a photo out of his shirt pocket and held it to where she could see it, just out of her reach.

Donna leaned forward, peering at the photo, and her stomach dropped. It was a Polaroid shot of her with Pam, in front of what looked like the fireplace in their living room. Both women in the photo were naked, and Pam was kissing her. Donna gasped. Her hand reached for it instinctively, but Stanley pulled it back, close to his body, and laughed. "Where did you get that?" Donna whispered.

"I took it the night that David and Pam first came to see us. I forgot about it until I was going through some stuff the other night." He grinned wolfishly. "So, are you having second thoughts now about coming home with me?"

Donna's mind was whirling. She shook her head speechlessly, bile threatening in her throat. "Stanley, why do you really want me to come back to you?" she whispered.

"Why?" He glared at her. "Do you think I enjoy the fact that folks are snickering behind my back that my wife left me?"

She looked down at the table. "So, all those letters, telling me that you loved me? You didn't mean a word of it, did you?"

"Oh, please!"

A thought hit her like a burst of thunder. "I know why you really want me back," she whispered.

"Why's that?"

"You want me there so you can go to those Choice parties! You want to be able to go down to Chapel Hill with me as your partner so you can screw whoever you want to!"

He stared at her.

"You don't care about me. You just want me to stay home and cook and clean for you and be a servant … and pay the bills … but most of all, you want to use me for *bait*!"

He looked around. "Keep your voice down!"

"No, I won't!" She jumped to her feet. "I won't let you threaten me, threaten my job, because you just want me for *bait* so you can do what you want! I won't have it—do you hear me, Stanley Porter! You can just … go to hell!" Donna grabbed her tote bag and ran out of the Diner, almost blinded by tears.

Donna ran heedless down the street until she got to her boarding house. She slowed as she went up the walkway, her mind whirling frantically. *Oh, God. Oh, God. Oh God. What am I going to do? What am I going to do?*

Cautiously, she let herself into the house. Thankfully, no one was around as she went down the hallway to her room and shut the door behind her. Donna sank down into her chair, letting her tote bag fall to the floor. She sat there as darkness fell, and the shadows in her room lengthened and then blackened. Her mind went around and around over the same thoughts with increasing despair. *Oh, God, Jennie. I understand exactly what you went through.*

She sat there for a while longer, and then her head popped up, as an idea struck her. She got to her feet and began going through a box of books by the wall. After several minutes, she pulled out a slim book, headed out into the hallway, picked up the telephone, and placed a call.

Chapter Fifteen

Donna was sitting alone in a booth, and she kept looking down at her watch as Clara came over to refill her mug again.

"Are you sure you're all right, Donna?" Clara asked as she poured a fourth cup.

"I'm fine," Donna said, looking up at her. "Why do you keep asking me that?"

Clara put her hand on her hip. "Well, if I may say so, it's probably because you've got those big, black circles under your eyes! You look like you haven't slept for a week."

Donna smiled wanly. "I'm OK, Clara, honestly, but thank you for your concern." Her eyes moved to the door.

Two women pulled open the door and stepped inside just as Clara moved away. They smiled and hurried forward when they caught sight of Donna standing there.

Donna opened her arms as the pair hastened across the room. Heads turned as the curious diners watched the three women embrace and settle down into the booth.

Donna could scarcely see through her tear-filled eyes. "Janice, Tina, I'm so glad you came!"

"How could we not?" Janice said as she scooted over to make room for Tina.

"Pam wanted to come too," said Tina. "She sends her love and says she would be right here if she could have gotten away, but she had to work today."

Donna bit her lip as the tears spilled over and began to run down her face.

"Hey!" said Janice. "Don't do that! I told you I'd come when you called me last night. I called Tina, and of course she wanted to come, and so did Pam, but she couldn't get away. So, Stan is giving you a hard time?"

Donna nodded and noticed several people trying to overhear what was going on. "Why don't we order us some lunch? After we eat, we can go over to where I'm living. It'll be more private there, and I'll tell you-all about what's going on." She used a napkin to blot her tears.

Janice said, "That sounds like a good idea to me. What's good here?"

"Almost everything," Donna said. "Lunch is on me. Let's have something to eat, and then we'll go to my place."

Tina nodded, and they all ordered food and sodas.

After Donna paid the bill, the three of them walked to the boardinghouse.

Mrs. Adams came out through the living room as they appeared at the front door.

Donna said, "Mrs. Adams, these are my friends, Janice and Tina. They're visiting me from out of town."

"Hidy, girls," said the old woman. "Glad to meetcha. You-all have a nice visit now." She nodded to them and disappeared toward the back of the house.

"She's my landlady," Donna said. "She probably heard the

door open and was just checking to make sure I wasn't taking a man back to my room."

"What's going on, Donna?" Tina asked as they went into Donna's room.

Janice and Tina took the chairs by the window, and Donna sat down on the bed.

"I've left Stanley," Donna said.

Tina nodded. "Yeah, that's what Janice said. I can't say any of us are sad to hear it, but we know there's a whole lot more to it than that. What's he trying to do to you?"

"He's trying to pull an Eric on me," Donna said. "He's threatening to disgrace me and make me lose my job!" Her tears started again when she saw the shocked looks on their faces.

Janice moved over beside the bed and put her arm around Donna. "Tell us all about it, Donna."

Donna said, "I lied to you about what I do. I'm a teacher. I could lose my job if Stanley tells the school board about—about Choice, and everything—about what we've been doing. He's threatening to do that if I don't go back to him. But that's not all!" Between fits of crying, she told them how Stanley had treated her and what had happened with Mitch and Jean.

"Mitch and Jean?" Janice said. "I've heard of them—and what I've heard isn't very nice. I wish you'd said something before they came up here to be with you. I would have warned you."

Tina said, "You say he whipped you with a paddle and wouldn't quit when you told him to?"

"Let me show you the pictures of my behind that my friend Pennie took the next day," Donna said. She got out the Polaroids that showed her bruised bottom.

Tina let out a low whistle when she looked at them.

"Man! He really beat you!" Janice said.

"I know. I was black and blue and purple for almost two weeks."

They looked at her awestruck.

Janice said, "You coulda had him arrested for assault."

"No. I really couldn't," Donna said. "How could have I explained any of that to the authorities?"

The three of them looked at each other.

"Well," Janice said. "When we get the word around, those two will *never* be invited to any of our gatherings."

"What did Stanley say when he saw what Mitch had done to you?" asked Tina.

"Not much." Donna made a face. "I think mostly he was sorry that I had interrupted him and Jean in the bedroom!"

There was a silence.

"But that's still not the whole story, is it?" asked Janice.

"No," Donna said. "Stanley's trying to blackmail me into coming back to him. He has a picture of me and Pam … er …"

"In a compromising position," Janice finished for her grimly.

Donna nodded. "He threatened to show it to the school board—and I'll lose my teaching job if he does—if I don't come back to him."

"That son of a bitch!" Janice said.

Donna's chin quivered again, and she nodded.

"OK, girls!" Janice said. "What are we going to do about this?"

"What *can* we do?" Donna asked.

"Oh, we can do *something*! You can bet your life on that!" said Janice.

"But what?" said Tina.

They were quiet for a few minutes.

"What about Stanley's boss?" asked Janice.

"What about him?" asked Donna.

"I dunno. Just tell me about him."

"Well, he's one of the community leaders," Donna said.

"Is he religious?"

"Yeah, I guess so," Donna said. "He's one of the deacons over in the Baptist church."

"I'll bet he wouldn't put up with having an employee who's a wife beater."

"But Stanley didn't—"

"His boss doesn't know that," said Tina, her eyes narrowed. "You have those pictures where you are all bruised from your beating. He won't know who actually was the one who beat you."

"That's right!" Janice said. "Where can we find Stanley?"

Donna said, "Well, I think this might be his Saturday to work. He works over at the used car lot section of the Ford dealership."

"Perfect!" Janice said. "Donna, let us borrow one of your photos. Tina and I are going to go pay Stanley a little visit at work. Maybe we can throw enough of a scare into him that he'll leave you alone."

"Oh, I don't know about that," Donna said. "I sorta doubt it."

"Don't you count on it!" said Janice. "Don't you know that bullies are the biggest cowards of all? I'll bet he'll just about pee his pants when he sees Tina and me."

"Well, you can give it a try," Donna said.

"See you after while!" said Janice. "Come on, Tina, let's go have us some fun! Donna, tell us how to get to that place where Stanley works."

"Wait!" Donna said. "I want to go too."

Janice and Tina exchanged a look. "Are you sure?"

Donna swallowed and gave a determined nod. "Yes. I think I have to. I'm tired of being such a pushover and having everybody tell me what's going to happen to me. I think I have to stand up to him myself for once in my life." She gave a shaky smile. "He won't dare yell and scream at me if he's at work and people are watching him."

"Let's go then," said Tina. "We'll go in first and corner him by pretending to be looking to buy a car. Then you come up to us with that photo."

"I'll tell him that I'm going to meet with Bill Carson and show him the pictures of my bruises—let on that he was the one who beat me and that was the reason I left him."

Tina said, "He'll already be off-balance by Janice and me being there. It should work."

ॐ

It was almost two hours later that the girls returned to the boardinghouse. They were giggling as Donna led them back to her room.

Janice said, "Oh, girl! Did you see Stanley's face when he caught sight of the two of us?"

"He turned absolutely white," Tina said.

"Really? I held back while you two found him," Donna said.

"Oh, yeah," said Janice. "We walked in and asked for him ... pretended we were looking to buy a car. I pushed him all the way back into a corner with these babies." She indicated her big bosom and laughed. "I told you one time that I could use these girls like most folks use a knife and fork!"

"He was scared spitless!" Tina said. "He kept looking around at the other salesmen. They were checking us out and trying to hear what was going on."

"That was when you walked up and waved that photo at him and asked if Bill Carson was in today," said Janice. "He lost what little color he had left when you did that."

Donna said, "When I asked him if he thought Mr. Carson would keep an employee who beat his wife, he was speechless. I've never seen him before when he couldn't think of something to say."

Janice said, "I don't think he's going to try to pull that on you again."

"Not after we mentioned Eric's name to him and told him that we didn't think anybody at Choice would appreciate what he's trying to do to you."

"I thought he was going to throw up when I mentioned the club," said Janice. "He tried to shush me. He knows better than to let it get around about the swinging."

"Oh, Lord!" Donna said. "Everybody in there was trying to hear what we were saying. Did you see that? I hope nobody did."

"No, no, it's good!" Janice said. "I think we threw enough of a scare into him that he'll back off."

"I sure hope so," Donna said.

"Well, anyway, it was fun," said Janice. "Now, I guess Tina and I ought to head on back home. It was really good to see you again, Donna."

"I can't tell you how much I appreciate what you did," Donna said as she hugged them. "Coming up here to help me out…thank you! Thank you so much."

"If you need us again, don't you fail to give us a call," said Tina. "That's what friends are for. Will we see you again at one of the socials?"

Donna shook her head. "No, I don't think so." Her eyes filled with tears. "You know how much you all and Pam mean to me, but …"

Janice smiled. "You just don't much like the lifestyle, do you?"

"I hate it!" Donna tempered her words by reaching out to them and touching their arms. "I just … you all are such great people, but …"

"You don't want to swing."

"No." Her tears began to flow. "No. Not ever again."

"Don't worry about it," said Tina. "We'll still be friends. Call us if you need us, OK?"

"I will," Donna said.

They hugged again, and Janice and Tina departed.

Chapter Sixteen

Donna pulled her jacket more closely around her as she waited on Mrs. Adams's porch. It was a cold Saturday morning in November. She was nervous. Harry Collins was picking her up for a date, but she had a feeling that this one was going to be different from the previous times when he had taken her out to dinner and or to a movie in Madiera. He had told her that he wanted to show her his farm, and although he had always been the perfect gentleman in all ways during their previous times together, for some reason, this was making her uneasy. She couldn't say why, but she had a bad feeling about today.

At last, the crunch of gravel in the driveway signaled that Harry's big Caddy had turned in.

Donna plastered a smile on her face and hurried down the porch steps.

Harry put the car in park, got out, and hurried to meet her. His lips met her cold cheek in a peck of greeting. "You're looking very fine today, my dear," he said as he opened the passenger-side door.

"Thank you, Harry."

He closed the door and hurried around to climb in behind the wheel. He backed slowly down the drive, pulled out into the street, and headed out of town. "And did you have a good week?"

"I did. My little guys are coming along so well! Most of them are starting to read words nicely and see how putting them together tells a story. And they can read their numbers now. I introduced them to some simple addition this week. They're all so smart!"

He looked sidewise at her. "You really do love teaching, don't you?"

"Of course, I do!"

"Do you ever think about having children of your own, Donna?"

"Well, yes, I guess so." Donna was taken by surprise by his question. "I mean … of course I do … someday. I've always wanted to have children of my own."

He smiled at her. "I believe you'd make a fine mother."

Donna felt that sense of unease again. "So, where are we going?"

"We're going out to where I live," he replied. "I have a farm just a little way outside of town."

"What kind of farming do you do?" Donna asked.

Harry laughed. "Well, not much of anything anymore. I used to grow tobacco and raise a few head of cattle and some pigs, but I rent out my tobacco allotment now. I just have a couple of pigs for my own use and one milk cow."

"I see," Donna said.

Harry made a sharp left turn onto a dirt road, proceeded slowly past a few mailboxes, and turned into a driveway on the right side of the road. "This is my place."

Donna looked around at the sprawling farmhouse. It was painted white, and a wide porch surrounded the front and side. A big maple tree grew near the front of the house, and just beyond it, she could see what looked like a well-maintained barn. The huge yard was covered with close-mowed grass, although it had turned brown for the winter.

Harry opened the door, and Donna stepped out into the utter silence of the place. On the porch, he took out a key and unlocked the door. "Come on in the house."

Donna followed him into the house. The front door opened into small entryway with a stairway straight ahead. A small living room on the right held an overstuffed sofa and matching chair in front of a brick-front fireplace. There was a dining room table by a set of French doors. A wall with two closed doorways was on the left.

Harry took her elbow and led her to a big country kitchen in the back. The appliances looked old, and a small table was covered with a red-and-white checked oilcloth tablecloth. Straight-backed wooden chairs were pushed up under the table. Big windows with ruffled curtains over the sink let in the pale, November sunlight. Well-worn, but clean linoleum covered the floor. It was warm inside, but the air had a stale smell.

"Well, this is it. This is where I live," Harry said.

Donna looked around. "It's … nice."

"My bedroom is here on the main floor—we passed by it—and there are two more upstairs. My two boys stayed up there, growing up."

Donna stepped forward and peered out the big windows over the sink.

"That's the barn you see out there, across the yard. I got about twenty-five acres here. It runs all the way back yonder until it hits the creek."

"It's nice, Harry."

"I know it ain't fancy, but I try to keep it clean and neat. Of course, my Della kept it a lot nicer, 'fore she died."

"How long has your wife been dead, Harry?" Donna asked.

"Almost four years now," he replied, his eyes reflecting his sadness.

"I know you miss her," Donna said.

"Yes, I do," he said softly. "Every single day of my life." He raised his head abruptly. "But come on, I want to take you out to see the barn and the pigs." He took her elbow again and urged her toward the back door.

They went on a walking tour of the nearby outbuildings, and Harry directed her attention to points of interest. Finally, they walked back into the house and entered the kitchen.

"Well, this is my little kingdom, Donna. What do you think?"

"It's a very nice place, Harry."

Abruptly he put his arms around her and drew her to him, lowering his lips to hers.

Startled, Donna simply stood there, accepting his kiss.

He raised his head and looked down at her sorrowfully. "This is not working, is it, Donna?"

Donna took a small step backward. "What do you mean, Harry?"

He gave a small shake of his head. "I know you and your husband are separated. Do you hope for a reconciliation, Donna? Do you still have feelings for him?"

"Lord, no!" Donna said.

"Well, I didn't get that impression, but I needed to ask. What is it, Donna? Am I just too old for you? I know you probably want to have children. My boys are grown and have left home, but we could start another family if that's what you want."

Sadness washed through her. She reached out and caressed his cheek. "You are such a good man, Harry."

His chin dropped. "You just don't feel it, do you?" His face brightened. "Maybe it's just too early. You need more time for us to get better acquainted … for us to get more at ease with each other." He looked at her longingly and slowly shook his head. "I know that Stanley must have hurt you—whatever it was that happened—but all men are not the same. I would never hurt you in any way. Oh, my dear! You are such an innocent!"

If only you knew, thought Donna bitterly. She shook her head.

"Or maybe it *is* me!" Harry looked at her sharply. "I'm just too old for you!"

"No. That's not it, Harry."

"You just don't feel anything for me, do you, Donna?"

"Oh, Harry, I do. I like you very much. You are such a sweet, kind man."

A little smile lifted the corners of his lips. "And I'm just a foolish old man. My Della was so full of joy and love. I guess I was looking for someone to replace all that in my life."

"Harry—"

He held up a hand. "No, it's all right." He took a deep breath. "I was going to suggest that we fix us a lunch, here in my kitchen, together, but I believe it would be best if I take you back home now."

Tears sprang to her eyes. "Harry, I am so sorry—"

"No, no! I don't want you to pretend to feel something you don't feel." He gave her a rueful smile. "Well, shall we get in the car and head on back now?"

"I guess so," Donna said.

They drove back to Phillips in near silence.

"I'll see you in church," Harry said when he pulled up the driveway at the boardinghouse.

Donna opened her own door and smiled. "Absolutely, Harry. I'll be seeing you." She carefully shut the car door and walked into the house.

Chapter Seventeen

Once again, Donna's life shrank to a daily routine of five days a week of school, the occasional teacher meeting, and church with the Whites on Sunday mornings, followed by a midday meal with them most Sundays. She felt neither happy nor unhappy; it was more like she was in a state of suspended animation. Her social life was reduced to near zero.

Pennie called one Friday evening and asked if she'd like to get together on Saturday to run a couple of errands and maybe drive over to Madiera for a movie.

Donna accepted eagerly.

Donna climbed into the passenger seat of Pennie's car at ten on Saturday morning. "Hi, girl."

"Hi, yourself! How's everything going?"

"OK, I guess," replied Donna. "So, what are we doing today?"

"Do you want to ride over to Madiera? I just have one stop to make. I picked up a present for Brett to give to his little sister Carol for her birthday today. He's working today, and I told him I'd drop it off."

"Sure," Donna said.

"It's the Carpenters' new album: *Close to You*. Carol is crazy about the Carpenters, and Brett couldn't find it in any of the stores up here. I picked it up for him in Winston-Salem after I got off work. It's so popular that it's real hard to find. She's going to be thrilled."

"Good," Donna said. Brett was Pennie's on-again, off-again boyfriend. "So, Brett's working today?"

"Yeah. Evidently Cavanaugh's business is booming. He doesn't usually have to go in on the weekends."

"Where did you say he works?" asked Donna, starting to pay more attention.

"Cavanaugh Excavation—you know, for Quinn Cavanaugh. They dig basements and put in septic tanks, stuff like that. Brett does the bookkeeping for them. He does the invoicing and gets the checks ready to sign."

"Oh, yes," Donna said. "I had Benjie Cavanaugh in my class last year."

Pennie drove up Commerce Street, past the Hillside Motor Court, and a mile later, she turned into a big gravel parking lot in front of a long, corrugated metal building. Several big pieces of earth-moving equipment were parked behind the building. A pickup truck and a Chevrolet car were pulled, headed in, near the steps at a doorway in the middle of the building. A small sign was attached beside the door: "Office."

"Just be a minute," Pennie said, taking a square, flat package from the back seat. "Unless you want to come in with me?"

"No, I'll just wait here," Donna said.

Pennie tripped up the steps, opened the door, and disappeared inside the building.

A moment or so later, a growling rumble filled the air. A helmeted figure on a big, black Harley rolled to a stop near the car, and he got off the bike and looked over at her. He was dressed in a black leather jacket, low-heeled boots, and faded jeans. He removed his helmet, and when he did, Donna recognized Quinn Cavanaugh. He raised his hand in greeting, and she gave a little wave in reply. She rolled down her window as he approached, smiling. "Mrs. Porter?"

Donna smiled tentatively. "Hello, Mr. Cavanaugh."

"To what do I owe this honor?"

"Oh, my … my friend Pennie is just dropping something off for Brett."

"I see."

"How is Benjie?" Donna asked to fill the small silence that ensued.

"Benjie's doing just great. Still loves school."

"Good. I'm so glad."

There was another silence.

"Um … it's a beautiful day," Donna said.

His lips curved upward. "Sure is. Too pretty to be working." He shrugged. "But here I am. Are you enjoying your day off, Mrs. Porter?"

"Please … it's Donna."

"Quinn." He had his helmet cradled under his left arm, and he took hold of the fingers of his right glove with his teeth, pulled it off, and extended his hand through the open window.

Donna automatically took it, and his long fingers curled around her hand. Her heart gave a strange lurch at the contact with his warm skin. "What would you be doing if you weren't working … Quinn?"

"On a day like today? I'd be flying."

"Flying? You mean … like in an airplane?"

"Just like that," he said. "I have my own small plane."

"Oh, that sounds wonderful!"

"It is. That's exactly what I plan to do tomorrow. Would you like to join me?"

"What?"

"Would you like to go flying with me tomorrow?" His pale blue eyes fastened on her big brown ones.

"Seriously?"

"Never more serious. Would you like to?"

"I … yes! I would," Donna said to her own surprise, her breath catching in her throat.

"Good! I'll pick you up after you get out of church tomorrow, say about one o'clock, and we'll go up." He turned away and took a step toward the building.

"Wait! I need to tell you where I live," she said.

He turned back and smiled wickedly. "I know where you live."

The office door opened, and Pennie came out. She regarded him curiously as he stood aside for her to pass, and then he turned and walked inside. "Who was that? Was that Quinn Cavanaugh?"

Donna nodded.

"Well, are you ready to go to Madiera?" Pennie asked.

"Yes," Donna said, her heart pounding.

ॐ

Donna begged off lunch next day, and the Whites dropped her off at Mrs. Adams's place immediately after church. She hurried to her room, changed into jeans and a warm shirt, took her place by the front window, and watched the street. It was another crisp, sunny day.

Promptly at one o'clock, the big pickup that had been parked in front of Cavanaugh Excavating rolled up the driveway.

Donna hurried to get her jacket and handbag. She opened the

front door just as he was crossing the porch. "Hi," she said breathlessly. Her heart was beginning to hammer again.

"Hello, yourself. Are you ready to go take a ride?"

"I am," Donna said.

They made their way to a tiny airfield just outside of town.

Donna looked around as they pulled up to a little building. "You know, I've passed this place dozens of times, but I never really paid much attention to it before."

"It belongs to a friend of mine," Quinn said. "He lets me keep my plane in the hangar here, along with his."

"That's so nice of him."

"It is."

They got out, and Quinn unlocked the gate. They walked toward the big hangar behind it. "Have you ever been up in a small plane before?"

Donna shook her head.

"Oh," he said with a grin. "You're in for a treat." He undid a padlock and pushed up a huge door in the side of the hangar that reminded Donna of an oversized garage door. "Just wait here a few minutes while I pull it out and do my checklist."

Donna watched Quinn as he hand-towed the plane outside, walked slowly around it, and took his time doing his preflight check. A short time later, he pulled it into position at the head of the runway, climbed up, opened the door, and motioned for her.

Donna walked over to the plane, and he helped her climb up inside. She sat down beside him. Glancing back, she saw two more seats behind them in the tiny plane.

She watched him as he took a few more minutes to check several gauges and other things she had no idea of the significance of and finally he started the engine. It sputtered and then settled into a steady roar as the propeller began to rotate. Quinn taxied forward, lining the plane up at the end of the short runway. He made a point of checking her seat belt, did something that increased the sound of the engine, and finally began to move them forward. "Ready?" he asked, looking sidewise at her with a grin.

She returned the grin. "Ready!"

The little aircraft gained speed, and the wheels left the ground.

Seconds later, Donna was looking down at the treetops and buildings below. She looked over at Quinn, who was stealing glances at her as he increased their altitude, and said, "Oh, this is fun!"

"It is, isn't it?" he replied, banking slightly as they rose. "Look. There's the river down there."

"I see it!"

They turned slightly and increased altitude until they leveled off and cruised for several minutes in a northwesterly direction.

"Oh, this is great!" Donna said as she took in the view.

"I know," Quinn replied. "I do this as often as I can. It's a great way to leave all your problems behind and just relax."

"I'll bet Benjie loves it too. You take him up, don't you?"

"You bet! He's been flying with me since he was a toddler."

"Oh, that's wonderful!"

Quinn tilted the wing on his side downward and quickly reversed the maneuver.

Donna was looking straight down through her window. She looked over at him, and he was grinning. She laughed as he leveled the plane again.

After several more minutes, they approached the steeper foothills of the Blue Ridge.

Quinn banked sharply, but instead of straightening up, he continued the bank.

Suddenly, they were upside down, but he steadily continued the maneuver until they righted again. Quinn looked over at Donna to gauge her reaction.

She threw her head back, and a peal of laughter erupted from her throat as she looked over at him, eyes sparkling.

He grinned widely. "Like that?"

Her response was another joyous peal of laughter.

Quinn chuckled and began a wide turn, taking them in a big circle. They flew for another half hour and then headed back to the airport.

He touched down smoothly, and they taxied back up to the hangar.

Donna's legs felt rubbery as she stood on the ground again. "Can I help you do anything?" she asked as Quinn began towing the plane back toward the building.

"Nope, I've got this," he replied. "I'll come back one evening this week to wash her down and refuel. You go on back to the truck and sit down. I'll just be a little while."

Donna did as he asked.

He joined her shortly, locking the gate behind him, and got in behind the wheel. "Hungry?"

"I could eat a horse," Donna said.

"Good. Me too." He drove back down the two-lane, but instead of heading back toward town, he headed over to the interstate and turned east—toward Winston-Salem. "Did you enjoy your first small-plane flight?"

"Oh, I really did!"

"Me too. That's one of my favorite things to do."

"What are some of the others?" Donna asked.

"Oh, that's for you to find out," he said with a grin.

"Maybe I will."

"I hope so. What do you want to know?"

"I know you own your own business," she said. "Let's see ... it's something to do with excavating, right?"

He laughed. "I dig holes in the ground."

She smiled at him. "Just like a little boy in a sandbox?"

"Yep. Just like that. Still like my toy trucks and my airplanes. How about you? What do you do—besides make little boys fall madly in love with their teacher?"

Donna shook her head. "Nothing much. I live a very dull life. I read a lot."

He cast a sidelong look her way. "Uh-huh. You've got a wild side buried inside there somewhere, baby doll. I see it peek out once in a while."

She shook her head. "Not me."

He smiled knowingly. "You aren't a vegetarian, are you?"

"Heavens no," Donna said.

"Good. I was thinking about a nice, thick steak. How does that sound to you?"

"Like it better be close by," Donna said.

Quinn chuckled.

ॐ

It was just turning twilight as they drove back to the boardinghouse.

Quinn opened the passenger door of his truck for her, and he walked her to the front door of the boardinghouse.

Donna stopped on the wide porch and turned to him. "I had such a good time, Quinn."

"Me too, Donna." He took the key out of her hand, turned it in the lock, and opened the door with a flourish. He gave her another one of his wicked grins and patted her cheek. "Take good care of those little ones this week."

Donna's eyes widened. "Oh, I will," she said as he turned and headed down the steps. Her fingers touched her face, tingling where his fingers had caressed it, and she felt a pang of disappointment. *No attempt at a good-night kiss? No I'll call you?* She heard the engine of the truck start, and the lights bathed the driveway as he backed toward the street. Donna turned and walked into the house, and she realized she was smiling.

Chapter Eighteen

Donna got another long, rambling letter from Stanley during the first week of December. Although she knew better, she read through it. It went on and on about how badly they needed to get back together so they could spend Christmas together "in our happy home."

A pang of sorrow shot through her. *Christmas?* She hadn't given the holidays a single thought, but now she was consumed by the thought of spending them alone. *What am I going to do?* That night, she called her parents in Florida, and both of them urged her to come down.

"We'll pay for your ticket," her mother said. "Just let us know when you'll be getting here. We'd love to have you with us."

Her father got on the line and seconded her mother's suggestion.

Donna gratefully accepted their invitation.

"Neither of your sisters can come," her mother said. "They're too busy with their own families now."

"Well, I won't be," Donna said, trying not to sound bitter.

"Be sure to bring your bathing suit," her mother said. "There's a pool here at the retirement village."

"Will it be warm enough to do that?" asked Donna. She had worn her overcoat to school that day.

"Oh, yes!"

Donna smiled, and a small ray of anticipation pierced her dark mood. She checked the school schedule and called the airlines to make her reservation.

The morning after school let out for the Christmas holidays, Donna drove down to the long-term parking garage at the Greensboro airport and boarded her flight to Florida.

Christmas was strange and somewhat unsettling. Although Donna's parents welcomed her with open arms, and she felt cocooned in their love, she felt very out of place in their new world of palm trees, golf carts, and elderly residents. They had a small, artificial tree set up in their tiny living room, and on Christmas morning, they unwrapped the gifts they had purchased for each other.

Donna couldn't get into the Christmas spirit in a community of bingo games and elderly women who talked about grandchildren and volunteering while their husbands avidly discussed their golf scores in minute detail. She was the youngest person around, and although everyone treated her with friendly hospitality, she was ready to return to Phillips and her students long before her return date arrived. The New Year's celebration was held at the clubhouse in the retirement center, and very few of the attendees made it until midnight. Noisemakers were distributed, and the New Year was ushered in by little tin horns, paper blow-out whistles, and nonalcoholic punch.

Her parents asked her about her separation from Stanley over lunch one day, their eyes full of concern.

Donna kept her answers to their questions brief, and they thankfully did not insist on hearing about it in great detail. They lovingly assured her that they would always be there for her—no matter what she decided to do. Donna felt her eyes swimming with tears, and she hugged both of them before directing the conversation back toward safer ground.

જ⑤

It was cold and windy when she returned to Greensboro, retrieved her car, and headed toward Phillips. As the miles flew by, she wondered what her future held in store—and even if there *was* a future for her in the small town where she was born and had grown up. But if not there, she wondered, then where? She felt hollowed out and gloomy as she drove up to Mrs. Adams's house and returned her car to its hiding place in the shed.

Chapter Nineteen

Donna was making her way down the sidewalk, walking home from school on a cold Friday afternoon, when she heard a throaty rumble.

A big motorcycle passed her on the opposite side of the street, made a U-turn, and came to a stop by the curb just in front of her. Looking quite formidable astride the bike, Quinn Cavanaugh lifted the face protector of his helmet and grinned at her. "Hi, Donna. You feel like taking a ride?"

Donna stopped dead, staring at him. "Quinn! I ... I can't do that."

"Why not?"

She looked down at herself. "Well, I'm not dressed for it."

He shrugged. "So go get dressed. I'll wait for you."

Donna opened her mouth and closed it again. "I ..."

"Go on! Just put on a pair of jeans and something warm—a jacket and a long-sleeved sweater. Do you have a pair of boots?"

Donna looked down at her feet. "No."

"Well, put on some heavy socks and sneakers."

She did not move.

"Don't you want to go?"

Donna looked at the challenge in his eyes as he stared at her. "Yes!" she said decisively, surprising herself.

"All right!" He gunned the motor. "Go on. I'll wait for you in the driveway."

Donna hurried, almost running down the street. She rushed to her room, tore off her dress, and scrambled through the dresser drawer for a heavy sweater and some socks.

Less than ten minutes later, she was ready.

Mrs. Adams was looking out the window at the driveway; the growl of the Harley could plainly be heard.

"I'm just going for a ride," Donna said as she hurried past her landlady. "I'll be back soon."

Mrs. Adams glared disapprovingly at her as she left.

Quinn handed her a helmet as she approached and waited while she fastened it. "Hop on!" He closed the face protector on his own helmet.

Donna threw her leg across the bike behind him, as he gave her an assist with his arm, and she put her arms around his waist and held on for dear life as he rolled out into the street and took off.

He went down the street at a moderate speed, but as they crossed under the stoplight at Commerce and Main, he increased the speed—and he really began to open it up as they left the town limits.

The wind was icy and cutting, and she held tight to him as they sped along the highway. He felt so safe and solid as she rested her head against his back and clung tight.

Several miles out of town, he turned off on a barely discernable dirt road going into some woods, reducing speed as he navigated up the overgrown center of the road between the deep ruts on either side. He halted the bike when they reached a blockade of barbed wire.

"End of the road," he said. After she slid off, he swung his long leg off and stabilized the Harley.

Donna stood there in the absolute quiet, her legs and pelvic area still quivering from the pervasive vibrations of the ride.

Quinn held out his hand. "C'mon," he said.

"Where are we going?"

He motioned ahead. "Over the fence. We're going to walk up there a little way."

She followed him as he scrambled over the obstacle and held out his hand to help her over. "Should we be going up there?" Donna asked as he steadied her as she climbed over. "Won't we be trespassing?"

"Probably," Quinn said with a smile.

Donna looked around nervously as they walked down the over-grown roadway. Even though it was winter, and the high weeds were dead, it was difficult walking. They went around a bend, and Donna saw a strange, tall metal structure up ahead. "What's that?" she asked.

"It's an old fire tower," he said. "Hasn't been used in years. Come on." He walked over to the metal ladder that ran straight up the side of the skeletal tower for what looked to be fifty or sixty feet. "Hop on. We're going to climb up."

"Is it safe?" asked Donna.

Quinn shrugged. "Probably so. Let's find out."

Donna looked at him, put her foot on the first rung, and began climbing. She held on tight with both hands as they got farther and farther from the ground. Although the metal was rusty, it seemed solid enough. She felt Quinn right behind her as she ascended.

The wind got sharper and colder as they climbed. Finally, the top half of Donna's body rose above the floor of a small catwalk, about a yard wide, which ran around the round center of the tower. A railing, made of metal rods about an inch or so in diameter, was built on each side of the opening at the top of the ladder. Donna held onto it tightly as she stepped out onto the narrow floor. A waist-high railing circled the outside of the catwalk. She looked out over the treetops and felt a surge of vertigo. She stepped backward and leaned against the side of the enclosed center of the watchtower.

Quinn stepped up beside her and slipped his arm around her waist.

She leaned against him, feeling much better.

He took a deep breath and looked across the trees. "Isn't this great?"

Donna followed his gaze.

The sun had disappeared, and long shadows were beginning to form. The cold air was fresh and invigorating, and there was an absolute silence around them. No sounds of human habitation—voices, car sounds, machinery—could be heard.

"It is kind of nice." She tried to peer through the grimy glass of the window behind her. "Can we go inside?"

"No. It's all padlocked up tight," he replied. "If we did, it would be tampering with government property."

"Oh."

"I just like to come up here sometimes," he said. "Sit on the catwalk, look out over the trees, get away from people."

"I hear what you mean," Donna said.

"Yeah. It can be a bitch, sometimes, dealing with people."

Donna nodded, her head just level with his shoulder.

He shifted his body against her and turned her to face him.

She looked up at him as his head bent to her, and his lips grazed hers, his breath warm in the chill air. Her arms went automatically around him as his lips moved gently against hers, softly, inquiringly, and then he shifted position slightly, and his lips claimed her mouth.

Donna felt a thousand fireworks exploding through her, and she opened her lips to receive him. She was melting. She pressed herself closer to his lean, hard body, losing herself as his tongue slipped inside her mouth, caressing hers, and a surge of heat began in a molten ball somewhere deep in her pelvis and spread deliciously through her. His arms tightened around her, and the kiss deepened.

Suddenly Donna's body stiffened, and she jerked her mouth away.

Quinn went very still in response, and his eyes narrowed. "What is it, Donna? What's wrong?"

She bit her lip and tried to pull away. "Nothing … I … nothing, Quinn. I just can't do this." Her eyes avoided his.

"Whoa, whoa." He loosened his arms around her, but he still held her firmly. "It's all right, Donna. It's all right. Just relax. What's wrong? Nobody's going to hurt you."

She bit her lips with embarrassment, trying to twist out of his embrace. "I'm sorry. I'm so sorry." She rocked her head back and forth.

"Shh," he murmured. "It's all right, baby doll. It's all right. I'm going to let go of you now, OK? Just remember where we are. I don't want you to fall off of here, OK? Relax … I'm letting you go, now, OK?"

As his arms loosened, Donna sank down to a sitting position on the catwalk. Hot tears flowed out of her eyes, and the wind gusts whipping against her body made her shiver.

Quinn sank down beside her, one arm draped loosely around her shoulders.

She looked up at him, her teardrops making rivulets down her face. "I'm sorry, Quinn."

"Shh, it's all right. Just relax. Nobody's going to hurt you, OK?"

"OK." She fumbled in her jacket pocket, brought out a tissue, blew her nose, and rubbed angrily at her wet cheeks. "I am so embarrassed."

"There's absolutely no reason to be embarrassed," he said. "Tell you what, though. Light's fading. It's beginning to get dark. It might be a good idea for us to climb down off of here. Are you OK to do that?"

"Sure, I am," she said, moving her legs as though to stand.

"Take it easy. I'm going to get on the ladder first. Let me get a few steps down, and then you get on as well. Can you do that?"

"Of course, I can," Donna said.

"OK, let's go then."

It took several minutes for them to make their way to the ground.

Donna felt relieved when her feet touched solid earth. Her legs felt rubbery and unsteady. She started to walk away, heading toward the overgrown road.

His hand caught her arm, stopping her. "Hey! I said it was all right, OK?"

Donna looked up at him. She met his eyes and nodded. "OK," she said.

They walked back to the Harley.

ॐ

When she awoke next morning, Donna's first thought was of what had happened atop the fire tower the night before, and she squirmed in embarrassment, remembering her reaction to his kiss. *He's going to think I'm completely nuts.* She threw back her covers and got out of bed. They had not spoken a dozen words after they climbed back on the Harley and drove back to the boardinghouse. When they stopped in the driveway, Donna had taken off her helmet and handed it word-lessly to Quinn before she turned and scampered into the house.

"See you later, baby doll," he had called after her.

She had just kept going.

Donna washed her face and brushed her teeth. Clad in jeans and an old sweatshirt, she made her way into the kitchen and made a pot of coffee and some toast. It was later than she usually slept, even on the weekend. She heard the murmur of voices in the parlor and recognized them as old Mr. Nichols and Mr. Parsons, the two gentlemen who rented the upstairs rooms. They were having another of their lively discussions—probably about politics. One was a diehard Republican, the other a lifelong Democrat, and they loved nothing better than their daily disagreements over something the government had done—or had refused to do. Down the hall, she heard Mrs. Adams's vacuum cleaner. Donna began tidying up after herself in the kitchen.

The vacuuming got louder as it got closer, moving toward the front of the house.

She heard a knock, and the vacuum stopped. She heard Mrs. Adams's voice, and the deeper one of a man, and then the front door slammed shut.

"Donna? Are you up?" Mrs. Adams called out.

"Here I am," Donna replied, walking toward the front of the house.

Mrs. Adams thrust her hands forward, holding an object in them. "Here, girl. These are for you."

Donna took a few steps forward and stopped.

Mrs. Adams was holding out a small oblong container covered with colorful foil, cradling three dark blue hyacinths, obviously expensive, having been forced into bloom this early in January.

"For me?" Donna whispered.

The old lady nodded and smiled. "Go on, Donna. Take them. You must have got yourself a beau." Her expression darkened. "Hope it ain't that guy I saw you with the other day in the pickup truck. You're a lady—and you need to get you a nice man who wears a suit and tie."

Mr. Nichols and Mr. Parsons were standing in the parlor doorway watching as she took the flowers, lowered her head, and inhaled their delicate fragrance.

"Well, who are they from?" Mrs. Adams asked. "Who sent them to you?"

"I don't know. Let me see." Donna put them down on the hall table and slipped the small white envelope out of its holder. She opened it and read, "Until our next adventure."

"Well?" Mrs. Adams said.

Donna smiled. "The card's not signed." She walked past them and carried her flowers back to her room.

Chapter Twenty

On Monday, Donna walked home slowly after school. She fixed herself a sandwich in the kitchen, ate it, and went back to her room. She leafed through a magazine, killing time and building up her nerve for what she planned to do. Time moved slowly as she glanced from time to time at the little drugstore alarm clock by her bed. When the hands on the clock moved from six to six-fifteen, she took a deep breath, wiped her palms on the sweatpants she had changed into, and crept down the hallway to the telephone. Glancing furtively around, she dialed the number she had memorized earlier.

"Cavanaugh Excavating, how can I help you?" said a deep male voice.

"Is Quinn Cavanaugh in?" Donna asked softly.

"Who's calling?"

"Uh … this is just a friend," Donna said. "Tell him it's an old friend of his."

"Hold on a minute." There was the sound of faint male voices in the background and then the sound of the receiver being picked up.

"Hello?"

"Thank you for my flowers," Donna said softly.

"Well, hello there!" His voice changed, deepened, and he laughed. "I'm glad you liked them."

"They're lovely. They make my whole room smell beautiful."

"Good. They reminded me of you—all delicate-looking and sweet-smelling, but a lot stronger than they seem."

"Oh!" Donna did not know what to say.

"Yeah." She heard a chair creaking, pictured him settling back in it, stretching out those long legs of his. "Your week starting off all right?"

"Yes," Donna said, searching for something to say. "Is yours?"

"Oh, yeah, it's going to be a busy one. Listen, I was wondering if you'd like to go somewhere with Benjie and me this upcoming weekend. They're putting on this children's show down in Winston-Salem on Saturday, and I promised I'd take him to see it. What do you say?"

"Oh, I don't know …"

"Come on … Benjie would love it. He still talks about you all the time—unless you get enough of being around the kids all week?"

"No! That's not it at all. I just don't want to …" Donna tried to think fast, but nothing came to mind. "Are you sure you don't want to just have a father-son day with Benjie?"

"He'd love having you come with us," Quinn said. "The play's at ten o'clock, and I told him we'd go have lunch at Mayberry afterward … you know, the place where they make the ice cream?"

"I do know the place," Donna said. It was a big, open restaurant decorated in a great deal of pink and white, attached to an ice cream factory, where restaurant patrons could sit and watch the ice cream being made through tall glass walls looking out into the factory. "They have good food."

"Then you'll go?"

"All right. If you're sure it will be all right with Benjie."

"I'm sure. Pick you up at nine o'clock on Saturday?"

"OK. I'll see you then." Donna hung up the phone, feeling disquieted. *Why is he asking me on a date that includes his little boy?*

ॐ

Their outing on Saturday was a huge success. Benjie was delighted to see her, bouncing up and down with excitement as they piled into the pickup and headed out. The children's play proved to be excellent, well-executed, and professionally done. At Mayberry's, they sat in one of the booths along the big U-shaped bar and ate big, juicy hamburgers accompanied by thick shakes, laughing, and talking about the play.

"So, how's school going this year, Benjie?" asked Donna. "You're in Miss Bigelow's room, aren't you?"

"Yes." He ducked his head, playing with the straw in his milkshake.

"You like Miss Bigelow, right, champ?" Quinn said, tousling his hair.

"Not as much as I did Mrs. Porter," he said, looking at Donna.

Donna laughed self-consciously.

"Sure, you do," Quinn said. "I guess every little boy gets a crush on his first teacher." He looked at Donna with a twinkle in his eyes. "In this case, I can't blame him."

"What do you do after school?" Donna asked Benjie. "I know your dad works late."

"I go to Grandma's. Grandma keeps me after school."

Quinn said, "That's my mom. He gets off the bus at her house, and she fixes supper for both of us."

"Dad's always late," Benjie said.

"Hey! I have to work and make money for you. You know you like it at Grandma's house."

"I know," Benjie said, eyes cast downward, drawing swirls in his drink.

"Well, we do a lot of things together, don't we?" Quinn said. "You liked what we did today, didn't you?"

Benjie nodded, still not looking up.

Quinn met Donna's eyes over the table, giving her a "what can I do?" look.

She smiled at him.

"Well, Benjie, are you about ready to head on back up the road?" Quinn asked.

"I guess so," said Benjie.

"Maybe we can throw the baseball after we drop off Mrs. Porter. Would you like that?"

"Yeah, I guess so." Benjie suddenly brightened. "Can she come home with us and watch?"

"I guess so," Quinn said.

Donna said, "I don't think so, Benjie."

Benjie looked crestfallen. "Please? Why can't you come?"

Quinn and Donna looked at each other.

"Can you?" Quinn asked quietly.

"Well, maybe just for a little while."

Benjie grinned happily and grabbed Donna's hand as his father paid the check.

When they got back to Phillips, Quinn drove them to a small house beside an unpaved street on the west side of town, not very far from his business on Commerce Street. He pulled up the gravel drive outside a detached garage, and they got out of the truck and walked up to a small, enclosed porch on the side of the house near the garage. An open porch with fat columns and a porch swing ran along the front.

Quinn unlocked the door and led them into a small—but very clean—kitchen.

Benjie grabbed Donna's hand and tugged. "Come and let me show you my room, Mrs. Porter."

She glanced over her shoulder at Quinn, and he smiled and shrugged.

Benjie led her back to a small room with a single bed. A Superman spread hung crookedly over it, and one wall was dominated by shelves filled with a small collection of miniature cars, a baseball and glove, board games, and other paraphernalia. A small desk in the corner held a stack of books and a spiral notebook, and a pair of slippers and a single sneaker were scattered on the floor.

"It's a very nice room, Benjie," Donna said. "I like it."

"Look, Mrs. Porter." Benjie pointed to a bulletin board over the desk. "There's a picture I made last year while I was in your room."

"I see, Benjie," she said.

"Your room's not very tidy, Benjie," Quinn said. "I thought you said you cleaned it up before we left this morning."

Benjie looked stricken.

"It looks fine to me, Benjie," Donna said.

Benjie's smile reappeared.

"Come back out to the kitchen," Quinn said. "I'll fix us something to drink. What would you like?"

"I want a Coke!" said Benjie.

"I knew *that*, sport." He looked at Donna inquiringly. "I meant Mrs. Porter."

"A Coke sounds fine to me too," Donna said.

They gathered around the small table in the kitchen.

Donna slipped out of her coat and hung it over the back of the wooden chair.

Quinn fetched glasses of soda for Donna and Benjie and a bottle of beer for himself. "Welcome to our bachelor pad." Quinn saluted her with his bottle.

"It's an honor to be here," she said.

Just then, a big gust of wind rattled the windows.

Quinn looked up. "I guess it might storm today after all. Maybe we'll have to wait a while to throw that ball around."

"Let's play a board game at the table in here," said Benjie. "Can we, Dad?"

Quinn looked at Donna inquiringly.

"What game?" she asked.

"Battleship!" cried Benjie. "Do you know how to play Battleship, Mrs. Porter?"

"No, I don't."

"Well, what do you know how to play?" he asked.

"I used to play Chinese checkers. Do you have that one?"

"Yes!" Benjie ran out of the room.

"I'm sorry, Donna," Quinn said softly. "I didn't mean to get you into this …"

"It's fine," she said. "I'd love to play board games with Benjie."

The little boy hurried back into the room with the board and marbles, and the three of them spent the next few hours playing at the table.

Late in the afternoon, they took Donna back to Mrs. Adams's house.

Chapter Twenty-one

Donna pulled up the driveway at her boardinghouse in her car, Pennie following closely behind hers.

Pennie rolled down her window as Donna jumped out of her vehicle and headed back toward the shed, preparing to open the door and drive inside.

"Just leave the car there!" Pennie said. "Come on and jump in with me—we're going to be late!"

Donna gave a backward look, and then she changed directions and hopped into Pennie's car.

"It'll be OK, don't you think?" Pennie said.

"I guess so," Donna said as they backed out into the street.

For a couple of months, Donna had been driving herself to church on Sundays. Although the Whites had assured her that it was no inconvenience for them to pick her up, after a while, Donna had felt guilty and insisted that she really should drive herself, particularly since her car sat idle during the week as she walked to school. Her car would benefit from being driven.

Donna knew in her heart of hearts that Stanley was aware of where she lived—Phillips was such a small place, after all—but she still felt better keeping a very low profile. He had not made very many attempts to contact her, other than the long letters he kept writing to her, in which he alternated between begging her to come back to him and accusing her of "breaking up" their "happy home."

Today, several members of their Sunday school class were joining members of a church in Madiera for a get-together at the fellowship hall in the neighboring town. The sermon had lasted overlong today, and Pennie and Donna were hurrying attend the function; Pennie had volunteered to drive them over there.

It was a fun outing; they met several new people their age, and everyone enjoyed the camaraderie at the potluck lunch. They lingered afterward, talking, and listening while one of the members from the Madiera group played his guitar for them.

Pennie and Donna were in a cheerful, mellow mood as they pulled back into Mrs. Adams's driveway at four o'clock that afternoon.

Donna opened the door of Pennie's car, looked at her car, and gasped.

"What is it, Donna?"

Wordlessly, Donna got out and walked swiftly toward her car. She stared at it in disbelief. The front and back tires on the passenger side were totally flat. She walked behind the vehicle and saw that the same thing had happened on the driver side. She stopped, her hands dropped to her sides, and her shoulders drooped.

Pennie got out of the car and walked up beside her. "Oh, my goodness!"

Donna looked up at her friend, shock written all over her face. "Stanley!"

"Oh, my Lord, Donna ... do you think so?"

"Who else could it be?" Donna turned toward the back porch.

"What are you going to do?" Pennie said.

"Call the sheriff," Donna replied.

A sheriff's car pulled up thirty minutes later. A big man in an impeccably pressed beige sheriff's uniform came up the walk, walking slowly, but with purpose. He rapped on the door and touched the brim of his hat when they opened it. "Ladies, I hear you've had some trouble here. I'm Davis Brown, deputy sheriff. Want to show me what your call was about?"

Donna nodded silently, and they all came outside, walked across the porch, and rounded the corner of the house.

Deputy Brown let out a low whistle when he saw the car. "So, when did this happen?" He squatted down by the car to get a better look.

"Between twelve-thirty and four o'clock this afternoon," replied Donna.

He looked up at her. "In broad daylight, eh?"

Donna nodded.

He looked over at Mrs. Adams. "Nobody saw or heard anything?"

"No," Mrs. Adams said. "If I hadda, you can bet we'd know who that son of a biscuit was! On my property!"

He bent over and felt the tire. "Looks like somebody gave it a stab, here on the side, maybe with a thin-bladed knife." He rose to his feet, walked to the front tire, bent over, and peered closely at it. "Yep. Got one here too." He straightened up and ambled back over to stand with them. "You told us you and your husband are separated—this have something to do with that?"

"I … I can't say one way or the other," Donna said.

"Domestic matter," Deputy Brown said.

"Does that make it all right?" Pennie asked sharply.

Deputy Brown turned to her. "No. Of course not."

"So, what should I do?" asked Donna.

"Not too much you can do. Your insurance cover this?"

Donna looked at him blankly.

"What kind of car insurance do you have? Comprehensive or liability?" When she did not speak, his gaze softened slightly. "Call your insurance agent in the morning. Ask if this is covered. Maybe you won't be completely out of pocket for four tires."

"Meanwhile, what are you going to do?" Donna asked.

He shook his head. "I'll write up a report on this. We'll ask around and see if anybody—maybe one of the neighbors—saw anybody messing with your car. I wouldn't count on it."

Pennie said, "So … he just gets away with it?"

Deputy Brown shrugged. "Has anything like this happened to you before?"

"No," Donna said.

"Well, I'd keep my eyes open if I were you." He took a small notebook out of his pocket and began making notes.

Pennie caught Donna's eye. "I am so sorry. If I hadn't been in such a hurry for us to get started—"

"It's not your fault," Donna said.

"Well, I still hate it," Pennie said.

Donna sighed deeply. "Me too."

*C*hapter *T*wenty-two

On a sunny Saturday morning in May, Donna sat up in bed, awakened by a knock at her door.

"Donna? You awake?" Mrs. Adams asked.

"Uh, yes. What?"

"You got a telephone call," Mrs. Adams said.

"Be right there." Donna pushed back the covers, reached for her robe, and glanced over at her alarm clock. *Seven thirty-five. Who could be calling so early in the morning on a Saturday? Who would be calling me, period?* She slid her feet into her slippers, a pang of anxiety darting through her, and hurried past Mrs. Adams to pick up the telephone.

"Hello?"

"Good morning, baby doll. Did I wake you up?"

Relief washed through her. "Oh, hi. Yes, you did. But that's okay."

Mrs. Adams swept down the hallway—with a dark look in her direction.

"Sorry about that."

"That's OK." Donna stifled a yawn. "What's up?"

"I just dropped Benjie off. I put him on a bus with a bunch of Cub Scouts, and they headed off for an overnight camping trip. Wondered if you might like to do something with me today."

Donna shifted the receiver to a more comfortable position and smiled. "Maybe. What did you have in mind?"

"Oh, I don't know. Just something casual. It's a real pretty day. Why don't you put on your jeans and let me pick you up?"

Donna only hesitated for a few seconds. "Sure."

"Good. I'll be there in a few minutes," he said.

Donna put down the phone and hurried to brush her teeth and put on her clothes.

He pulled up at the house a short time later. "Had your coffee yet?" he asked as she got into the truck beside him.

"No."

"OK. We'll go by my place, and I'll make a pot."

Quinn unlocked the door, and Donna followed him into the kitchen. Almost as soon as she sat at the kitchen table, he had the coffeepot gurgling. He opened the refrigerator, pulled out butter and eggs, and put a frying pan on the stove. "You like your eggs scrambled, right?"

"Well ... yes."

Using an economy of motion, he melted the butter and broke the eggs in a skillet. He beat the eggs, reached into a cabinet for mugs, and placed a steaming mug of coffee in front of her. Quinn ladled the eggs onto two plates, buttered the toast, and set a plate before her. "Will there be anything else for milady?" He took silverware from a cabinet behind him and handed it to her.

"That looks like everything I need," Donna said. "It smells delicious."

He sat down and picked up his fork. "We aim to please."

"So ... cooking is part of your resume?"

"Has to be," he replied. "Benjie and I don't have a maid—or a cook."

"This is good." She drank some coffee.

As Quinn stood up to clear the table, the telephone rang. He frowned and picked up the call.

Donna gathered their dirty dishes, stacked them in the sink, and listened to Quinn's brief monosyllabic conversation. After a moment, he hung up the phone and uttered a soft curse.

"Is there anything wrong?" she asked as he came back into the kitchen.

"No. Just a small hitch in our day. Would you mind if we run by one of my work projects for a few minutes? There's something I have to take care of."

"No. That's fine," Donna said.

They locked up and headed up the interstate. A few miles up the road, he turned off at a construction site and stopped beside a large area that had been bulldozed and leveled. Several men in hard hats were standing near a backhoe.

"Wait here. I'll be back in a few." Quinn walked toward the men.

They greeted him and began talking and gesturing, and one of the men handed him a large blueprint.

Quinn gestured toward the backhoe, and another man walked over and climbed onto the big machine. The backhoe fired into life and began rolling as Quinn got into the truck.

Donna looked at him. "Problem solved?"

"Yep," he replied.

"So … what's the plan now?" asked Donna.

He glanced over at her and smiled. "Want to go up?"

"Up?" Donna looked at him for a moment, and then her face lit up. "You mean, up in your plane? Flying?"

"Yep, flying. Do you want to?"

"Oh, yes! I'd like that very much," Donna said.

Quinn drove them to the little airport. They parked, and Donna trailed around after him as he got the plane out and prepared it for takeoff. She happily buckled herself into her seat beside him, he taxied down the runway, and they were airborne.

"What kind of plane is this, Quinn?" Donna looked around at the interior, paying more attention than she had on her first flight.

"It's a Cessna 172," he told her.

"How often did you say you bring Benjie up with you?"

"All the time. I'm starting to teach him to fly."

"Really?"

"Really. You want to get the feel of it?"

"Me?"

He glanced sidewise at her. "Yeah, you. Why don't you put your hands on the yoke?"

"What's the yoke?" asked Donna.

He chuckled. "I guess you'd call it the steering wheel. That thing right there in front of you. It's called the yoke in an airplane."

"Oh." There were two of them—one in front of each of the seats in front of the plane. Donna placed her hands on the instrument, and after a moment, she clasped it more firmly and glanced at Quinn.

"Good," he said. "Now look down at the floor. See those two pedals? Those are called rudders. If you know how to use the yoke, the rudders, and the flaps, you can pretty much fly the plane while it's airborne."

"Humph! I know there's a lot more to it than that," Donna said. "Look at all those gauges. There're probably a million things you have to learn to be able to fly."

"Maybe not quite a million, but I could show you some of the basics if you want me to. Do you?"

"You know what? I do!"

Quinn proved to be a terrific teacher, and he led Donna through some simple actions during the next hour, his voice calm and even as he let her get the feel of handling the plane. Her nervousness faded as he patiently led her through some simple steps, and she started to really get into it, thoroughly enjoying herself.

"OK," he said at last. "Ready to take her in?"

"I guess so." She started to release her grip on the yoke.

"No, no," Quinn said. "I want you to continue to hold on and watch what I do as we fly back to the airport. Sort of see what I do and get the feeling of taking her down. One of these days, maybe I'll be sitting beside you as you land her."

A warm feeling ran through her. "Really?"

"Sure. Why not?" Quinn casually banked in a circle and headed back toward the airport.

Donna watched closely, trying to absorb every detail as he smoothly put them back down on the runway and rolled toward the hangar. When they had it back inside and securely locked away, he turned to her and looked down at her, his expression serious. "OK, baby doll. Where do you want to go? I can take you out to lunch someplace—and we can figure out something or other to do to spend the rest of our day—and then I'll take you home. Or we can go back to my house. We can fix us something to eat there, and we can have some private time, getting to know each other. It's entirely up to you."

Donna looked up at him, and she suddenly had a hard time breathing. His pale eyes studied her, calm and waiting, but there was invitation in their smoldering depths that made her want to throw herself at him. At the same time, she wanted to run away as fast as she could.

"Well?" he asked, his lips curving in a lazy smile.

The tip of her tongue wet her suddenly dry lips, and her knees felt weak. "We … we could go fix us a sandwich at your house, I guess," she whispered.

"Good! Good choice." His hand lightly touched her back as they walked toward his truck. He opened the door for her, went around and got in, and started the engine.

Donna's heart pounded as they drove away, fear and excitement warring inside her. She looked at his hands on the steering wheel, his long, slim fingers relaxed and competent, and her eyes moved over his profile, strong and totally male, devilishly handsome. She was quite aware of what she had tacitly agreed to, and while terror tightened her chest and made breathing an effort, a ripple of heat snaked through her hips—and she felt an unfamiliar dampness between her legs.

"What?" she said, realizing that he had spoken.

"I just asked if you like ham and cheese. I know I've got some of that—or I can stop and get something else if you want me to."

"No. Ham and cheese sounds fine to me," Donna replied.

"Good." He flashed a grin at her.

Moments later, they pulled up in his driveway, and he let them in through the back door. Quinn wasted no time before opening the refrigerator and pulling things out.

Donna moved beside him, and they built the sandwiches to-gether. Quinn got out the sodas, and Donna plated the sandwiches and put them on the table. Donna nibbled at hers, watching him eat. Quinn devoured his sandwich, pausing only to drink from his soda between bites. He picked up his napkin, looked at her inquir-ingly, and raised an eyebrow. "It's not to your liking?"

"No, it's good. I guess I'm just not that hungry." Donna looked down with dismay at the half-eaten sandwich on her plate. The knot in her stomach refused to let her take another bite.

"No problem." He rose and began putting away the leftover food and condiments. When he finished, he turned back to her and smiled. "Let's go sit in the living room. I'll take care of our dishes later."

He draped an arm around her, guided her into the other room, and indicated that she should sit beside him on the sofa. He circled her shoulders loosely with an arm, and his fingers lightly caressed her upper arm. "So, did you enjoy your flying lesson?"

Donna looked at him; his face was bland and innocent, his expression unreadable. "Yes, I did. I enjoyed it very much."

He nodded. "I'll take you up again … real soon."

"I'd like that," Donna said.

They sat in silence for several minutes, and Donna was starting to wonder if she had read his intentions entirely wrong.

Quinn said, "Something … or somebody … hurt you real bad, didn't they, Donna?"

Startled, she opened her mouth to protest.

He put his fingers on her lips, smiled tenderly, and shook his head. "Whatever it was, it made you shut down."

"No! That's not true at all."

"You just built yourself a wall … all the way around your feelings."

She shook her head, looked at him uncomfortably, and dropped her eyes to stare downward.

"Donna!" he said sharply, startling her.

"What?" She looked up at him, and his pale eyes drew her in.

Slowly, he lowered his head toward her. He caught her chin in his fingers, tilting her face, and his lips brushed hers.

A shiver of desire went through her, and he lightly moved his lips over hers, barely touching them. He moved away when she would have returned his kiss, interrupting the contact. "Baby doll?" he whispered. "Do you trust me?"

"I … yes. I guess so. I think I do."

"Come on." He started to rise, pulling her with him. "I want to do something for you. I want to give this to you."

"What?"

He pulled her to her feet and guided her to his bedroom. The bed was against the wall, neatly made and covered with a plaid bedspread.

He tugged at her shirt and raised it over her head.

She feebly resisted as it came over her head and down her arms.

He kissed her again, and his lips moved over hers, lingering and devouring their softness.

She surrendered to the kiss, and her arms circled his neck.

He lifted his head, and she opened her eyes, gazing at him. "Let me," he whispered. His hands went behind her to the clasp of her bra, unsnapping it, and he pulled it down her arms. He bent and took one nipple into his mouth, sucking and tonguing it, and then the other.

Donna heard a soft moan escape her as she closed her eyes, and her head arched back.

Quinn's hands moved down to where her jeans fastened, and he unsnapped them, pulled down the zipper, and the garment parted as he inserted his hands, pushing it downward, over her derriere. He hooked his fingers into the top elastic of her panties and tugged them downward.

Donna's eyes popped open. "W-wait."

Quinn scooped her up with a smooth movement and deposited her onto the bed. He stared down into her eyes. "Just trust me, baby doll," he said softly. "Will you trust me? Please?"

Donna looked up at him. Her breath hitched as he continued to stare down into her eyes, waiting. She relaxed slightly and gave a tiny, helpless nod.

"You trust me?" he asked.

"Yes." She gave him a tenuous smile, her lips trembling.

Quinn took hold of her jeans and pulled them down her legs, discarding them beside the bed. He gently pulled on her panties, and his eyes locked with hers.

Donna lifted her hips, helping him ease the panties down and off.

He lowered himself beside her on the bed, fully clothed, and gave her a slow, thoughtful kiss. "Don't move," he whispered. "I want you to just lay still and let me love you." Donna looked at him questioningly. "Close your eyes, baby doll," he murmured. When she did, he lowered his head and began kissing her small, round breasts, moving back and forth from one to the other until the nipples hardened under the demands of his lips and roving tongue. He trailed a line of kisses down the center of her body, stopping to kiss and tongue her navel.

Donna shifted her hips and made a sound that was half giggle, half moan.

He continued his downward path, and when he reached the edge of her patch of pubic hair, he shifted position, moving to kneel on the foot of the bed. He grasped her ankle and lifted first one leg and then the other, bending it at her knee, placing her foot close to her buttock, fully exposing her crotch to his avid view.

Donna's body stiffened, and she opened her eyes again.

"Uh-uh! Close your eyes. Relax, baby doll." He caught her eyes and gazed at her until she obeyed him—then he lowered himself, moved his face to the junction of her legs, and began ravaging her hungrily.

Donna jolted and moved to sit up the instant that his mouth touched her.

He simply raised up, pushed her shoulders back down to the bed, and hovered over her. "Trust me." He swayed forward above her so that his lips claimed hers again.

After an initial hesitation, Donna responded hungrily, her hands grasping his head, pulling him closer.

He abruptly broke the kiss and pulled away from her. "Not yet." He looked down at her. "You lie back and let me love you another way first. I want you to close your eyes. Don't move or do anything. Just feel what you feel—and just go with it. All right?"

Her breath came in shallow gasps. Donna nodded and closed her eyes tight.

Quinn moved back down and arranged her the way he had positioned her earlier, and then he lowered his mouth to her again. His tongue entered her, exploring the warm folds and finding the hard little button of her clitoris. His tongue began caressing it repeatedly.

Almost at once, her hips pushed back against him, and she let out a wordless cry.

His tongue ravaged her relentlessly.

She was suddenly very wet and slippery, and as ripples of sensation began to radiate through her, Donna tried to pull away.

Quinn's strong hands held her hips firmly in place, his tongue working, teasing, and demanding.

Suddenly, Donna's whole body stiffened, a cry burst out of her throat, and she slowly went limp.

Quinn raised his head.

She took a deep breath and looked down at him. She raised one arm and then let it fall weakly back to the surface of the bed. "What happened to me?"

Quinn crawled up beside her and smiled. "What do you think happened?"

"I don't know," Donna said.

"You really don't know?" Quinn asked.

"No."

"How do you feel?"

Donna took a deep breath and smiled. "Oh, I feel wonderful. I feel all warm and lazy and relaxed. Sort of like I'm floating in a warm bathtub. Or maybe like all the bones have been removed from my body." She looked sharply at him. "Quinn! What did you do to me?"

"Baby doll, you just had a huge orgasm. Do you mean to tell me that that has never happened to you before?"

"No," Donna said. "It never has."

Quinn looked at her flushed cheeks and languid expression. He shook his head in wonder and hugged her to him. "Well, I sure am glad I was the one who gave it to you."

"Me too." After a long moment, she said, "So that's what all the fuss has been about all this time—and I've missed it?" She pulled back from Quinn. "Do you think you could make me do it again?"

"Well, I certainly hope so," he replied with a chuckle.

Donna cuddled up close to him. "Can we try to make it happen again today?"

"You better believe it."

They had been quiet for a long time. Quinn kissed her forehead as she half-dozed beside him. He rose, freeing himself from her circling arms. Donna opened her eyes to watch as he stood beside the bed, unbuttoning his shirt. Her breath caught as he peeled it off, revealing broad shoulders above a tapered, muscular chest that was covered with an intricate tattoo that extended over his shoulders, down and over his bulging biceps. He unfastened his jeans, bent to remove them, and then pulled his briefs down and off, revealing a long, sinewy body and an already half-erect penis.

She watched with fascinated awe as he bent over to remove his footwear, one after the other. As he climbed back onto the bed, she reached out to touch the pattern of ink on his chest.

"I got that while I was in the service," he murmured. "Does it turn you off?"

"Oh, no," Donna said. "I like it!" She traced the pattern with her fingertips, and a flicker of heat ran through her lower abdomen.

"Good." He gathered her tight against the radiating warmth of his body, and his mouth claimed hers, lazily at first, but with an increasing demand and a hunger that Donna found herself responding to. His long, muscular body pressed tight against her, and she felt something long and sinewy become much more so as his erection grew and pulsed against her. His hands moved down to cup her buttocks and press her even closer, and his tongue explored the recesses of her mouth. He pulled her buttocks even farther apart, and she felt him insert a finger from behind her inside her still-moist vulva. He broke the kiss. "Oh, God, baby doll, I could just eat you alive!" He rolled her onto her back and slid down her body. He pushed her legs apart, lifted her hips to straddle his head, and moved to take her with his mouth, his tongue sliding inside her.

Donna cried out as it found its target, sensation again radiating through her.

He slid his body upward, between her legs, splayed on either side of him, until she felt the heat of his erection touching her. From somewhere, he produced a condom, and he rolled it onto himself.

She looked up at him, towering over her, strangely aroused by the faint menace of his strong body above her. She made an almost meowing cry and reached up her arms to him. When he kissed her, she tasted her own juices on his lips.

He lifted his body slightly, parted her with his fingers, and inserted just the tip of himself inside her. "Are you ready for me, baby doll?" he whispered, rocking slightly. His fingers caressed her around the tip of his penis, slipping inside her and rubbing her clit, watching her face when she gasped in response. "Oh, yeah! Oh, baby doll, you are so wet! Will you let me go inside you? I want you so bad!"

"Oh, yes!" Donna cried, and her hips lifted of their own accord against him. "Oh, yes! Oh, yes!"

He thrust himself deep inside her.

She surrendered herself to the sheer sensations that engulfed her, carrying her aloft on a wave that rose and rose. As he thrust into her again and again, the wave came crashing deliciously down over her with a starburst of feeling that she had never before experienced. She clutched at his sweaty shoulders and cried out wordlessly, feeling him climax inside her even as her own body convulsed again and again with roaring sensation.

"Quinn?" Donna murmured sometime later, opening her eyes.

"Hmm?" he replied from where his head rested on the pillow, collapsed against her, his arm loosely holding her.

She moved her hand to his shoulder, lightly caressing it.

He opened those incredible pale eyes and focused on her with an indolent smile. "Hi." He shifted, raised his head, and gave her a soft kiss on the cheek. "You want to get under the covers and take a little nap?"

"I don't know," she said softly.

"Come on," he moved off the edge of the bed, and she obligingly followed him. He pulled back the bedspread and sheet and gestured for her to climb back in, stretching out beside her and covering them both, hugging her close.

To her surprise, Donna felt herself drifting contentedly off to sleep.

When she opened her eyes again, Donna felt, more that saw, Quinn lying next to her, propped up on his elbow and staring down at her.

"Hey, sleepyhead," he said.

Her eyes widened. "What time is it?"

"Almost dinnertime," he replied.

"Oh, my goodness!"

"Relax, baby doll. You don't have any place you have to be, do you?"

"Well ... no."

"OK, then." His hand moved under the covers, caressing her waist, moved up to cup her breast, and his thumb rubbed lightly over her nipple.

Her hand snaked up to grasp and hold his wrist.

He looked down at her quizzically.

Donna felt her cheeks go hot. "Quinn ..."

"Shh," he whispered.

Donna was very much aware that she was lying naked in bed with this very attractive almost stranger. "Quinn, listen, I ..."

"Relax, Donna," he said. "It's OK."

She pushed his hand away, sat up, and covered her face with both hands. "No, it's not. It's not OK."

"Talk to me, Donna." His hand grasped her wrist and tugged. "Tell me why you're getting upset. Please."

Donna lowered her hands and looked at him. "I ... I just don't know what to tell you. I want you to know that ... what we did today ... that just wasn't something I usually do."

"Don't you think I know that?" he asked softly.

"No! I mean besides ... I never have, uh, reacted to a man like that before. Ever." She peeked up at him.

He nodded. "I think I know that too."

"And I certainly don't go jumping into bed with people I barely know!" She felt the blood draining from her face as she realized what a lie this was. She *had* jumped into bed with strangers, however unwillingly! On a regular basis! Her heart shrank. How would anyone ever believe that? Or understand why?

He threw back his head and laughed. "Baby doll! That's exactly why I like you so much! You're the perfect, modest little lady on the outside, but you've got a wild streak hidden inside you that's a mile wide. You just don't want to admit it—not even to yourself." He shook his head. "We're a lot alike, you and I. We're not afraid to jump in and do things we want to do. And we don't want to get stuck in the straight and narrow, in a rut somewhere."

"There's no way you can know something like that about me!" cried Donna. "I … I mean … maybe … I could be a little bit like that … but you couldn't know it. I barely know you."

He smiled. "Well, I'll tell you what. You just take all the time you want to, getting to know me. We've got all the time in the world."

Donna felt her face flame again. "Quinn … about, you know, um, what we just did together …"

He grinned at her. "What about it, baby doll? It was pretty damn spectacular, I thought."

She wouldn't meet his eyes. "That's what I wanted to ask you … I mean … is it always like that for you?"

He reached out and took her face between his hands, forcing her to look at him. "I won't lie to you, baby doll. I do like having sex. Always have. I enjoy making love with a willing woman. I like it a whole lot. But what we had today, well, that was special. I have to tell you … it went *way* beyond special."

"Oh," Donna said. *Maybe there is a chance, just a tiny one, but a chance, that he could understand. Maybe I can tell him. No,* she thought. *This is so new, so treasured. There is no way I can take that chance.* Her stomach clenched.

"What do you say we get out of here, get dressed, and go have dinner someplace? How does that sound to you?"

"OK. As long as it's not over to the diner. I eat there all the time, and to tell you the truth, I'm sort of tired of it."

"Deal! How about we ride over to the Barbeque Barn? Could you go for some barbecue?"

She nodded.

"All right, then!" He swung his long legs out of bed. "Let's get our clothes on and go eat."

⅗

They drove over to Madiera and parked in front of the Barbeque Barn. Since it was still early, the restaurant was only about halfway filled.

Quinn held the door open for her, and as they walked to an empty booth, Donna was aware of the looks they were getting from some of the diners.

"I guess it'll be all over town that you and I had dinner together tonight," Donna said to him as they settled into the booth.

"Does that bother you?" Quinn asked.

"Not at all," Donna said. "Does it you?"

He laughed. "I've been the subject of gossip for so long that it would be news if they weren't talking about me. Now, what sounds good to eat tonight?"

They took their time with dinner. Donna found Quinn to be easy to talk to and well-versed on any subject she brought up. The restaurant filled as they lingered over their meal, sipping coffee afterward as they talked and laughed together.

Quinn glanced over at her as they drove back toward Phillips. "Would you consider coming back to my house for a while?" he asked.

Donna darted a quick look at him. "I don't know," she said softly.

"You aren't still afraid of me kissing you, are you?"

"No."

"Then come back with me. We won't have this opportunity often." He reached over and touched her arm.

Donna shivered, and her breath caught in her throat.

"Are you afraid I'll want to make love to you again, Donna?" he asked.

"I'm afraid you won't," she whispered.

Quinn's foot pressed down harder on the gas.

The kitchen door had barely closed behind them when they started kissing. Clothes were unfastened as they rushed back to the tumbled bed in Quinn's room, and they made love feverishly.

Quinn soon brought her to another stunning orgasm.

Donna refused to spend the night with him, and Quinn drove her back to Mrs. Adams's house before it got scandalously late.

Chapter Twenty-three

Donna and Pennie were seated in a restaurant on Stratford Road in Winston-Salem at midday on a Saturday in May. They had driven down to Thruway Shopping Center for a morning of shopping.

Donna leaned back in her chair as the waitress left with their orders, and she took a deep breath and smiled.

"I really liked that dress you tried on in Thalheimers," she said. "I wish you'd bought it."

Pennie wrinkled her nose and looked thoughtful. "I don't know … I might still go back and get it if I don't see something I like better. I'm glad you bought the shoes. They're so cute!"

"Yeah. I really didn't need them, but you're right. They were just too cute to pass up."

The waitress arrived at the table with their drinks.

Pennie took a sip and looked over at Donna. "There's something I wanted to ask you."

Donna looked back at her, eyes wide and guileless. "Ask away!"

"I guess this is none of my business …"

"What?" asked Donna.

"Well, I heard talk that you were seen going out with Quinn Cavanaugh." Pennie grimaced. "It's not true, is it?"

Donna looked surprised. "Well, yes. As a matter of fact, Quinn and I have gone out a few times. Why? What's wrong with that?"

"Oh, Donna!" Pennie looked dismayed. "Why on earth would you go out with him?"

"What's the matter with Quinn?"

"Donna!" Pennie leaned forward, and her brow creased as she spoke. "Everybody knows that he's always been so wild—riding motorcycles and stuff like that! And everybody knows he's a womanizer! He had his little boy with some girl who was just as wild as he was, and then just as soon as she had the baby, she took off with another man—and left it with Quinn. I think his mother ended up having to help look after it—"

"I know that! And he's not a baby anymore. I had Benjie in my class last year. He's a darling little boy."

"I'm sorry! He probably is, and I sure didn't mean to imply anything bad about the poor little guy! But that's not the point I'm making. I just don't want to see you get mixed up with a man like that."

"Doesn't Quinn Cavanaugh own his own business? Isn't that where your boyfriend works? That sounds to me like he's pretty solid and responsible."

Pennie shook her head, and her cheeks turned pink. "That's true, but Brett tells me that he goes out with a whole string of women—one girl right after another—and he never keeps the same one very long. I just don't want to see you get your heart broken again. That's all."

Donna smiled. "I really appreciate you trying to look out for me, Pennie, but I really do like Quinn. We have fun together, and a lot of the time, we take Benjie with us when we go somewhere. Why, just last weekend, the three of us went to see a movie together on Saturday afternoon—and out for hamburgers afterward. And as for the motorcycle, he's taken me for a ride. It was fun!"

Pennie looked miserable. "I'm sorry, Donna. I know that it's your business who you see ..."

The waitress arrived at the table with their food and put the steaming plates in front of them.

Donna looked across the table and smiled. "Pennie, you're my very best friend in the whole world. I appreciate that you're trying to look out for me—and I do love you for it—but Quinn's a good guy. All that stuff is way back in his past, and he's a great father to Benjie, from what I've seen. I'm not going to get hurt. There's nothing serious between us, and I just love his little boy absolutely to death! He's adorable, and I like to be around him—as well as his daddy! And don't forget that I'm still married to Stanley. So, I'm sure not looking for anything else serious in my life right now. OK?"

Pennie picked up her fork and gave her a dubious look. "OK. If you say so. Speaking of Stanley, how's that going? Is he still sending you those letters, begging you to come back to him?"

Donna sighed. "Not lately. But my year of separation from him will be over in less than a month. Then I can file for divorce."

"Well, that's good, isn't it?"

"Yes and no." Donna looked solemnly at her friend, her eyes wide and troubled. "I'm scared to death of what Stanley might do when I do file for divorce."

"What do you think he'll do?"

"I don't know, but I feel like he'll try to do something. It's not that he loves me; he just doesn't want to lose something he thinks is his. I'm almost like a piece of property to him, and he thinks it makes him look bad if I don't want to be with him anymore. And he sure can be mean and spiteful. Remember the cut tires on my car? I know he did that; I just can't prove it."

"I sure do remember that, but you *are* still going to file for divorce, aren't you?"

"Of course, I am, but I'm still scared."

"I don't blame you," Pennie said.

They ate in silence for a few minutes, and then Donna raised her chin and looked over at Pennie. "Hey! We're not going to let Stanley spoil our day together, are we? Where do you want to go when we finish eating?"

Chapter Twenty-four

After church, Donna accompanied the Whites and Pennie back to their house.

Mrs. White had a roast slow simmering in the stove.

They enjoyed the meal together, and Donna excused herself shortly after the dishes were done.

Pennie gave her a knowing look as she gathered up her things and headed toward her car.

Donna averted her eyes and felt a blush heat her face.

She stowed her car in Mrs. Adams's shed, hurried into the house, changed into her jeans, and made her way down to the front door. She did not have to wait long.

A few minutes later, Quinn's pickup pulled up the driveway.

Donna slipped out the front door and walked out to meet him.

He opened the door for her, and Benjie slid over to make room for her.

Quinn got back in and backed down to the street.

"So, what are the plans for today?" she asked.

"Well, I sort of promised Benjie that I'd throw him a few balls so he could practice his hitting. Maybe we could go over to the ball field at the school for a little while."

Benjie was staring up hopefully at her.

"Sure, that sounds good," Donna said.

Benjie's face lit up.

"Maybe your dad can be the pitcher—and I can be the catcher."

"Really?" Benjie asked.

Donna gave him a big smile and ruffled his hair. "Really."

"Thanks, Donna," Quinn said as he turned toward the school.

When they got to the field, other people were already using it. There was a man she did not recognize with a boy who looked to be about ten years old. Jerry Miller, from Benjie's class, was tossing a ball back and forth to his older brother.

Quinn took Benjie's ball, bat, and glove out of the truck, and the three of them walked over toward home plate.

Jerry stopped throwing and waved to Benjie.

Quinn nodded to the other man. "Mind if we join you folks?"

"Sure thing," the man said. "Glad to have you."

Quinn looked around. "You boys want to take turns hitting? I can throw you some pitches."

There were affirmative responses, and Quinn started toward the pitcher's mound.

The four boys clustered around home plate. "Maybe you can practice running to first too." Quinn looked at the other father. "Would you mind tending first base?"

"I'm Tom. Tom Woods." The man extended his hand. "I'd be glad to."

As Tom trotted toward first base, Donna walked over to the boys.

"Hey, Mrs. Porter," said Jerry.

"Hey, Jerry. I'm going to catch for you guys, but I know you won't need me because you're going to hit every single ball that Quinn throws, aren't you?"

They all grinned.

"OK, let's get you-all lined up," Quinn said. "Who's going to be the first batter?"

"Benjie. He's got the bat," said Brady.

"OK, the rest of you line up and get ready!"

They sorted themselves out and began playing.

After an hour or so, Donna was ready to call it quits.

Quinn called out, "OK, you guys! One more bat for each of you."

The boys grumbled a bit, but the next batter took his place, and Donna resumed her position behind him.

After the round, Quinn and Tom Woods walked toward home plate.

"Good job, boys," Quinn said.

"Nice to meet you folks," said Tom.

"You too," Donna said. "Whew, I need to go over yonder to the water fountain."

"Let's all of us do that." Quinn lightly clapped Benjie on the back. "Good job, sport."

They drank water and ambled back to Quinn's truck.

"Where to now?" Quinn asked.

"I want some ice cream," Benjie said.

"Hmm, where can we get ice cream?" Quinn asked.

"Well, it's Sunday, so the counter at the pharmacy is closed," Donna said. "And the Burger Chef doesn't sell ice cream—except in milk shakes."

Quinn opened the door for them. "I have an idea. Why don't we just swing by the grocery store? I'll run in and get us a gallon, and we can take it home with us and eat it there? That OK with you, Benjie?"

Benjie nodded happily and climbed into the truck.

A short time later, the three of them were sitting around Quinn's kitchen table with bowls of ice cream in front of them.

As they were finishing up, a car drove up the gravel driveway.

"Who can that be?" Quinn asked.

Benjie ran to the back door and looked out. "It's Grandma," he announced over his shoulder.

Donna looked toward the door as it was pushed open, and a tall, rangy woman with short, gray hair came in with a covered dish in her hands. Her sharp eyes swept over the room, narrowing when she saw Donna sitting at the table.

"I thought you were coming by today for dinner," she said, looking at Quinn accusingly.

He shook his head. "Nope. I didn't tell you that."

"Well, I made chicken pie for Benjie. It's his favorite, and I told him that I'd make it for him this week. When you didn't show up, I brought it over here so he could have it for supper."

"Thank you, Ma. I appreciate it, but you didn't have to do that." He looked over at Donna. "This is my mother. Ma, this is Donna Porter."

Donna started to get to her feet. "Hello, Mrs. Cavanaugh. It's a pleasure to meet you."

"Hello," the woman said shortly, barely sparing her a glance. "Quinn, take this pie. Give it to Benjie for his supper." She handed the dish to Quinn, turned, and swept back out the door.

Donna stood in astonishment as she heard the slam of a car door and the motor starting. "I don't think your mother likes me very much." She sank back down onto her chair.

He gave a short laugh. "Don't mind her. She never likes anybody that I … uh …"

"That you date?" Donna finished for him.

He grinned. "Yeah," he admitted.

"Why did Grandma rush off?" asked Benjie, still standing by the kitchen door.

"I guess she was in a hurry," Quinn said. "C'mon, sport. Let's get these dirty dishes in the sink. See? Grandma brought us chicken pie for supper."

Quinn and Benjie washed their bowls and put them away. When they finished, Quinn suggested that they play a board game. Benjie happily went off to find one, and they played several rounds as the afternoon passed. After that, Quinn portioned out the chicken pie as their main dish for dinner.

Donna helped with the dishes, and they watched TV for a while before Quinn announced that it was time for Benjie's bath. After a token protest, the boy disappeared from the room.

When they heard water filling the bathtub, Quinn moved over beside Donna on the sofa and gave her a kiss. "You've been awfully quiet this afternoon since we got back. Is there anything wrong?"

"No," Donna said. "I've just got a lot on my mind—that's all."

He gave her a penetrating look. When she said nothing further, he tightened his arm around her shoulders and drew her closer, his hand rubbing and caressing her upper arm.

Donna sighed, rested her head against him, and feigned interest in the TV program.

A short time later, Benjie appeared in the doorway, clad in his pajamas.

"Did you hang up your towel?" Quinn asked.

Benjie nodded.

"OK, sport. Say good night then. You need to get to bed so you can get up early for school tomorrow. There's just a few more days left."

"Good night, Benjie," Donna said.

"'Night." The boy reluctantly turned and moved out of the room.

A few minutes after Benjie left, Quinn said, "So … are you ready to tell me what's wrong?"

"Nothing!" Donna responded too quickly.

He continued to look down at her.

"I guess we do have to talk …"

"What about?" Quinn asked softly.

She stared down at her hands, twisting her fingers together. "I need to tell you something. I need you to know about something I was doing—what Stanley and I were doing—before I left him."

"No!" Quinn put his fingers over her lips and turned her face up toward him.

Her eyes widened when she saw the stern look on his face.

He smiled, moved his fingers, and caressed her face. "I don't care. All I care about is what's between you and me … right now. Everything that happened before that doesn't matter. All that stuff that happened before we got together—whether it was you *or* me—all it did was make you and me who we are now. Just tell me one thing, OK?"

"OK. What?"

"Have you been honest and truthful with me since we've been together?"

"Well, of course I have!"

"Then that's all I want—and all I want to know."

"But—"

"No buts about it, baby doll." He captured her lips with such sweet tenderness that tears sprang to Donna's eyes.

She put her arms around him, drew him closer, and reveled in the feel of his hard body and the delicious smell of him. As reality intruded, she pulled away.

"What, baby doll?" he whispered.

"Oh, Quinn! I'm just so scared," she said.

He held her firmly, refusing to let her turn away. "What are you scared of Donna?"

She closed her eyes, and teardrops squeezed their way out. "It'll soon be time for me to file for my divorce from Stanley—and I just know that he's going to do something awful when I do."

Quinn pulled her face against his shoulder and caressed her back. "Why do you think that?"

"Because … because he's already threatened to make me lose my job." She pulled back and looked up at him, her face wet with tears. "You see … he has this picture of me, and he threatened to show it to the school board. If he does, I'll lose my job. And then what will I do?" She dropped her head back to his chest and wept.

"Don't you worry," Quinn whispered. "He's not going to do any such thing. He wouldn't do something that stupid … shh, baby doll. Don't you worry about him. That's not going to happen."

"What makes you so sure?" Donna's voice was muffled against his chest.

"Trust me! It ain't gonna happen!" Quinn rubbed her back softly until she took a deep hiccupping breath and stopped crying.

"I'm sorry," she whispered, rubbing at her wet face.

"Nothing to be sorry about. Let me go get you some tissues."

She forced a smile. "Thank you."

"Do you want something to drink?"

"No. I'm good," Donna said, sniffling.

When he handed her the tissues, she blew her nose loudly. "I'm sorry."

"Nothing to apologize for." He sat back down beside her, put his arm around her, and pulled her close.

They sat silently as the TV played, neither of them watching it.

Finally, Donna stirred. "I guess you'd better take me home soon."

"Will you be all right?"

"Of course."

"OK, let me look in on Benjie. If he's fast asleep, it will be all right to leave him while I drive you on home.

"OK," Donna said.

Quinn went to look in on his son.

"When can you file for your divorce?" Quinn asked when he pulled up to the boardinghouse.

"Around the end of June," she replied.

"And you're going to file as soon as you can?"

"Absolutely," Donna said.

"OK." He grinned in the darkness. "I'll be thinking of some way that we can celebrate."

She felt the first real smile of the evening lift her lips. "You do that!"

"You better believe that I will." He smiled and opened his door.

Chapter Twenty-five

Quinn finished reading the final page of a lengthy contract and laid the document down on his desk. He rubbed his tired eyes, reached for another paper from the stack on his desk, and frowned. "Have we worked this job for Hugh Thompson into the schedule yet?"

Brett, sitting at the adjacent desk, wrinkled his forehead. "No, I don't think so. The schedule's pretty full for the next couple of weeks."

"Get it in there. Hugh's jobs always take priority; he backed me when I was starting out and I needed it. Make it happen, OK?"

"Yes, sir," said Brett.

The telephone rang, and Brett picked it up. "Cavanaugh Excavating."

"Can I tell him who's calling?" Brett said. "Hold on." He covered the mouthpiece. "Boss, I got some guy named Stanley Porter on the phone, and he's asking for you."

Quinn's eyebrows rose. "Oh, really?" He picked up the phone in front of him and gestured for Brett to hang up. "Hello?"

"This Quinn Cavanaugh?"

"It is," Quinn said.

"Well, this is Stanley Porter. I expect you know who I am since I hear you're running around with my wife!"

"Soon-to-be-ex-wife, I believe," Quinn said dryly.

"That's not what's going to happen," Stanley's voice rose. "She's going to change her mind and come back to me!" He took a deep, shuddering breath. "But in the meantime, I got something you need to see. It's going to make you think twice about going out with her."

"I can't imagine what that would be," Quinn said. "I'm not interested in anything you got to show me."

"Wait! Don't hang up! I promise that you really need to see this. It's really in your best interest for you to."

Quinn frowned. "So how do I see this … whatever it is?"

"Come and meet me here at the car lot at the Ford place … where I work," Stanley said. "I promise you won't be sorry you did."

"And when am I supposed to meet you?" Quinn asked.

"How about in thirty minutes? We're just getting ready to close. I'll wait for you by the entrance to the used car lot."

Quinn glanced over at Brett, who had his eyes down on the papers in front of him, appearing not to be listening, but Quinn saw him sneak glance over at him as he paused in his conversation.

"OK," Quinn said. "You got my attention. I'll see you in thirty minutes." He walked across the office, took his key ring from his pocket, unlocked a file cabinet, and pulled open the top drawer. Reaching inside, he pulled out a handgun and slid it in his waistband at the back of his pants.

Brett was staring at him openly. "What's going on, boss?"

"Nothing serious." Quinn slipped on a light jacket and headed toward the door. "Just a minor problem I need to take care of. You go on and finish up for the day. Lock up when you leave."

⚜

Darkness was falling as Quinn drove slowly down Main Street. The Ford dealership looked closed for the evening; subdued lighting illuminated the interior of the building behind the big, glass windows, but no people appeared to be moving around inside. He made a slow right turn on a side street.

Two rows of new vehicles gave way to used cars parked in neat columns, displayed for maximum view for passersby. Under a streetlight, a driveway led to the side of the business. A man was standing on the sidewalk.

Quinn's senses were on high alert, and he felt his military training kick in as he eased his truck to the curb and slipped the truck into park.

The man turned his attention toward Quinn's vehicle.

Quinn opened his door and stepped slowly onto the street; his eyes fixed on the waiting man. He moved deliberately around the front of his truck, his eyes scanning the street for movement, listening for sounds that would indicate the presence of others.

"Quinn Cavanaugh?" said the man loudly. "That you?"

Quinn recognized the voice of the caller. "Yeah. You Stanley Porter?"

"That's me." The man took a couple of steps closer.

Quinn watched Stanley intently, still highly aware of the immediate area around them, and he stepped up on the sidewalk. His eyes swept over the man, alert for any sudden movements. It was quiet except for the occasional car passing by the front of the dealership. The side street was deserted.

Quinn ran his eyes over Stanley. He was slim and a few inches shorter than Quinn, and Quinn judged that he probably outweighed him by thirty pounds or so. *I can take this guy*, he thought, and a small amount of tension left his shoulders.

Stanley shifted nervously from one foot to the other and cleared his throat. "Glad you decided to meet me."

"What's this that you think I need to see?" Quinn asked.

"Well, I know you've been going out with Donna, although I can't think what you see in that cold bitch." He backed up a step when Quinn took a menacing step toward him. "Look, man, she comes across all sweet and innocent, but she's not what you think she is. I can prove it to you. You're not going to want to have anything to do with her when I show you this."

"Show me what?"

Stanley pulled something from his shirt pocket. "Take a look at this."

His eyes fixed on Stanley's, Quinn reached out and took the photograph. He spared it a second's glance before staring at Stanley again. "This the picture you been blackmailing Donna with?"

"W-what?" Stanley said.

Quinn's eyes bored into him. "Yeah. Donna told me that you threatened to show a picture of her to the school board to make her lose her job. This the one?"

Stanley's face slackened. "I don't know what you're talking about. That's a lie."

"Oh, yeah? I don't think so." Quinn took a step forward.

Stanley stepped backward. "No, man! That's wrong. All I wanted to do was show you that … to let you know just what kind of person she is. I wouldn't threaten her job. That's crazy. If she told you that, she's lying!"

Quinn grinned, looking wolfish in the streetlight's harsh illumination. "Do you know what I do, Stanley?"

"What?"

"Do you know what I do … for a living?"

"I … I'm not sure. You own some kind of excavating company, isn't that right?"

"Yeah, Stanley. I dig holes in the ground for a living … big holes."

Stanley frowned. "What does that …"

Quinn's smile widened. "Septic tanks are kind of my stock in trade. I install a lot of septic tanks in my business. Do you know what a septic tank is, Stanley?"

"I guess so. Sure."

"We go in to where a new house is being constructed," Quinn said. "We dig a big old hole in the ground, out a distance away from where the house is being built, and we dump a load of gravel into it and smooth the whole thing out. Then we bring in this huge tank—looks kind of like a big, rectangular bowl—and we drop it into the hole. It's a big ol' thing … maybe fifteen or twenty feet across and about ten feet deep. We level it, slide the top on it, and then we push the dirt back over it, covering the whole thing up, except for the end where the plumbers are going to attach the sewer lines that lead out from the house."

"What's that got to do with anything?" asked Stanley.

Quinn stepped closer to him. "Well, see, Stanley, here's my point. Let's play a little pretend game. Let's pretend that I wanted a man to just disappear, without a trace, without anybody ever seeing or hearing from him again. What if—by accident, of course—he happened to get tossed into a hole that had been dug out for a septic tank? What if the tank got dropped in right on top of him, and the whole thing got covered up with dirt?" Quinn made a little disparaging twist of his lips. "What happens if the body starts to rot under there, and smell bad, you might ask? Well, look where it is—right underneath a septic tank. And what is it that's in that tank? Raw sewage, right? And sewage stinks." Quinn shook his head. "Who would ever think anything about it—even if it did start to smell a little bit?"

Stanley stared at him with shock written over his face. "What are you saying?"

"This the only print of this picture you got, Stanley?" Quinn asked sharply. When Stanley did not reply, he continued. "Well, if it isn't, you better destroy any others you got! And if anything—any-thing at all—happens that threatens Donna's job, well, let's just say that I'm going to hold you, and you alone, responsible!" He glared fiercely at Stanley.

Stanley held up a hand as if to ward off a blow. "Wait! What if … what if something happens … what if the school board hears something from somebody else?"

"You better hope that never happens, Stanley. See, it doesn't matter where it comes from. In my mind, you'll be responsible! You stay away from her! Don't talk *to* her. Don't talk *about* her! Don't ever have anything else to do with her or try to hurt her in any way. Do I make myself clear? Do you understand?" Quinn glared at Stanley.

"I understand," Stanley said weakly.

"Good!" Quinn reached out and clapped his shoulder.

Stanley winced.

"Now get your ass outta here before I change my mind. You get my drift?"

Stanley hesitated and then scurried away.

Quinn stood beside his truck until he heard a motor start. He watched Stanley drive out of the car lot and speed away. He let out the breath he didn't realize he had been holding and sat behind the wheel of his truck. He knees felt weak. He raised the photo and took a good look at it under the glow of the streetlight.

In the photo, Donna was on a blanket with another woman in front of a fireplace. Both were obviously naked, their limbs en-twined, and they were kissing.

Quinn studied the photo with a genuine grin on his face. He chuckled. "I sure wish I could keep this, baby doll, but I'm sure you'd be happier if it was gone so none of those holier-than-thou old fogies on the school board will ever get their hands on it." He reached into the glove box and pulled out a Bic lighter; regretfully, he brought the flame to the corner of the photo, watching as it blackened and curled. When only a corner remained, he snuffed the fire out.

He started his motor and began the short drive to his mother's house to pick up Benjie.

Chapter Twenty-six

Donna raised her fist and knocked on the front door. She heard footsteps inside, and the door swung open.

Thelma White's face lit up in a welcoming smile. "Hello, Donna. I wasn't expecting to see you today. Come on in out of this heat. Pennie hasn't got home from work yet." She stood to the side as Donna entered the house.

"I know it's too early for her to be home yet." Donna stopped in the little entryway. "I just sort of wanted to be with someone today. Is it all right that I came over?"

"Well, of course it is." Mrs. White's face filled with concern. "Is something wrong, honey?"

"No. Actually, I guess you might say something's right." Donna's face crumpled. "I just came from over at the courthouse in Madiera. My divorce was finalized today. I just didn't want to be by myself right now."

Mrs. White wrapped her arms around Donna in a warm hug. "Of course, you didn't. You did exactly right, coming over here. Now come on in and sit down. Let me go fix you a great big glass of cold sweet tea." She kept an arm around Donna and led her to the living room sofa. "Now you just sit down. I won't be but a minute."

She returned carrying two glasses, the ice cubes clinking, and the outsides of the glasses fogged. Handing one to Donna, she sank down beside her on the sofa. "Now, you just sit here and tell me all about it. Did Stanley try to act the fool over there?"

Donna shook her head, accepting her tea. "He didn't even show up."

Mrs. White raised her brows. "Really?"

"That's right." Donna sipped and stared at her drink. "The whole thing was over in about ten minutes. They called our case, and me and my attorney walked up to the front. I was sworn in, and the judge asked me a few questions. Marshall Owens—that's my attorney—told the judge that the divorce was uncontested, and a few minutes later, the whole thing was over." She looked at Mrs. White with a wan smile. "I was a free woman."

"I'm surprised that Stanley wasn't there," said Mrs. White.

"Me too," Donna said. "I really expected him to cause some kind of uproar."

"Well, I'm glad he came to his senses, and I'm glad this whole thing is over for you."

I'm not so sure it's over, thought Donna. She shivered. *He'll try something.*

They drank their tea and made light conversation for a while.

Mrs. White smiled at Donna and said, "I was just about to start dinner. Want to come on out to the kitchen and keep me company while I get it started?"

"Sure thing."

They carried their empty glasses out to the kitchen.

As they were chatting at the kitchen table, the back door opened.

Jack White came in and planted a kiss on his wife's cheek. "Hey there, Donna. What a nice surprise to see you!"

"Hello," Donna said.

"Donna's going to stay for supper with us," said Mrs. White.

"That's great! Glad to have you!" he said. "I'm just going to go in and get cleaned up. Be back with you girls in a few minutes."

When he came back, he helped himself to a glass of the tea and sat down with them. "Ah, that hits the spot. So, Donna, are you enjoying your time off from teaching?"

"I guess so. I'm just resting up from the last few days of school. It was pretty hectic, as usual, that last week, getting all the paperwork done and taking care of getting the year closed out."

"I'll bet it was," he said. "So, what are you doing with your time now that school is out?"

"Donna got her divorce today."

"Oh!" His eyebrows rose. He reached over the table and covered Donna's hand with his. "Good for you."

Donna smiled at him.

Mrs. White got up and tended to the pots on the stove. "Why don't Donna and I go set the table? We'll be ready to sit down when Pennie gets home."

"Yeah," Mr. White said. "Why don't we eat in the dining room tonight? This is a special occasion."

Mrs. White said, "I think Pennie's here."

Donna looked up from slicing a big bowl of fresh tomatoes from the Whites' garden.

"Is that Donna's car in the driveway?" Pennie asked as she came in the back door.

Donna wiped her hands on a dishcloth. "Hey! Yes, it's me."

"Donna's having supper with us tonight," Mrs. White said. "We were just waiting for you to get home."

"Oh, good!" Pennie looked at Donna questioningly.

"Let's just carry this food to the table," said Mrs. White. "Pennie, go get washed up and come on and sit down."

As they were enjoying Mrs. White's fresh vegetables, Donna looked over at Pennie. "My divorce was finalized today."

Pennie set down her fork, and a wide smile lit her face. "Oh, good. Did everything go all right?"

"It really did," Donna said. "Stanley was nowhere to be found. He didn't bother to show up."

"Well, that was good, right?"

"I guess so," Donna said. "It made things go quicker, anyway. The whole thing was over in less than fifteen minutes."

"OK. But?"

"Well, it makes me nervous," Donna said. "It's not like him. I was really expecting him to be there and to try to cause trouble."

Pennie narrowed her eyes. "Maybe Quinn had something to do with it."

"Quinn?" asked Donna.

Mr. White said, "Quinn who?"

"Quinn Cavanaugh," Pennie said. "He's the owner of the company that Brett works for. Donna's been dating him."

"I didn't know that." Mr. White looked at Donna and then turned back to his daughter. "Why do you think this Quinn character would have anything to do with Stanley's actions?"

Pennie said, "Well, I don't. It's just that Brett told me that Stanley called Quinn on the phone, about a month ago, and he thinks that Quinn went out to meet him right afterward." She looked over at Donna's surprised face. "Didn't you know about that?"

"No. I didn't," Donna said.

"Quinn didn't mention it to you?" Pennie asked.

"No!"

Pennie shrugged. "Well, that's what Brett told me. Maybe you ought to ask Quinn about it."

"I'm going to." Donna frowned. *Wonder what that was about?*

Chapter Twenty-seven

Quinn called the following day and said, "Want to take a ride with me on the bike this weekend? Don't we have something to celebrate?"

"You mean my divorce?" Donna said.

"Yep. You up for a ride up into the mountains? It'll be nice and cool up there. We can get away from this heat. And the weathermen promise we won't get rain for the next few days. What do you say?"

"That sounds awfully tempting," replied Donna.

"Good! Plan to stay overnight."

"Wait! What do you mean … *overnight*? Where will we stay?"

"Oh, I have some friends who won't mind if we stay with them. My mother says she'll keep Benjie. We can leave on Saturday morning. You game?"

"What do I need to take?" asked Donna.

"Toothbrush, change of undies." Quinn chuckled. "I travel light. Nothing more than what will fit into the little storage bin on the bike. How about it, baby doll?"

"I'd love it!"

"All right! I'll pick you up at ten o'clock. You need to wear jeans and long sleeves, so you don't get windburn."

Donna's heart pounded at the thought of a trip on the back of his Harley. "I'll be ready."

॰॰

Donna hurried out of the house on Saturday morning when she heard Quinn's Harley coming up the driveway.

He shut off the motor, took the small paper bag she held out to him, and stowed it. He gave her a quick kiss and handed her a helmet. "Ready to go?"

"Yes, I am," she said.

He straddled the machine, and she hopped up behind him, clutching his waist as they started off.

It was a beautiful summer day as they sped up the interstate, heading west, toward the mountains. Donna reveled in the vibrations of the powerful machine between her legs and the feel of Quinn's hard body against hers, partly blocking the rushing air as they seemed to almost fly up the highway.

They encountered a few miles of heavier traffic near North Wilkesboro, but they soon left it behind. When they reached the Blue Ridge Parkway, Quinn turned south. They continued along the beautiful scenic route for several miles, and the sweeping curves provided a glorious ride.

Just past Blowing Rock, Quinn left the parkway and pulled up in the gravel parking lot of a small café. He parked amid several cars and pickup trucks. "Ready for some lunch? I've been here before, and they serve good food."

Donna looked around. "I *am* hungry." Her legs were still quivering from the ride. She removed her helmet, as Quinn had done, and followed him as he strode toward the entrance. He held open the heavy screen door, and she stepped inside.

It was cool inside, and ceiling fans circled lazily overhead. Several tables were spread across the tile floor, and a short eating counter ran along the back of the restaurant. Neon advertising signs illuminated the wall, wooden booths ringed the walls on either side of the front door, and natural daylight poured in through the high, narrow windows above the booths. A few of the tables and about half of the booths were occupied.

They found an empty booth and slid in.

A waitress handed laminated menus to them. "What can I get you folks to drink?"

"Coffee." Quinn looked at Donna. "Two coffees," he amended at her nod.

The waitress walked away, and Donna turned her attention to the hand-printed menu. A short list of entrees was listed, along with a long list of vegetable selections.

"I think I'll have the pork chops," Quinn told the waitress when she brought them their coffees. "Along with the mashed potatoes and green beans. What do you want, Donna?"

"That sounds good."

"Be sure to save some room for dessert," the waitress said. "We've got homemade peach cobbler today."

"We'll remember that," Quinn said with a smile.

The food was delicious, and Donna felt stuffed after she finished almost all the ample portions on her plate. Quinn ordered a dish of the cobbler and insisted that she try a bite or two as they sipped on the coffee refills that the waitress kept them supplied with; it was excellent.

"How much farther is it to your friends' house?" Donna asked as they climbed back on the bike.

"Not much farther—maybe another hour or so," Quinn replied as they got back on the road.

True to his word, about an hour later, Quinn turned off the twisting main highway at the edge of a small town and drove down a shady street that wound up and down gentle hills, large, impressive homes set back on manicured grounds on either side of the street. He slowed at the driveway of a three-story Victorian home, set well back from the street, the turrets and sweeping porches framed by century-old trees and a profusion of multicolored flowers in perfectly kept beds. He came to a stop in front of the portico dividing the house from what looked to be an attached three-car garage and shut off the engine.

"Oh my God, Quinn. Is this where your friends live?" Donna asked.

"Yep. Live here, work here. This is their bed-and-breakfast," he replied.

A blond man about his age, his tight T-shirt revealing a rippling muscular physique, came out a side door and rushed toward them. The man grabbed Quinn in a bear hug as he stepped off the bike and pounded him enthusiastically on the back. "Good to see you, man!"

Quinn was laughing and pounding him in return. "Matt! How's the world treating you?"

They broke apart, and Quinn turned toward Donna, as the man gave her a head-to-toe look.

"Matt, I want you to meet Donna Porter. Donna, this is my old service buddy, Matt Duncan."

"Hello." Donna held out her hand.

Matt enfolded it in both his big hands, grinning. "Really good to meet you."

"Where's Sally?" asked Quinn.

A blonde woman, obviously very pregnant, walked out of the same side doorway, smiling broadly.

"Sally!" Quinn enfolded her in an enthusiastic—but very gentle—hug. He stepped back and looked down at her. "You guys didn't tell me about this! When's the big day?"

"September 1," said Sally. "I can't wait."

"Sally, this is my friend Donna Porter," Quinn said. "Sally's this big lubbock's wife—and the best decision he ever made!"

"You better believe that," Matt said. "You-all, come on in. I'll show you to your room."

"We're staying here?" Donna asked as Quinn took the few things they'd brought with them out of the bike, and they all started toward the doorway.

"We are," he said. "I called Matt and told him that I wanted to reserve his best room for us this weekend."

"Nice bike," Matt said.

"Thanks. You still got yours?" Quinn asked.

Matt shook his head. "Nope. I had to sell it when we bought this place. We put every penny we could into the property, but it was worth it … never a regret."

"This is beautiful," Donna said, admiring the rich furnishings and antiques as they walked through the house.

"How many rooms do you have available to rent?" asked Quinn.

They passed by a sitting room and a lovely, curved stairway.

"Seven," said Sally. "There are two on this floor, four on the second, and there is a big suite on the third that will sleep six or seven people. Matt and I also have our quarters up on the second floor. It's a big house."

"This is your room." Matt threw open a door near the end of the hallway. It was exquisite, thought Donna, as she saw the little brick fireplace painted white, a paisley loveseat facing it. The big, four-poster bed was covered with a downy-looking hunter green and white comforter, and several pillows were propped up against the headboard. A small table with a dainty lamp was on either side of the bed, and the hardwood floor had homey-looking braided rugs scattered around the room. A big window near the fireplace looked out over the grounds, all sweeping, perfect lawn, big trees, and bright accents of bedding flowers, a walkway curving through them. She caught a glimpse of a clawfoot tub through an open doorway on the other side of the bed.

"This is so beautiful," Donna said.

"We're so glad you like it," said Sally.

"Why don't you guys relax for a while? Sally and I are making dinner for you. Quinn and I can catch up while we eat. We were thinking that we could barbecue and have dinner together out on our back porch—if that's OK with you guys."

Quinn looked at Donna, and then he nodded. "Sure, bro. Sounds good to me."

They freshened up after their long ride and then left through the door at the end of the hall to stroll down the little pathway through the peaceful grounds, before returning to their room, simply enjoying the quiet of their surroundings.

At some point, they heard a car drive up and the sound of footsteps and voices. At seven, they walked through the house in search of Quinn's friends.

They walked through the large kitchen and saw them out in the backyard directly through a large, enclosed back porch. A table on the porch was already set for four. Matt waved to them from where he was presiding over a big grill in the yard.

"Almost ready," Matt called, waving to them.

"What do you-all want to drink?" Sally asked, walking over from beside her husband.

"Just water is fine," Donna said. "We're not big drinkers."

"Neither am I," said Sally, patting the mound of her belly.

"Hey, Quinn! Look inside that cooler by the door," called Matt. "Why don't you snag me a beer—and get one for yourself. I've just got to pull this stuff off the grill, put it on platters, and we'll be ready to eat."

Carrying the beers, Quinn went out to join Matt, and Donna followed Sally back into the kitchen, where she put ice and water into two tumblers. "Let's go out and sit down," Sally said, handing one to Donna. "We'll let the menfolk wait on us tonight."

A few minutes later, Quinn held the door open for Matt as he carried in a big platter, piled high with foil-wrapped packages. "This is my specialty," Matt said. "A full meal made on the grill—except for the banana pudding that Sally's got waiting in the refrigerator for dessert." He began placing the hot packets on their plates. Pulling open the crimped foil, one size revealed a steaming salmon steak, yet another held perfectly done asparagus stalks, and the third contained an ear of succulent corn on the cob.

"Wow, that's a real feast," Quinn said.

"Dig in!" said Matt. "If you need anything you don't see on the table, just ask."

They ate silently and with appreciation.

Matt said, "Donna, are you from Phillips too?"

"Yes. I'm a teacher there. I teach first grade."

"Whoa, good for you," Matt said. "How's that boy of yours, Quinn?"

Quinn's expression softened, "He's just great. He's a great kid. Growing like a weed."

"You ever hear from Becky?" asked Matt.

Sally kicked him under the table.

Quinn's face froze. "Nope." He picked up his ear of corn and bit into it.

Donna broke the small, uncomfortable silence. "Sally, what do you-all want: boy or girl?"

Sally gave a grateful smile. "Oh, we don't care, as long as it's healthy."

Matt said, "I'd kind of like it to be a boy, but I think Sally wants a little girl."

The uncomfortable moment had passed, and they relaxed.

Quinn said, "So … how many people you got staying tonight?"

Sally sighed. "Only two other couples."

"I think it's because we're kind of off the beaten path," Matt said. "Not enough people know we're here, but business is going to pick up."

"It better pick up pretty soon," Sally said darkly, looking down at her plate.

"It will, honey. We knew it would take a while," said Matt.

Sally's eyes glistened. "I know. I'm sorry."

Quinn looked sharply at Matt. "Is there a problem?"

"Oh, nothing we can't work out," he said. "There's just a big bump in the road that we've got to get over."

"What's that?" Quinn asked quietly.

Matt sighed. "Business is slow. Not enough people know about us yet. Everyone who stays here really seems to like us—and we've even had several repeat visitors—but we really need to grow a lot faster. We have this quarterly loan payment that's coming up at the end of the month, and frankly, I don't know how we're going to pay it."

"We've tried everything," Sally said. "The bank won't budge an inch or give us any kind of extension."

"We've got some of the money," Matt said. "Just not the full amount."

"How much are you short?" Quinn asked.

"About fifteen thousand dollars," Matt said.

Quinn sat silently for a moment. "OK, I'll send you a check for the fifteen thousand this week."

"What?" Matt looked at him in astonishment. "I … no! I wasn't asking—"

Quinn said, "I know that, bro, but you'd do the same for me."

"Well, sure, in a heartbeat. But …"

Quinn looked him straight in the eyes. "Don't give it another thought. My business is doing good right now, and I'll just have to shift a couple of things around. Don't worry about it. You can just pay me back when you're able to."

"Thanks, man!" Matt said.

"Oh, yes, Quinn," said Sally. "We just didn't know where we were going to turn to … and with the baby coming …"

Quinn smiled at her. "Us marines stick together. Now, didn't Matt say something about some banana pudding?"

Sally jumped to her feet. "You bet." She began to gather up their plates.

Donna got up to help.

After the dishes had been put in the dishwasher, the four of them talked for another hour or so.

When Quinn and Donna went inside, Donna sat down on the pretty paisley loveseat, feeling ill at ease.

Quinn sat down beside her and put his arm around her shoulders. "What's the matter, baby doll?"

She shook her head.

"Come on. There's something bothering you. Tell me about it."

She looked up at him, her eyes troubled. "I don't know, Quinn. I guess I'm just not feeling the way I thought I would."

"What do you mean?"

"About the divorce … before it happened, I thought I would be on top of the world. I thought I would want to party and celebrate, but I don't. I just feel sad."

"I understand," he said softly.

She looked up at him.

"I've been through it too." He pulled her gently to him. "It's more like a death than anything else."

Donna felt her eyes fill. "This wasn't the way it was supposed to be. I thought I would be married to Stanley forever, but it turned out that he wasn't the person I thought he was. He wasn't someone I could live with for the rest of my life."

"I know," murmured Quinn.

"I'm so sorry," Donna said. "I didn't mean to spoil this. I know you put a lot of planning in our special weekend together."

"Shh, it's all right," Quinn murmured, holding her.

They sat like that for a time. Donna wept silently, and Quinn just held her against him.

When she finally stopped, he waited a few minutes and then loosened his arms. "Come on, baby doll. Let's get into bed—no strings attached. I promise. Come on. Let's just get undressed and get under the covers. Let me just hold you, and we'll get some sleep. OK?"

Silently, she let him pull her to her feet, and he went over and pulled back the covers. He began taking off his shirt and jeans, hanging them over the back of a chair. When he was undressed down to his briefs, he lay down and opened his arms. "Come on, let's try to go to sleep."

Numbly, she followed suit—removing her clothes, but leaving on her bra and panties—and she crawled into the bed beside him.

He reached over, switched off the light, drew her to him, and held her comfortingly against his long, sinewy body. Donna closed her eyes and willed her body to relax.

She must have dozed off. Donna didn't know how much later it was that her eyes opened in the darkness. She stirred against Quinn's body. All her senses came wide-awake, and she moved a hand over the hard muscles of his chest. His breathing quickened, and she knew he was awake too.

She breathed in the scent of him, and a tiny ribbon of feeling curled deep inside of her. Stretching her face upward, she touched her lips to the bristly line of his jaw and moved her body microscopically closer to him.

The arm that he had casually draped over her tightened, and his lips found hers in the darkness. Her heart began to hammer as his mouth covered hers hungrily.

He reached over her and switched on the little lamp, and the room came into soft focus as he pushed the enveloping covers aside. Within seconds, she felt her bra unsnap, and his hands were caressing the small mounds of her breasts under the loosened garment. When he stripped the bra down her arms and away, a small cry escaped her lips as his mouth covered her nipple, and he sucked it gently until the tip became a hard nub. His mouth took hers again, and she arched against him, feeling the heat of his growing erection against her upper legs, straining against the covering material of his briefs.

Reaching down, she tugged at the waistband, wanting to feel the heat of his skin against her. Pulling slightly back, he stripped the offending garment down his legs, and his erection sprang free; in a continuing movement, he reached for her panties and pulled them so forcefully down her legs that the flimsy fabric tore. Donna reached for his erect penis, even as he pushed her legs apart and kneeled between them. His eyes ran over her scorchingly, and she felt his gaze move over her skin like a touch. His fingers went between her legs, parting her, and she felt her body ready itself for him as her wetness made her slick under his questing fingers. He made a groaning sound as he slid deep inside her, and Donna pushed her hips against him, welcoming him. She brought her legs up to circle around his hips as he plunged hard and fast into the scalding depths of her, over and over, until his whole body stiffened, and she felt his pumping climax inside her.

He sank down, rolling his body close beside her. "Oh, God, I'm sorry, Donna," he said weakly, catching his breath. "I couldn't wait … I wanted you so badly."

She caressed his cheek. "I loved it," she whispered.

A look of horror crossed over his face.

"What is it, Quinn? What's wrong?" she asked.

"I didn't take time to put on a condom," he said, starting to rise.

"It's OK," she told him softly. "I went to my doctor more than a month ago, and he renewed my prescription for birth control pills."

The relieved look on his face was almost comical. He took a deep breath and grinned at her. "You did, did you?"

She nodded.

He cupped her breast with his big hand and lightly pinched her nipple. "And why would you do a thing like that?" he teased.

Donna felt her face redden. "I thought it might come in handy," she said.

"You wild woman," he moved over her, and his lips claimed hers again. He propped himself up on an elbow beside her, the fingertips of his free hand tracing a path down her body, lightly tickling her stomach, moving lower to push through the patch of hair covering her mons, circling sensuously. His fingertips brushed against the folds of her vulva so lightly that she shivered, and the gentle massage soon sent currents of desire coursing through her.

She raised enormous brown eyes to him, and her hand began mimicking his movements, tracing the inked pattern on his chest, which moved her so erotically, moving downward to caress him as well.

"Shh," he whispered. "Lay still, baby doll. Let me touch you. I want to see you want me." He inserted two fingers inside her and began to stroke and fondle her, gently rubbing the little nub of her pleasure spot.

Donna's breath caught as he petted it, and her thighs involuntarily spread wider for him.

"That's it, my love." He captured the nipple of her closest breast in his mouth, nipping it with his teeth.

Donna gasped at the tiny pinch; she reached out and grasped his now half-erect penis.

He chuckled, drew out of her reach, positioned himself between the V of her legs. He moved his hands underneath her buttocks, lifted her hips up off the bed, and lowered his mouth to her, his tongue invading her, forcefully circling her clitoris until she cried out, her hands fisting in his hair. He continued what he was doing until she was squirming under his assault.

Finally, he leisurely raised his head and gazed down her body. "What do you want, baby doll?" His eyes took in her swollen nipples, the flush that had spread over her chest, and her half-closed eyes gleaming as she looked back down at him. "Tell me," he repeated, inserting a finger inside her and rubbing it against her swollen clit.

"You! I want you inside me," Donna cried, her head moving back and forth on the pillow in response to the spirals of sensation he was creating.

His erection tightened and throbbed as he looked at her; he repositioned his body between her legs, inserted himself into her, and slowly began to plunge into her depths, feeling her clutch and yield to him as he plundered her, the wet velvet of her inflaming him even as she grasped for his shoulders, pulling him to her.

This time, he lasted much longer, and she whimpered and cried out as he brought her up in a spiraling crest that culminated in a crashing wave of sensation as her entire body melted into a pool of slackened satiation.

As he felt her body undulate around him, Quinn let go as well, and climaxed.

Donna clasped him blindly, her eyes shut tight.

Quinn switched off the light and pulled the covers over them.

Minutes later, both of them dropped into a deep sleep.

જ⊚

The morning sun coming through the window brightly lit the room when Donna opened her eyes, squinting against the sudden glare. Quinn breathed deeply beside her. She heard voices outside the room, and it took a moment to orient herself.

Quinn opened his eyes and smiled at her with no hint of lingering sleepiness in his expression. "Hey, there, baby doll."

"Good morning," she answered. She yawned. "What time is it?"

"I have no idea."

"Should we get up?"

"Do you want to?" His hand moved to her waist under the covers, urging her toward him.

Donna sat up. "I think so. I think I need a bath."

He laughed. "You do, do you? Why don't we go in there and see if both of us will fit into that tub?"

"I doubt if we can," Donna replied.

"Well, let's try it." He threw back the covers, and Donna's skin prickled with the sudden rush of cool air. "Come on," he said. "This was your idea."

Donna laughed and swung her feet to the floor.

They ran the big, clawfoot tub halfway full of almost-hot water, and after several hilariously awkward attempts, they managed to maneuver their bodies into a seated position inside it, splashing each other, laughing, and playfully running a soapy washcloth over each other. When the water began to cool, they turned on the hot water faucet to prolong their playtime.

But as their bath cooled a second time, Quinn made his way to a standing position, pulled Donna up against him, and plastered their wet bodies together to share a lingering kiss. He stepped out onto the bathmat and lifted her out of the tub. Taking down one of the big, fluffy bath towels, he began drying her off, tenderly, as he would a child.

She stood passively as he attended to her, turning, lifting her arms, and letting him pat her dry.

When he finished, he began toweling himself off, his intense gaze fixed on her as she stood, watching him as though hypnotized. He let the damp towel drop, wordlessly picked her up, and carried her back to their bed.

This time, he laid her down sidewise across the bed, her buttocks just at the edge, and stood beside it, lifting her feet up on to rest atop his shoulders. Hard once again, he positioned his member at her opening and pushed slowly into her, his hands under her hips holding her in place. She was wet inside and ready for him again, and he took her fiercely and possessively. His climax came quickly, and he rolled up onto the bed, carrying her with him, their bodies still joined, Donna sprawled on top of him. He was breathing hard against her neck. "I didn't hurt you; did I baby doll?" he whispered.

She shook her head fiercely.

"I'm sorry," he said softly. "I didn't mean to be so rough." His hands caressed her silky back. He smiled apologetically at her when she raised her head and gazed down at him. "You make me half-crazy; I want you so bad!"

"I want you too," she whispered.

"My sweet little baby doll." He held her close, and a distant look came into his eyes. "Do you remember the first time I saw you? I walked into the doorway of your classroom with Benjie, and there you stood, behind that desk, talking to some other parent, a perfect little figure of a woman, all prim and ladylike, and then we looked at each other, and I saw something hiding back in your eyes, all wild and daring, and *in that moment*, I knew I wanted you, with every ounce of my being!" His lips twisted ruefully. "And when I found out that you were married, I backed off." His lips curved upward. "Later on, when I heard that you and your husband had separated, all bets were off!"

Donna caressed his face with her fingertips. What she saw in his pale blue eyes looking up at her melted her heart.

"It was magic," he whispered. "I knew from that first moment that I had to make you mine."

Donna closed her eyes and whispered, "But you're wrong about me. I'm so dull and boring. I'm going to disappoint you …"

He gave a bark of laughter. "You're kidding. I take you up in my plane and go into a barrel roll to see how you'll react, and you just laugh! Like a kid on a roller coaster!" He shook his head, smiling. "You're something else, baby doll! Come on. It's probably getting pretty late. I hate to say this, but maybe we'd better get dressed and start back down the mountain."

They dressed and gathered up their few belongings.

Matt was tidying up the front parlor and saw them as they walked down the hallway toward the front of the house. "Hey, did you two finally decide to get up?" He gave them a knowing look.

"Yeah," Quinn said, returning his grin.

"Well, come on back to the kitchen. We stopped serving breakfast more than an hour ago, but the coffee's still hot—and I think maybe we saved you some bacon and eggs."

Sally was puttering around the kitchen when they all walked back there. "Good morning," she said cheerily. "Did you sleep well?"

"Oh, yes," replied Donna.

"Well, sit down. Matt will pour you some coffee. It won't take me but a minute to fix you some fresh eggs."

"No, don't bother," Quinn said.

Her smile lit up the room. "It's no bother! Really. I can do this in my sleep." She was already putting a pan on the stove.

"Sit down," Matt said as he put mugs of coffee in front of them and poured one for himself.

They sipped the fragrant brew, and Sally put plates of food in front of them.

"So, your business is doing well?" Matt asked.

"Oh, yeah. In fact, I might have to hire another couple of men."

"I'm really glad to hear it, man. You deserve it."

Donna said, "How are you going to manage things here? I mean … after the baby comes."

Sally replied, "We have a couple of high school girls lined up to help us out with the housekeeping, right after it's born, and we know an older lady who wants to do the cooking when we need her. We'll make out all right."

"And we can't thank you enough, Quinn … for your offer," said Matt.

Quinn waved a hand dismissively.

"It's so lovely here," Donna said. "I'm going to tell everyone that I can about it."

"Thank you," said Sally.

As they finished eating, Quinn turned to Donna. "Are you about ready to go?"

"Yes. Thank you so much for having us. I really enjoyed meeting you both." Donna gave them a warm smile.

"You have to come back up here real soon," said Sally.

"Let us know when the baby comes … if we don't see you before then."

"We sure will!"

They got back to Phillips late in the afternoon after stopping outside North Wilkesboro for a light lunch.

Quinn stopped the Harley in Mrs. Adams's driveway and dug Donna's little bag out of the saddlebag.

She took it and handed him her helmet.

The moment stretched out between them.

"Are you going to get Benjie now?" Donna said.

"Yeah. Back to reality."

Donna looked at him, and her lips parted.

Quinn grinned his devastating grin, bent his head, and gave her a quick kiss. "I'll call you." He secured his helmet, turned the bike, and roared away.

Chapter Twenty-eight

Donna transferred her groceries from the cart to her back seat. She shut the door, and her hand was on the driver's side door latch when someone grabbed her waist from behind, pulling her back against their body. Just as a hand clamped over her mouth, she recognized her ex-husband. *Stanley!*

"I have a gun in my pocket, Donna," he hissed, his mouth an inch from her ear. "If you scream, I'll shoot you. I swear!"

Her body rigid with shock, she let him pull her backward, past two parked cars, to his own vehicle. He released her mouth just long enough to use his free hand to pull open the passenger-side door to his car and gave her a hard shove. She banged her head against the top of the door frame as he gave her another push, and she landed awkwardly on the seat. He slammed the door shut and ran around the car before she could recover enough to react.

Sliding in behind the wheel, he jammed the keys into the ignition. As the motor roared to life, he turned his head toward her and pulled a pistol out of his jacket pocket. "Sit still and keep quiet, Donna, or I'll shoot you. I mean it." He backed the car out of the slot and took off with a screech of tires.

"What are you doing, Stanley?" she managed to blurt out as he turned down the highway. "What do you want with me?"

"You'll see soon enough!" His eyes went back and forth between her and the highway, and he turned down the street toward their former home.

Donna felt tendrils of fear running through her. She braced herself as he made a fast left turn toward his house.

He stopped the car in front of the garage door and pointed the pistol at her. "Get out of the car, Donna. Don't you try to run off on me. Just walk real slow with me. We're going to go inside the house."

"Stanley, have you gone out of your mind?" Donna struggled to keep her voice steady.

"Just do it, Donna." He held the gun on her as she opened the car door and walked toward the front of the car. He got out, grabbed her arm roughly, lowered the weapon, and pushed her toward the front door. He pushed her across the living room and down onto the sofa.

She saw a coil of rope on the coffee table.

He stared down at her. "You ruined everything, Donna."

She swallowed and looked up at him. "What are you talking about?"

"Everything was just great—until you ruined it all!"

"What? What did I ruin?"

"You turned all of them against me—that's what you did! You made up all those lies about me. You told them to Janice and Tina, and all of them, and they repeated your lies to Olga and Frederick. I've been blackballed from Choice! They told me that I can never go to a party again!" He scowled.

Donna gasped. "I didn't lie!"

"Yes, you did! But you're going to fix it!"

"Fix it how?" She shrank back from him.

"I found out that there's a party down at Chapel Hill tomorrow night. You're going down there with me, and you're going to tell them that it was all a lie! You're going to convince them to let us back in … so we can swing with everybody again!"

"What are you talking about, Stanley? Are you completely crazy? Are you saying that you plan for us to drive down to Chapel Hill and crash the Choice party?"

"That's exactly what I'm saying! We're going to walk in, and you're going to tell them that it was all a big mistake. You're going to tell them that we're back together and that none of that stuff that Janice and Tina told them was true! You're going to convince them to let us back in!"

"I'm certainly going to do nothing of the kind!"

"Oh, yes, you are!" He gave an ugly grin. "I'm keeping you right here until tomorrow, and then we're going to drive down there. You'll do what I tell you if you know what's good for you!"

"Oh, no, I won't!" Donna tried to get to her feet.

Stanley grabbed her again and twisted her arm behind her. "I thought you might be like this, but I was prepared!" He grabbed the rope, pushed her across the room to a chair, and forced her to sit down. He wound the rope around her arm and tied it to the chair.

Donna struggled and kicked, but he held her in place and tied her other arm. Pushing his weight against her, he captured her legs and tied them securely. In moments, she was trussed securely.

"I'm going to scream," Donna said. "Stanley, you untie me—right this minute! Do you hear me?"

He laughed. "Scream all you want to. You know we live far enough away from the nearest house that nobody's going to hear you!"

"Stanley!"

He calmly walked over and turned on the TV. "Guess I'll see what's on—watch the news, maybe, and then go get me some sleep. I'm going to leave you there, like that. You'll see it my way by the time we need to leave tomorrow."

"Stanley Porter, you untie me right this minute!"

He ignored her.

Donna talked and pleaded, trying to reason with him, but Stanley just sat there and watched TV. After the national news program went off, he switched off the set and went to the bedroom.

Donna kept railing at him for a while, but if Stanley heard her, he paid no attention.

He switched off the light in the bedroom, and the house went completely dark.

Donna struggled against the rope, but she was fastened securely. After a while, her head drooped, and she dozed off in a fitful sleep.

She lifted her head painfully when Stanley came down the hallway, whistling cheerfully. She could tell that it was morning from the light shining through the windows.

He stopped and looked at her. Without speaking, he came over and checked the ropes. He nodded and walked out to the kitchen.

In a few minutes, Donna smelled coffee brewing. She heard him moving around, and then he reappeared with a mug of coffee. "You ready to do what I tell you? Are you going to be my sweet little wifey when we get down to the Holiday Inn?"

Donna glared at him.

"Oh, well," he said. "You'll change your mind." He left the room and puttered around the house.

The time crept slowly past. She ached all over from being confined to the chair. Her mind raced, trying to figure out how to get out of this mess, but no solution came to mind.

She must have dozed off again; she started at a sudden noise near her, and her head came up as she saw Stanley standing near her, staring down at her. "What?" she croaked. Her mouth was so dry.

"I was just thinking that we need to get ready to go pretty soon." He grinned at her.

"We can't," Donna said.

"Why can't we?"

"Well, I can't go to a party dressed like this. I need a pretty dress to wear."

He frowned. "You're right. You need to dress up and look sexy—so we can get with one of the good couples."

"That's right," Donna said. "All I have here is these jeans. I guess we'll just have to forget about going to Chapel Hill. Why don't you just untie me and let me go?"

"Oh, no!" he shook his head adamantly. "I can fix this. I'll go get you something to wear." He walked over to the front door and locked it. He headed toward the kitchen and grinned at her. "I'm locking you in, so don't you get any fancy ideas … and I won't be gone long."

Donna bent her head, and tears flowed down her face as the car started. When the sound faded, she looked over at the telephone, in its usual place on a small table, about ten feet away. She tried to move the chair toward it. Hunching her body and rocking the chair, ignoring the screaming pain in her cramped muscles, she was able to move an inch or two at a time. The carpet made progress difficult, but she kept at it, repeating the motion over and over again.

After what seemed like hours, the chair was beside the little table, but another problem presented itself. She had no idea how to get to the telephone—or how she would use it even if she could reach it with her arms so securely tied to the chair. In desperation, she hunched the chair into contact with the telephone table, jarring it. Finally, the telephone moved to the edge of the table, and one final jar made it fall to the floor.

"Now what?" she asked aloud, perspiration running down her body. She rocked the chair back and forth, harder and harder, until it tilted over. The jolt when it hit the floor made her cry out with pain. The bottom part of the telephone was about a foot away from her head. She could hear the faint hum of the dial tone. Inch by painful inch, she wriggled and jerked her body closer to her goal. At last, she was able to insert a finger in the telephone dial, and she blindly counted the little holes with her fingertip. She inserted the tip of a finger and began to awkwardly make it move, dialing a familiar number. She heard the sound of a phone begin to ring. "Oh, please, oh, please be there."

Chapter Twenty-nine

The telephone on his desk at Cavanaugh Excavations rang insistently. It was almost noon on a Saturday in September. The steady increase of business over the summer had not let up, and Quinn was spending a rare Saturday at his desk, catching up on the stack of paperwork on his desk. Quinn frowned at the interruption and reached for the phone without raising his eyes. "Cavanaugh," he said tersely.

"Quinn? This is Pennie White. Have you seen Donna this morning?"

"What? No, Pennie, I haven't. Why? What's wrong?"

"Probably nothing," Pennie said. "It's just that ... well, Donna and I made plans to get together this morning. She was going to come over to my house, but she didn't show up. I thought maybe she forgot. When I called over to Mrs. Adams's place, she told me that Donna wasn't there."

"She probably just forgot and went off to do something." Quinn looked back at the columns of numbers on the page in front of him.

"I thought so too—until Mrs. Adams told me that she went to the grocery store last evening. Mrs. Adams hasn't seen her since. Her car's not in the shed."

"Are you sure?" Quinn frowned.

"Yes! I'm at her house now. I came over here to see for myself.

This is so not like Donna. Mrs. Adams made a snide remark about how maybe she went off with that boyfriend of hers, but I didn't think you two had plans."

"No," Quinn said. "And you're right—this doesn't sound like Donna."

"Where can she be?"

"Maybe she just forgot about your plans this morning. She's probably just running an errand or something and let the time slip up on her."

"Maybe ... I think I'll drive around a little bit ... see if I can see her."

"Why don't you do that?" Quinn ended the call and frowned as he went back to his paperwork.

ॐ

Less than thirty minutes later, the phone rang again. "Quinn, it's Pennie. I just drove by the parking lot of the grocery store, down here at the shopping center, and Donna's car is parked here."

"Did you find her inside the store?"

"No! That's the problem! The car wasn't locked, and there was a sack of groceries on the front seat. I looked at the ticket, and they were bought last night. Quinn, she had sandwich meat in the bag and a carton of milk. Donna would never just go off and leave her groceries in the car to spoil!"

"You're right. Where are you now, Pennie?"

"I'm calling from the pay phone outside the grocery store. Quinn, I'm getting worried."

"Stay where you are, Pennie. I'm coming over there." He was reaching for his truck keys when the phone rang again.

"What?" he barked.

"Quinn?"

"Donna! Is that you? Where are you?" He gripped the receiver to his ear so tightly that his knuckles whitened.

"Quinn … please help me … can you come get me?"

"Donna! Baby doll, what's the matter? Where are you? What's happened?"

"It was Stanley … he took me. He tied me up. Please help me."

"He took you where? Baby doll, talk to me! Where are you?"

"I'm at Stanley's house. The house where we used to live together."

"Where is this house? Tell me where it is."

"It's out on Oak Grove Road … Pennie can tell you exactly where it is. You can ask her. Please hurry … he's not here right now, but I think he'll be back soon." She sobbed.

"Hang on, baby doll! I'm coming!"

"He's got a gun," Donna said in that faraway voice.

"I'll be there a quick as I can," Quinn said. "Hang on! I'm coming!" He threw the receiver down and dashed out the door.

Minutes later, he pulled into the grocery store parking lot.

Pennie was standing beside Donna's car.

Leaning over, he threw open the passenger-side door. "Get in quick! We need to go, right now!"

"What's happened?" Pennie scrambled into the vehicle.

"Donna called me right after we hung up! I think Stanley kidnapped her. He's got her at his house. Can you tell me how to get there—the fastest way?"

"Yes! Go back across under the interstate and turn on the first street!"

Quinn's tires squealed as he turned out of the parking lot. "I'm not exactly sure of the details. She said he tied her up, and he's going to be back soon. I don't know if he hurt her or not!" Quinn kept his eyes glued to the road, his face a stone mask.

"Oh my God! Did you call the sheriff?"

"No! I didn't take the time."

"Turn left at the next road."

They skidded, and Quinn accelerated again. "She said he was gone, but she thought he'd be back soon. How much farther is it?"

"Right up ahead. It's that little brick ranch house up yonder on the right."

Quinn braked and pulled into the driveway. No cars were visible outside, and the garage door was closed.

As soon as the truck halted, they ran to the front door.

"Locked!" he said.

Pennie tried to peer inside the big picture window. "I can't see anything—the curtains are shut."

Quinn ran around toward the back of the house, and Pennie ran after him. He crossed the little patio and smashed a window.

Pennie almost crashed into him as he stopped in the kitchen.

Donna was still tied to the chair. The telephone was beside her, and the receiver was off the hook.

Quinn bounded into the room, righted the chair, and fumbled with the ropes. "Baby doll! Talk to me. Are you hurt?"

Donna burst into tears. "I'm all right ... now that you're here."

"Get me a knife from the kitchen! Hurry!" Quinn said.

Pennie opened the drawers and brought back a small knife with a serrated blade.

Quinn began sawing at the ropes.

Donna fell against him as he enclosed her in his arms.

"Are you OK? Did he hurt you?" Quinn asked.

Pennie stared at them with her hands pressed over her mouth.

"I'm all right." Donna looked at her bleeding and bruised wrists.

"Thank God!" Quinn said. "Can you stand up?"

"I think so … but let me go to the bathroom. He had me tied to that chair since last night. I'm going to die if I don't get to go pee."

They helped her walk toward the bathroom.

"What happened?" Quinn asked.

Donna got her jeans down and sat down on the commode. "Oh, that's so much better," she said after she had relieved herself. "We've got to get out of here! He could be back any minute. He has a gun!"

"Don't worry about that," Quinn said. "Pennie, why don't you see if you can get the phone to work and call the sheriff's office."

Donna swayed against him when she tried to take a step.

"Can you tell me what happened?" Quinn asked.

"Well, I was just coming out of the grocery store last night. I put my groceries on the seat, and as I was closing the door, he grabbed me. He put his hand over my mouth and told me not to scream." She shuddered.

"The phone's working," Pennie said. "I got a dial tone! I just dialed the sheriff's office, and it's ringing."

"He made me get in the car," Donna said. "He showed me the gun and told me he'd shoot me if I screamed or refused to go with him."

"Why did he do such a thing?" asked Quinn. "What possible motivation did he have to do a thing like this?"

"He was talking crazy," Donna said. "He tied me to the chair. When he left, he told me he would be back soon. I moved the chair toward the phone and knocked it onto the floor. I had to make the chair turn over and get my hands close to the dial." Her eyes filled with tears again. "It took me forever to dial your number with my hands tied. I was so glad when you answered. I could barely hear you."

"But you did it, baby doll. I'm very proud of you."

Pennie said, "They've already got Stanley in custody! He broke into Donna's room. Mrs. Adams heard him in there, and she called the sheriff. The sheriffs office wants to know if we can meet them over there?"

"How about it, Donna?" asked Quinn. "Do you feel like you can do that—or do you need to go to see a doctor?"

"I'll be all right," Donna replied. "Let's just get this over with."

They walked slowly out to Quinn's truck, and he helped her inside.

Pennie crawled in and held Donna as Quinn drove toward town.

Her body sandwiched between Quinn and Pennie; Donna leaned her head against the back of the seat. Pennie cradled her, and she felt the warmth and comforting solidity of Quinn. She felt incredibly drained, and her limbs were heavy and weak.

Donna's eyes popped open as Quinn slowed the truck.

Pennie said, "Look at that! There are two sheriff's cars."

Quinn pulled in behind one of the sheriff's cars.

Mrs. Adams was standing on the sidewalk with Sheriff Hill and a deputy.

The sheriff looked at Quinn as he approached. "You're Quinn Cavanaugh?"

"I am," Quinn said.

"I thought I recognized you, Mr. Cavanaugh." His eyes swept over Pennie and lingered on Donna as Pennie helped her out of the vehicle. "And who might you ladies be?"

"I'm Pennie White. I'm the one who called you earlier."

"Ms. White?" He nodded. "And you're Mrs. Porter, the wife?"

"Ex-wife!" snapped Pennie.

The sheriff gave a small, mirthless smile. "*Ex-wife.* I stand corrected." His eyes swept slowly over Donna. "Are you all right, ma'am?"

"She's been better." Quinn's hands balled up into fists at his sides. "Can you tell us what's going on here, Sheriff?"

He kept his eyes on Donna as he said, "It seems that your landlady heard noises coming from your room. Lucky for us, she was smart enough to call it in instead of playing hero and barging in on the situation. Deputy Hobson over there found your *ex*-husband trashing your room and pulling the clothes out of your closet."

Donna put her hands over her face and swayed.

"You sure you're all right, ma'am?" Sheriff Hill asked.

Donna lowered her hands and looked him in the eye. "I'm fine."

"I'm going to get you to a doctor," Quinn said. "You need to be checked out."

"He kidnapped her," Pennie said. "She was tied to a chair all night!"

Sheriff Hill pulled a notebook out of his pocket and scribbled some notes. "And it was Stanley Porter, your ex-husband, who did this to you?"

Donna nodded.

He looked at her over the notebook. "Well, I'll tell you what, ma'am. You look all in. We've already got enough charges to hold this character. You look like you need to be looked after. Why don't we hold off on taking your statement until tomorrow? You can come over to the office and give it to me in the morning." He looked at Quinn and Pennie. "We'll need statements from both of you as well, but they can wait until tomorrow. I'm going to finish up here and take this guy in." He gestured toward his car.

Donna saw Stanley in the rear of the sheriff's car, and a deputy was standing on the sidewalk beside it. She felt her face twist in dismay.

Pennie put her arm around Donna's shoulders. "Let's take you to my house. We need to get you something to eat and to drink—and let you rest."

"Good idea." Quinn turned back toward his truck.

"Come on, honey," Pennie said. "You look like you're about to fall over."

They got back in the truck and went to Pennie's parents' house.

Mrs. White took over like a drill sergeant. Donna was enthroned on the sofa, and cold water and hot soup were placed in front of her in no time.

Donna gratefully sank down into the soft pillows and drank the water. When a mug of hot soup was urged into her hand, she felt like nothing had ever tasted so good. Her stomach growled in approval, and she realized how hungry she was. As she finished, she looked up at everyone. Her vision blurred, her eyes filled with grateful tears, and she smiled.

Mrs. White said, "All right! Donna's got to get some rest now. Pennie, get her one of your nightgowns. We're going to put her into bed."

"Pennie, I'll take you over to the shopping center to get your car," Quinn said.

"I'll go with you," said Mr. White.

"What about Donna's car?" asked Pennie.

They all glanced at each other.

Quinn said, "We probably need to call Sheriff Hill and tell him where it is. I don't think we told him that part of the story. He might want to take a look at it before we move it."

Mrs. White said, "Why don't you men do that? We'll get Donna to bed."

"The phone's in here," said Mr. White.

Quinn made the call. "Sheriff Hill is sending a deputy to the shopping center to go over Donna's car. He said not to move it until after they look it over, take pictures, and whatever. He's already sent a car over to Stanley's house."

"OK," said Mr. White. "I guess we can go get Pennie's car now."

Pennie came back into the room. "We put her to bed. She's already asleep. When I think about what almost happened …"

Quinn's face went stony. "I know."

Mr. White put his hand on Quinn's shoulder. "Come on, son. Let's go get Pennie's car."

🕊

Donna opened her eyes, disoriented, and looked around the bright, sunny room. She frowned. *Where in the world am I?* The memory of the past two days came crashing into her mind, and she realized that she was in the cheerful extra bedroom at Pennie's parents' house. As she threw back the covers, her eyes fell on the clothes she had worn since Friday now neatly laundered and stacked on a chair.

She padded toward the door in Pennie's too-long nightgown, opened it, and peered down the hallway. She thought she heard someone moving around and headed toward the sound.

Pennie came around the corner and said, "Hey! You finally woke up?"

"What time is it?" asked Donna.

"Going on eleven," Pennie said. "Want some coffee? I'll get you a cup."

Donna said, "No … not just now. I'd rather have a big glass of water. I feel parched all the way down."

Pennie nodded. "You're probably dehydrated. I'll get you a glass, and then I'll make us a fresh pot of coffee. Do you want to take a shower?"

"A hot shower sounds like heaven," Donna said.

"OK! You know where the bathroom is. I'll bring you a cold bottle of water. Oh, Momma laundered your clothes—they're in your room."

"Your momma's an angel!"

"Sometimes." Pennie laughed. "I'll get your water. There should be towels and soap and stuff laid out where you can find them." Her voice grew fainter as she moved away toward the kitchen. "Everybody's gone to church. When you get out of the shower, I'll fix you some breakfast."

Donna went back and picked up the little stack of her clothes. She walked to the bathroom and started the water in the shower. She glanced down at her arms as she stripped off the nightgown. The skin on her forearms was striped with angry-looking red marks. *Must be from all that straining at the ropes that I did when I was tied up.* She stepped into the shower and let the hot water beat down on her.

Pennie came into the bathroom and handed her a glass of water around the shower curtain.

Donna took it and drank it down thirstily.

"Are you hungry?" Pennie called out over the sound of the running water.

"Starving!"

"Good. Momma made a big batch of biscuits this morning and fried some country ham. She told me to feed you when you woke up."

Donna's mouth watered. "Did you say they went to church?"

"Yep! I volunteered to stay here and babysit you. We didn't want to wake you!"

Donna laughed and turned off the shower. "Hand me a towel, will you?"

Pennie scrambled some eggs to go with the ham and biscuits and made a fresh pot of coffee.

Donna finally pushed back her plate and sighed. "I'm stuffed."

"Oh, I forgot to tell you that Quinn called. He said he'll pick us up whenever we're ready to go over to the sheriff's office in Madiera to make our statements."

Donna's smile faded. "I guess we have to do that."

Pennie looked at her sympathetically. "Shall I go ahead and call him now?"

Donna nodded and rubbed the red marks on her arms. "Yeah. Go ahead."

Chapter Thirty

Donna reached up into the cabinet and put away the dishes she had just washed and dried in Quinn's kitchen. He and Benjie had left her there, cleaning up the kitchen, while they went to the store for some items needed for the meal they planned to cook later.

The door opened, and Quinn and Benjie came in with bags of groceries.

Quinn captured her in and embrace and gave her a long, steamy kiss.

Donna laughed at this simple normalcy as Quinn righted one of Benjie's bags that threatened to fall over.

Benjie said, "Guess what! We saw Billy Mathis and his momma at the store, and he told me that he's got a new puppy. He said I could come and see it. Can I? Can I go right now?"

Donna looked at Quinn. "Do you want to take him to see the puppy?"

"He lives just down the road! I could ride down there on my bike. Please, Daddy? Can I?"

Quinn and Donna looked at each other, and Quinn smiled. "Well, that's true. It's just down the road, about a quarter of a mile or so. All right, Benjie. Go ahead—but just for an hour! We've got plans here—don't forget."

"I won't! I'll be back in an hour. I promise." Benjie headed for the door.

"Be careful!" Donna and Quinn said in unison. They looked at each other and laughed.

Quinn stowed away the last of his purchases and gathered up the empty bags. "I heard something else while I was out. Thought you'd want to hear this."

A flicker of apprehension ran through her. "What?"

"Nothing alarming." He pulled out a chair and sat down. "I just found out that Stanley had a hearing, and the judge released him on bond—with the stipulation that he has to see a psychiatrist down in Winston-Salem twice a week. Deputy Sheriff Brown said that he thinks that Bill Carson let him come back to work over at the car dealership … as a salesman."

Donna sat down. "That's good."

"I guess so." Quinn's eyes lingered on her. "You don't seem too surprised to hear that part of it."

"Why? What do you mean?"

"Well, I guess everybody just assumed that he'd be fired."

"That would have been a bad thing," Donna said. "He needs to have a job—something to do, to keep his mind occupied. Plus, he has bills to pay."

"True enough."

The silence between them grew.

Donna looked up to see Quinn's gaze lingering on her. "What?"

"Why do I get the feeling that you know more about this than you're letting on?"

Donna felt her face redden. "I didn't know that he was out on bond."

He continued to look at her.

Donna fidgeted. She took a deep breath. "I might have gone down to the dealership and talked to Bill Carson."

"You did?" His eyebrows rose in surprise.

She bit her lower lip and stole a glance at him. "I felt sort of sorry for Stanley, and I knew that if he lost his job on top of everything else, well, I just didn't know what he would do. So, I went down there, and I asked Mr. Carson if he could find it in his heart to give him another chance."

"What did Bill Carson say?" Quinn asked quietly.

"He said he'd think about it. He told me that there was no way that Stanley could still be the used car manager, but he'd think about keeping him on." Donna looked at Quinn. "I used to have feelings for Stanley. I didn't really love him, but I couldn't just stand by and see everything be taken away from him."

Quinn looked at her with a strange expression. "You're quite a woman, Donna Porter. You've got the biggest heart I've ever seen."

"You're not mad at me?" she asked.

"No, baby doll. I'm not mad at you."

There was another silence.

"There's another reason," she said softly.

He raised an eyebrow.

"If he lost everything, he'd look for someone to blame. That would be me."

"You've got to be careful," Quinn said. "He's out of jail now, and he could still be a danger to you. You don't know what he might try to do."

"I know."

"Come here."

Donna got up and walked over to him.

His chair scraped across the floor as he pushed it back and put his hands on her waist. He turned her and pulled her down onto his lap.

She put her arms around his neck.

"I need you to stay here with me—so I can protect you," he murmured.

"You know that can't happen." She smiled.

"There's one way that it could. Marry me, Donna."

Donna sucked in a deep breath—not sure she'd heard right.

His icy blue eyes were fixed on her, passion stirring in their depths. "When that happened to you … when Pennie and I saw you, tied to that chair …" He closed his eyes briefly, then fixed them upon her again. "Let's just say that it was a real wake-up call for me. I realized how much you mean to me. I love you, Donna. I want you to be my wife."

She stayed silent.

His arms tightened around her. "I want you in my bed at night, sure I do, but I also want you sitting here with me at this table while we make our life decisions. I want to support you in the work that I know you love, and I want you to be part of mine as well. I want us to be a family: you, me, and Benjie." His breath hitched. "I want to go off to work every day and know that you'll be here when I come home."

"I'm not going anywhere, Quinn," she whispered.

"Then you'll say yes?"

She smiled at him through the tears that began trickling down her face. "Maybe so." She stroked his cheek. "But there's a couple of things that I need to have happen if I do."

"What's that, baby doll? I'm at your mercy!"

"I want you to start going to church with me—and I want Benjie to come too and go to Sunday school. I had to give all that up when I was with Stanley, and it really means a lot to me."

Quinn laughed. "Some of the old biddies at church will probably faint dead away when bad-boy Cavanaugh walks in, but you're right. Benjie needs to be getting that kind of influence in his life. That's fine with me. I can do that. You said a couple of things. What else?"

Donna's face grew troubled. "It's your mother. Quinn, I know how close you are to her—both you and Benjie—but she really dislikes me!"

"She'll come around," he said.

"When? Ten years from now?"

Quinn nuzzled her neck. "Oh, much sooner than that, I'd expect. All we'd have to do is present her with another little grandson or a granddaughter—a little brother or sister for Benjie. She acts hard-hearted, but she's got a real soft spot for a little baby!"

Donna swatted at him. "I'm serious." She wiped the tears from her cheeks. "She really does hate me."

"No, she doesn't. A big part of it is her being protective of me. I tell you she'll come around when she sees how much I love you—how much Benjie and I both love you. Then, when she gets to know you, she'll learn what a wonderful person you are, and she'll grow to love you for you."

Donna shot him a skeptical look.

"Now, I asked you a question, Donna, and I need to know why you're not giving me an answer. Are you trying to tell me that you don't want to marry me because you don't love me?"

"Oh, no, Quinn! I do love you—I love you so much that it hurts."

"Well, what then?"

The tears began anew. Donna turned her head away. "There's so much about me that you don't know, Quinn."

"Listen to me, Donna! I know that something happened to you while you were married to Stanley. Whatever it was, it just shut you down inside. I'm just so thankful that I could help you get past it, so that you opened yourself up to me, let yourself feel again! But believe me when I tell you that *I don't want to know what it was that happened!* If I did, I might have to do something about it. And that something might ruin all our chances for a happy future!" A dark look ran over his face and then disappeared. "I don't want to dig up the past—I just want us to go forward. I asked you once to trust me, Donna. Will you trust me on this as well?"

She dipped her head. "Yes, Quinn, I will," she whispered.

"So!" he almost growled. "Are you going to say yes to me or not?"

"Oh, yes, Quinn! Yes! I will marry you." Donna threw her arms tightly around his neck.

"Well, thank God for that! This had to be the world's longest proposal!" Quinn was grinning inanely. He gave her a resounding kiss and set her on her feet, rising. "Where is that boy of mine? He needs to get back here. Forget about fixing lunch—we've got someplace we have to go!"

"What are you talking about?" Donna looked at him with confusion. "Go where?"

"Why, we're going to go to find us a jewelry store—and I'm going to buy you a big, sparkly diamond ring and put it on your finger before you change your mind. I want all the world to see it and know that you're mine!"

Donna laughed; her face was still wet with tears. "You're nuts! You know that?"

He picked her up and swung her around. "I know it." His face grew serious. "How soon can we do this? You don't want a big, fancy church wedding, do you?"

"No," Donna said. "I had one of those once before—and you see how that turned out?"

"We can go over to the county seat on Monday morning and see about getting our license. I think we may have to get blood tests, or something, but we can have this done by the end of the week, for sure. Is that all right with you?"

"But school's going to start soon. I have to be at an all-day meeting for the teachers on Monday morning."

"OK! You get off at three, don't you? I'll pick you up at three o'clock, and we'll ride over there and find out what-all we have to do."

"I have to tell Pennie and her parents!" Donna said, catching his excitement. "Maybe she can stand up for me and be our witness."

"I think we'll need two witnesses. I can ask Brett, from my office," Quinn said. "Aren't he and Pennie going out together?"

Donna nodded. "Yes, they are. I'm sure my minister would perform a little service for us in the church. I would like that. Pennie won't be working next Saturday. Can we see if we can do it then?"

"It's all settled then," Quinn said. "Let's go pick up Benjie and get this thing rolling."

Donna laughed. "You don't waste any time, do you?"

He stopped still and captured her with his piercing gaze as he caught her around the waist, holding her lightly. "Not where you're concerned, baby doll. I don't want to waste another single minute of the rest of our lives."

If you loved *Choice*, then you won't want to miss *Glitter*, the next in the series, coming soon!

Becky Cavanaugh grabbed her chance to take her incredible voice and overpowering ambition to Nashville, deserting her brand-new husband and infant son in the process. Within weeks, Becky Barnes, her new persona, had a hit on the charts, and "Tarnished Rose" could be heard on every radio station in America. Then—nothing. The harder she tried, the more elusive her next hit became. As quickly as she rose, she disappeared from view, her gigs and appearances becoming harder and harder to find, her moment of fame but a distant memory.

Now why is she back? Why has Becky come back to Phillips?

Glitter

ELIZA GRACE HOWARD

Chapter One

The woman set down the cheap suitcase on the concrete surface of the street and straightened up, her eyes fixed on the small house on the other side of the street. In the near darkness, where the only illumination was from a streetlight fifty feet or so down the street on the far side of the next house, the house across from her looked forlorn and somewhat unkempt. The windows were dark, and the front lawn looked in need of a mowing behind the short picket fence along the front. It was more decorative than useful, and the plantings bordering the fence inside the yard were tall and ungainly. The short gravel driveway on the right side of the property, which led up from the street, was empty.

The woman's hand moved to the small of her back, and she rubbed it absently as she stared intently at the house. After a moment, she picked up the suitcase and walked a few feet farther down her side of the street to where a large tree grew close to the pavement. There were no sidewalks here on Pine Street. Geographically, this was probably near the center of town, but here the houses were small, and the owners too financially insignificant to rate this amenity. The late-September air was cool and pleasant; no breeze was stirring, and there was just a hint of fall in the hushed atmosphere. She set down her burden, and her knees folded as she slowly sank to sit at the base of the tree. Leaning back against the trunk for support, she waited.

Not long afterward, a vehicle approached from down the street on her right, its headlights briefly illuminating the yard and front porch of the house as it turned up the short driveway and stopped at the side of the house. The woman's drooping eyes flew open, and she sat still, watching. As the driver-side car door opened, the interior light illuminated the slim figure of a woman as she emerged and then reached back into the vehicle to retrieve a tote bag. The woman approached the house, paused at a side doorway, and seconds later disappeared inside. A light came on, spilling out through both the doorway and a window near the back of the house. The door swung closed, eliminating the spill of light into the yard. Minutes later, a glow showed through the front windows as more lights came on in the depths of the house. Across the street, the woman got to her feet, picked up her suitcase, and walked un-hurriedly across the pavement toward the house. She bent over to unlatch a gate in the center of the short picket fence and let herself into the yard. She walked up the narrow gravel walk that bisected the yard, up a pair of concrete steps, and crossed the wooden planks of the porch.

The front entrance was covered by a screen door hinged in front of the sturdy wood one, with the twin panes of glass set too high up to see through. A pull on the handle of the screen door proved it to be latched shut, so the woman raised her fist and rapped loudly on the plank frame of the screen door. She had just raised her arm to knock a second time when she heard approaching footsteps. She blinked as the porch was suddenly bathed in dazzling light from an overhead fixture in the porch ceiling. The wood inner door was yanked open, and the woman who had been driving the car stood there, staring out at her visitor. Her eyes widened in recognition, and her mouth went slightly agape.

"What are you doing here?" she rasped.

The woman with the suitcase smiled through the screen barrier. "Now what kind of greeting is that for your long-lost sister?"

The surprise on the woman's face gave way to a frown. "I asked you what you want."

"I want to come in the house, for one thing," the woman said flatly. "It's been a long day. I've come a far distance, and I'm tired. Are you going to let me come in?"

There was a long, intense moment as the pair stared at each other. The woman inside moved her hand, and a click indicated she had unlatched the screen door. She stepped backward without saying a word.

The visitor pulled open the screen door and walked inside, past her sister. Her eyes darted around the small alcove behind the doorway and past it, to a small room on the right, furnished with a well-worn sofa and a pair of matching armchairs. A small, round table stood at either end of the sofa, each holding a lamp and a few pieces of bric-a-brac, and a low, wood coffee table sat in front of it. A small TV set sat out of sight of the entrance on a metal stand on the opposite wall, and an oval, braided rug covered the middle half of the oak floor. The sight and familiar smell of the house hit the woman like a blow to the midsection.

"It looks just like it always did," she said softly.

"What did you expect?" Her sister slammed the front door shut behind her, threw the lock, and switched off the porch light. "Did you think I was going to *redecorate*?"

"Clara ..."

"What are you doing here, Becky?"

Becky set her suitcase down. Her hand went to her forehead, and her lean fingers massaged between her brows. "Would you believe me if I said I don't honestly know?"

Printed in the USA
CPSIA information can be obtained
at www.ICGtesting.com
JSHW081623240923
48747JS00004BA/12